The Wind Reader

Dorothy A. Winsor

Inspired
Quill

Published by Inspired Quill: September 2018

First Edition

Chief Editor: Sara-Jayne Slack
Cover Image: Marco Pennacchietti
Cover Design: Venetia Jackson
Typeset in Minion Pro

Paperback ISBN: 978-1-908600-75-2
eBook ISBN: 978-1-908600-76-9
Print Edition

Printed in the United Kingdom
1 2 3 4 5 6 7 8 9 10

Inspired Quill Publishing, UK
Business Reg. No. 7592847
www.inspired-quill.com

Praise for Dorothy Winsor

Journeys: A Ghost Story, is a very good tale that, without any real surprises, still manages to surprise. There's a well-wrought aura of melancholy that permeates the story, even in the funny moments. Another author I'll keep an eye out for in the future.

—Fletcher Vredenburgh,
Black Gate Magazine

Dorothy A. Winsor is a meticulous writer who expertly balances intelligence and delight.

—Saladin Ahmed,
Hugo, Nebula, and Gemmell Awards finalist

[In Finders Keepers], the action is brisk, emotions are deep, and the moral message is subtle but strong, providing excellent depth for all readers, young and not so young. Great story – I loved it as an adult and think it is a wonderful book for older kids and young adults. Five Stars.

—Melinda Hills,
Readers' Favorite

For Richard

Chapter 1.

An Ill Wind

I F I HADN'T been dead sure about talking my father into this trip, I might think the Divine Powers had slowed the wind to punish me for nagging. The sailors swore we were making good time, and the lone sail bellied out overhead, but the *Rose of Rin* felt like it was standing still. My hair would turn gray before we docked. I'd grow a beard down to my knees, and I'd *still* be on this wallowing pig of a boat.

Bracing my feet against the slight sway of the deck, I scooped the last handful of salted codfish out of the basin, flung them on the platter, and wiped my palms on my trousers. The job left my hands reeking, but I couldn't complain because it was easier than my father's. He was working on repairs near the stern at the moment, his blond head easy to spot among the lowland sailors. Like most Uplanders, Da was short and slight, so you could miss the muscles in his back and arms. I hoped these lowlanders were learning some respect from seeing him tote a heavy bucket of tar as if it weighed nothing, while the sailor working with him dragged his feet.

I emptied the basin overboard. Maybe we would be in Marketon by nightfall, as the sailors claimed, and Da and I would be off this tub, ready to negotiate with the timber buyer. Ready to make a deal with him about *my* timber, a notion that made me smile. I inherited the trees when my grandfather died, and now that I was finally fifteen and old enough to manage my own property, I'd be hanged if I'd sit home like a kid and let Da sell it cheap in Merinoic.

"Boy!" Cook called. He didn't seem to realize I had a name or, more likely, didn't care. "Aren't you done yet?"

I'd stopped working for a moment. Can't have that. No sir. Not allowed. Platter of fish in hand, I ducked into the canvas shelter where Cook had laid an iron grill over the glowing coals. I plunked the platter down at what passed for Cook's elbow, a red knob protruding from the mass of black hair furring his arm.

"All the salt is out?" Cook asked.

"I changed the water three times. Why do we have to eat dried fish anyway? That seems—" I stopped myself in time from saying *stupid* "—odd to me."

As he arranged fish on the grill, water dripped into the coals, hissing and sending up puffs of steam. "You Upland farmers have some other way to preserve fish?"

"You could catch fresh fish." I waved toward the flat, brown water rippling away to either side. "We're on a boat."

"You don't say. You see anyone aboard with time to fish?"

I snorted. The captain didn't give us time to scratch our backsides.

Cook pointed to a wheel of yellow cheese. "Slice that. Then fill the ale tankards." He poked at the fish with a huge knife.

By the time I fetched the ale, the fish were ready, and Cook sent me running around the boat with fish, cheese, and ale for the sailors. At last, everyone else was fed, and I flopped onto the deck next to Da and the sailor he'd been working with. The man leaned back against a barrel, face flushed, dinner only half eaten, while Da lounged beside him, not even sweaty. Ha!

I cradled the shallow wooden bowl of food in my lap and tore into it. My stomach had been rumbling since mid-morning.

Da grinned at me. "Your ma will be happy to know you've taken up cooking."

"Don't tell her," I mumbled around a mouthful of fish, which was pretty good, if I did say so myself. All the salt was out. "The girls can do it."

"I thought you didn't like your sisters' cooking."

"Better them than me." I nodded toward the shore creeping past. "Will we really get to Marketon by dark?

We're hardly moving."

"Boat's low in the water." The deck hand spoke as if his tongue were too heavy. Keeping up with Da must have worn him out. I knew the feeling. "All that iron ore from your mountains," the man went on.

"Ore stolen from our mountains, you mean," I said.

The deck hand raised an eyebrow. "Your Lord Grimuld is the one shipping it."

"That's because Lord Grimuld is the one stealing it," I said. "At the market last month, the gossip was all about how he took a farm five leagues west of ours and had his men tear up the earth looking for it."

"You let him talk that way?" the deck hand asked Da. "The boy'll get himself in trouble."

"Boys become men, and a man needs to recognize wrong when he sees it. A cat can hiss at a king, we say." Da threw me a look I'd seen way too many times. "On the other hand, Clever-tongue, I've told you more than once that a man of sense talks when it'll do good but stays quiet when it won't."

I kept my eyes on my bowl and chewed hard on the remaining bit of my dinner. I'd heard Da say plenty about Grimuld. He'd been Lord of the Uplands only a year, and in that time, he'd not only stolen land but also tried to stamp out all the ways we revered the wind. Someone needed to talk about that. In my opinion, Da was too careful sometimes.

Farther along the deck, the captain was prodding

sailors back to work. As Da dropped his empty bowl into mine and stood, the deck hand grabbed the top of the barrel and dragged himself erect. Or maybe not quite. I peered up at him. Surely he was swaying more than the motion of the boat would account for, and his face was so flushed, it was nearly purple. He took a single step before his knees buckled and he sprawled face down on the deck.

At the *thunk* of his head hitting wood, Da whirled and sprang to crouch on one side of him, while I lurched to the other. The captain came running, followed by a crowd of sailors.

"Is he drunk?" the captain demanded.

Da shook his head and rolled the groaning man gently onto his back. He laid his palm on the sailor's forehead. "He's fevered."

My heart sped up.

Da rubbed his hand on his thigh, hesitated, then yanked the deck hand's shirt out of his belt to expose his belly. A red rash bloomed all around the man's navel. The captain took a step backward. "Mountain Fever," he whispered.

I staggered back a step. I didn't mean to but, Sweet Powers, Fever!

The deck hand's eyes flew wide open. "I have the Fever?"

"Put in to shore," one of the sailors said. "Get him off the boat."

Da looked up sharply. "Abandon him, you mean?

No."

"You get off and stay with him then." The sailor's voice shook.

Da looked at the captain, who was silent, gnawing his lip. I choked back the urge to tell Da to get away from the sick man. Or I would have if I'd been able to breathe. Last autumn, while out hunting, I'd stumbled on an empty house with dishes still on the table and a baby's rattle on the floor. That was what Fever left behind. That and graves in the meadow.

"There's a village a mile or so on," the captain said. "They'll have a healer. We'll leave him there." He jerked his head at the sailors. "Back to work." They wasted no time scuttling away. The captain strode after them.

"Go on back to Cook, Doniver." Da pulled the scarf off the sick man's neck.

"What about you?"

"Don't argue with me. Go right now. I'm just going to damp him down, see if I can fight that fever a bit." He moved to a nearby barrel, scooped water into one of the dinner bowls, and came back, dunking the scarf in the water.

"Come away when you're done," I said.

"Go!"

I ran back to where Cook stood, staring along the deck toward Da. When he stayed silent, I asked, "You want me to wash dishes?"

Cook shook himself. "Your father's a fool, you know

that?"

"He's brave," I said sharply.

He glanced at me. "Dishes." He lifted a shoulder to wipe sweat from his jaw, then went to fuss with the stores.

The thing was, part of me thought maybe Cook was right.

I heated water, collected forgotten dishes, and scrubbed them, trying to watch Da and the shoreline at the same time. Da moved back and forth, wiping the deck hand down and then standing near the railing. Where was that village? The sooner the sick man was gone, the happier I'd be.

At last, a scattering of thatched houses straggled into sight, and the boat nosed in to the small dock, where two men sat fishing. Da tried to heave the deck hand to his feet, but the man sagged on his arm and no one moved to help. For a moment, I rocked back and forth. I could do what Da told me and stay with Cook. No one would blame me.

No one but me.

I ran to the man's other side. At a close sight of him, the air went out of me. The rash had spread. Oozing blisters blossomed on his face.

"Get away," Da snapped.

"You can't manage him alone." It made me queasy to touch him, but I pulled the man's left arm around my neck. He moaned.

Da set his jaw. Between us, we wrestled the man to

where his fellow sailors had just thumped the gangway into place. They shuffled away as we got close.

"You there," the captain called to the two on the dock. "Get your healer."

The two villagers rose, their gazes on the deck hand, propped between me and Da. "What's wrong with him?" one of them asked.

The other's eyes rounded. He grabbed his companion's arm. "Fever!"

The first villager took a step backward. "Get him away! You can't leave him here!" He shouted toward the houses. "They want to leave a man with the Fever!" The second villager darted into the lane, shouting an alarm, sending up puffs of dust with every footfall.

Da and I stopped at the top of the gangway, the sick man hanging between us. "He'll get no help here," Da said. "The Powers only know what they'll do with him."

The captain rubbed his jaw. "Stone them." For a long moment, he was silent.

I braced myself against the deck hand's limp weight, the heat of his fever burning my side right through my clothes. *Hurry. Make up your mind*, I silently urged. *I don't want this man touching me.*

At length, the captain said, "Put him back where he was. We'll try the next village."

"Captain!" one of the other sailors protested.

"He's my wife's nephew," the captain said. "I won't leave him. Get the gangway up." He strode away, giving orders to sail on.

I helped Da lug the feverish man back to his corner of the deck and lower him in a boneless heap. Da looked up, deep lines between his brows. "I'll stay with him, but you keep away, Doniver."

"I could take a turn," I offered, unsure whether I wanted him to say yes or no.

"No, you couldn't. Go."

I felt a terrible relief. When Da used that tone, arguing was an invitation to big trouble. At the kitchen, Cook was nowhere in sight, so I ducked under the canvas shelter, then had to stop to take in what I saw. Cook lay on the deck, his shoulders propped against a sack of onions, his head thrown back. He turned glazed eyes toward me, and when he did, I saw the rash on his cheek.

BY THE TIME we reached the next village, two more men had collapsed. Word of what we carried must have galloped down the road more quickly than the *Rose of Rin* had sailed, because a knot of men with clubs warned us off from the dock.

Crouched between Cook and the deck hand, I watched the village slip behind us. *Maybe at Marketon. That's a big town. There'll be a sickhouse.*

When Cook moaned, I put a cup of water to his cracked lips, but he didn't even notice it was there. Where

I touched him, he felt hot enough to burst into flame. On Cook's other side, two more men lay stretched out. Another sailor bent over them, and one more had been willing to help too, but the captain said he needed everyone still on their feet to help sail the boat.

"Doniver."

I looked over my shoulder at Da, still tending the deck hand he'd worked with.

"Let the crew do this," Da said one more time. "You go see if the captain needs help."

For a horrible moment, my legs twitched with the urge to walk away. Instead, I forced myself to meet Da's worried gaze. "I can't. I'm fifteen. I'm a man. You've been saying I should act like one. Isn't that what you're doing?"

Da made a noise somewhere between a moan and a laugh, then gave a curt nod, and I turned back to Cook. A moment later, the first man who'd fallen sick rattled out a noisy breath and didn't draw another. I spun to find Da with his ear pressed to the man's chest. A moment stretched into forever before Da straightened and swept his hand down the man's face, closing his eyes. He rubbed his temples as if his head ached, which scared me, but he walked steadily enough to the side of another sick man, patting my shoulder as he passed.

I bent over Cook, heart racing. *Sweet Powers, we're people of the wind. Send us one now. Blow us along to Marketon. Someone there will help us.*

The day slowly faded, and the captain came and set

two oil lamps on the deck. Their flickering light cast an orange glow over the sick and well alike. When two sailors dragged another sick man into the light's circle, the dancing flames made them all seem to stagger. At least the night was warm, though Cook shivered even after I spread a blanket over him.

Finally, ahead on the right, the dark was pierced by the lighted windows of houses. I leaped to my feet so fast that I stumbled and had to steady myself before I hastened to the rail. "It's Marketon. I never thought I'd be so happy to see a place."

All the sailors along the rail were quiet.

"It's Marketon, isn't it?"

"Aye," the one next to me finally said. "They're waiting for us."

I snapped around so quickly I made myself dizzy again, but I still saw the torches held by the crowd on the dock. I still heard when a man shouted, "Keep off, *Rose of Rin!*"

"No!" My hands tightened on the rail. "They have to help us."

The sailor walked away. I turned to watch him vanish into the wavering dark. I took a step, and then I was falling, falling, falling.

"Doniver!" Da's voice cried, but it was somewhere far away.

HEAT FLAMED ON my skin. My blanket was on fire! I pushed but was too feeble to shake it off. My head pounded. Demons with tiny pincers for hands scrabbled up from my feet. I moaned and dove into the dark. I swam up, and the demons came after me again, red-faced and snarling with malice. The dark closed me in.

The darkness paled to gray, and I came awake because my neck itched with sweat. I smelled bread baking, which meant Ma already had it in the oven, and I was late for chores. Why hadn't anyone shouted at me to get up? I opened my eyes to see a thatched roof rising overhead and a wall on the wrong side of my bed. Something scraped on the floor, and I turned my head to see a small, dark-haired boy who'd just jumped up from a stool.

"Ma!" The boy darted through a doorway. "Ma! He's awake!"

When I tried to prop myself up on my elbow, my arm gave way, and I flopped back. Where was I? Abruptly, the image of the boat and the fevered men tumbled into my head. Da! Where was he?

"So you're awake." A tall, gaunt woman came into the room, wiping her hands on her apron. She put one of them on my forehead. "Good. Your fever's down."

I licked my dry lips. "Is my father here?"

She offered me a cup of water from the bedside table, steadying it as I drank. "He would have been on that boat?" She looked at the cup, rather than me. "No, lad, he's not here."

"Where is he? Did he go home?" That couldn't be right. Da would never leave me sick with strangers.

She set the cup back on the table. "I don't know."

"But—"

"Rest now. Rigan, my husband, found the boat. He'll be home in a while, and he'll tell you what happened."

Before I could protest, she was gone.

A WEEK LATER, I struggled up the rise to see the river stretched across my path. Just to my left was the small cove Rigan had described, its shore marred by the burned remnant of the *Rose of Rin*. For a long moment, I stared at it, breathing fast. The smell of phantom smoke nipped the inside of my nose. Then my shaky legs gave out, and I sank down heavily into the damp grass. I hugged my knees and thought about how we'd been on that boat only because I kept after Da until he gave in.

A step stirred the grass beside me, sending a tiny shower of dew flashing into the morning sun. I squinted up at Rigan, who stood looking soberly at the blackened boat.

"Are you sure they were all dead before you burned it?" My voice came out like a croak, and I swallowed hard.

"Aye. All but you."

When I could speak around the grief choking me, I opened my fists and let go of the last wisp of hope. "You were good to chance taking me in, Rigan. I thank you."

"My wife would have kicked me out if I'd left you, and truth be told, you lay in the barn for the first week. None of us is sick, so the Powers rewarded us." Rigan smoothed the grass with his toe. "We can't keep you, though. I'm sorry, but we have too many mouths of our own to feed."

"I know. I need to find work on a boat heading home anyway. My ma will be worried." Sweet Powers, how was I going to tell Ma that Da would never come home again?

Rigan grimaced. "I'm afraid you can't, not just yet. Fever's bad in the Uplands. King Thien put it under quarantine. No one's allowed in or out."

My heart burst into a frantic gallop. "Bad? Where? Our farm's near Merinoic. Is it bad there?"

Rigan shrugged. "Bad pretty much everywhere, I think." He squatted by my side. "Here's what we'll do. Next week, one of our neighbors is delivering a horse to a woman in Rin. He says he'll take you, too. You can maybe get some sort of work and wait for the quarantine to end. All the boats fetching iron start from there, so you'll have a good chance of finding one that'll take you on as a deck hand and carry you north."

"Rin?" I felt stunned to stupidity. The city of Rin lay to the south. I'd be going farther from home, not closer. And what would I do when I got there? Where would I stay while waited? How could I manage on my own in a strange city?

Rigan rose. "It's the best I can do, lad. I'm sorry." He

plodded away, head down.

I sat and stared at the burned boat, swimming in a watery blur into which the world slowly dissolved.

Chapter 2.

Lost

"COME BACK IN a few weeks," the sailor said. "Fever usually burns itself out in a month or so. Once it's done, we'll go north again and maybe need a cabin boy."

"But—" I found myself speaking to the sailor's back as he strode up the ship's gangway. "I don't have few weeks," I said to no one in particular. "Ma and the girls need me now." I backed away and counted the ships lined up along Rin's docks. Seven, not including the little fishing boats, and not one of them would take me home. Stone the quarantine. Stone King Thien for imposing it. Stone the Fever. Stone *everything*.

In the week since I arrived in Rin, I'd spent so much time alone that I was used to talking to myself, which was good because this late in the afternoon, not many folks idled on the docks outside the city's east gate. Who would want to spend time there anyway? The river reeked on account of the way city folks dumped their garbage in it. The only person in sight was a red-haired girl sitting on the edge of a dock and singing to herself. My oldest sister liked that song. She'd played it over and over on pipes she'd talked Ma into buying from a tinker, played it until I threatened to throw the pipes down the well if she didn't give it a rest. My vision smeared again until the boats in front of me all looked like they were covered in ashes. Pain swelled in my chest and throat.

Something rat-like rustled in the pile of fishing nets a yard from my feet, and I shuffled away until I blinked hard and saw it was just a ragged-eared terrier nosing around for food. My stomach cramped around empty air. *Good hunting, doggy.* I was hungry enough that if the mutt found a forgotten fish, I might fight him for it. How long since I'd last eaten? This morning? Or had that been yesterday? The days were blurring together.

The terrier barked, and a real rat scurried from behind the nets, heading for a hole in the city wall. The dog scrambled after it but fell with a startled yip when one of its hind legs tangled in a net. It struggled, and when that just pulled the net tighter, it let out a dismayed yowl. Another trapped creature. I could at least fix that.

"Easy now." I made my voice soothing, like I did when I talked to the goats or my littlest sister in a snit. "I won't hurt you. Let me help." I put one hand on the dog's back and untangled the net, the dog crying mournfully all the while.

Running footsteps pounded along the wooden quay. "Tuc! Tuc!" The red-haired girl came panting up. She was about my age, I saw. "Are you hurt?" she cried, clearly talking to the dog, not me.

As soon as I pulled the last bit of rope off the dog's paw, it spurted toward the girl, whining for sympathy. She picked it up and hugged it, which meant she really must love it because judging by the smell, it had rolled in dead fish. I was filthy, and I still wiped my hands on my trousers.

"Thank you," the girl said, drawling out her words. "Tuc gets himself into trouble sometimes. I'm Dilly."

"Doniver."

"I haven't seen you around before." She eyed my dirty clothes and carry bag. "Are you...lost?"

Yes. Oh, yes. So lost I may never be found. "Not really. I'm just staying in Rin until I can find a way home."

"Me too. I'm from Lac's Holding."

I'd guessed that from her red hair and drawl. My stomach chose that moment to rumble, and she cocked her head, listening. My face grew hot.

She stroked Tuc thoughtfully, then set him on his feet. "Rin's a hard place to be on your own. You should meet a friend of mine. He's working in the market, but he might be ready to go home by now."

An alarm drum thumped in the back of my head. Dilly was around my age and didn't look menacing, but I'd already found that "friendly" city people weren't always as helpful as a body might hope. Another reason besides hunger that the days were blurring together was that it was dangerous to sleep on the streets in the dark, so I'd taken to grabbing short daytime naps in an alley behind an alehouse. They weren't enough, and I was so tired, I couldn't think straight.

"Come on," Dilly said. "We can eat together. If we get along, maybe you can stay with Jarka and me until you move on." She took two steps toward the gate.

"I don't have coin." Empty belly squeezed tight, I followed her like a fool. Food. She had food.

"That's all right. I don't have coin today either, but Jarka will share." She maybe read the tight set of my shoulders because she added, "I'm not working for a kidnapper or anything. You helped Tuc, so we owe you."

I trailed her and Tuc through the gate into the noise and stink of the East Market. Gray flagstones paved the space, surrounded by buildings of dark wood and plaster—not a green thing in sight, unless you counted the moss scraggling between the stones. The voices of the late shoppers flooded the place with the usual blurred Rinnish speech. Lazy tongues, talking like words didn't matter. The Powers moved in breath like they did in the wind. Words and breath were sacred.

Dilly led me past the rag sellers to where a dark-haired boy of maybe sixteen leaned on a crutch. Jarka, I guessed. He was all sharp angles, with high cheekbones, a thin nose, and a bony elbow outthrust from his crutch. One of his feet was clubbed in, so he couldn't walk on it. I breathed out a reverent puff of air. Jarka was maimed, marked by the Powers, and they always gave some special gift to make up for what they'd taken. Someone with the Powers' mark could surprise you left and right. You had to be careful.

Jarka was talking to a woman with a marketing basket over her arm. Wait. Not talking. I had to look twice to believe it. Jarka was telling her what he saw when he peered into a box woven from reeds with gaps for the wind to flow through and stir the bright colored bits of paper inside. He was reading the wind, telling a fortune the way Uplanders did, the way city folks like Lord Grimuld stupidly thought was fake, when they didn't think it called on the Evil One. No problems guessing Jarka's gift then.

When the woman handed over a coin and left, Tuc pattered up to Jarka, who nudged him away with the side of his foot. "You stink, Tuc. Clear off before you drive away any customers." He beckoned invitingly to me. "Care to learn your future?"

"This is Doniver," Dilly said. "He saved Tuc from hurting himself on the docks. He needs food and a place to stay."

Jarka pulled himself up straight, his face growing shrewd instead of friendly. He was taller than he'd looked leaning on his crutch, with thin fuzz darkening the curve of his jawbone. He swept a narrow-eyed gaze up and down me.

"Just for a little while," I said, "until I find work and earn some coin. I'd haul my weight, I swear." I tried to keep desperation from my voice. This boy had the Powers' mark, and I hated looking needy in front of him.

"You an Uplander?" Jarka asked.

"How did you know?" I glanced at his wind box. I hadn't thrown the paper bits into it, but maybe he saw things about me anyway. What a horrible thought. I didn't want anyone else knowing why Da was on a death ship.

"You talk like they do," Jarka said, and I relaxed. "You're a long way from home."

"Not on purpose," I said. "My family needs me back as soon as I can get there."

"Huh." Jarka caressed the wind box. "You know, if you need coin, you could do this."

"I don't have the gift. I can't."

He shrugged. "If you did it right, folks would believe you could because you're from the Uplands."

"You mean fake it?" Ice slid down my spine. "Are you faking?"

"What do you think, farm boy?" Jarka cocked his head.

I wanted to move away before lightning struck us. "I don't want to fake wind reading. You invite the Powers' wrath if you do that."

"Take a look at you, me, and Dilly, and tell me the Powers haven't already sprinkled a whole lot of wrath on our heads."

He had me there.

"Doniver's all right, Jarka," Dilly said. "Tuc trusted him."

Jarka met Dilly's earnest gaze and smiled faintly. He pulled a string and collapsed his wind box, then shoved it into his bag. "Work's hard to come by right now, with half the sailors idle. If you can't find something else, I'll teach you to fake a good fortune. Come with us for now. Street trash has to stick together."

Street trash? Was that what I was now? I stayed where I stood. Was I someone who stuck close to a fake wind reader, a homeless girl, and a lop-eared dog? A knife-toothed animal bit fiercely inside my gut. I was whatever I had to be. Da was gone, everything except his memory burned away by Fever and a boat set on fire. I had to survive. Ma and the girls needed me. I followed Jarka, Dilly, and Tuc across the East Market into the slums of Rin.

"I'LL GIVE YOU this," Jarka said, as we sat in the evening twilight in front of the abandoned tailor's shop. His lame foot must ache tonight because he was rubbing it. "You held out longer than any normal person would. Two months? That's what I call Uplander stubborn."

As I worked the reed into the side of the emerging wind box, it snagged on one of my broken nails, tearing it further. I went to suck on it but stopped when I saw how dirty my hand was. "The Fever should be gone by now. It never lasts this long." Like I'd been doing for weeks now, I swallowed down the panic I felt every time I thought of Ma and the girls. The longer I was away, the more they'd be struggling. Unless they were dead.

A man up the street shouted at the woman he lived with. Jarka tensed and turned his head but didn't get up to interfere.

"Maybe it's ended, and we just haven't heard yet." Dilly handed me another reed, then dragged the back of her hand under her nose. We'd all been sick with the same cold for a week. Share and share alike, that was life on the streets. When it came to things like sickness and lice, anyway. And weather, I added to myself, as thunder rumbled in the distance. Tuc shoved his nose under Dilly's palm so she'd pet him. "It's good you've been letting Jarka teach you, though," she said.

It wasn't, but it was the only path left. Pictures flickered through my head. Me at dawn, standing in line among men twice my size, all looking for work. Me, hired for a day's work delivering fire wood, and nearly tripping over a woman lying in the gutter. I'd started to set my load down so I could see what the matter was, but my boss for the day shoved his own load into my back. "Keep moving," the boss said, and I stumbled on, looking back over my shoulder. In the Uplands, you fed strangers. You took them in. But this was Rin.

I tucked the end of the last reed into place, stood, and hitched up the trousers riding on my hipbones. "It's done." *Just like me. I am so very, very done.*

"It looks good," Dilly said.

"We'll try you out tomorrow," Jarka said.

"I WANT TO stop at the book seller's table," Jarka said as we entered the East Market the next day.

"Fine." I was in no hurry. The thought of what I was about to do made me faintly sick. *I won't lie. As long as I don't lie outright, it will be all right.* Folks would have to figure out for themselves what my words meant. Inside my head, Da's voice made me flinch: "The rock solid center of a man is his honor, Doniver. You lose your honor, you lose yourself." I swallowed, trying to ease the pain of wishing, and followed Jarka across a market full of shoppers. It was crowded enough that a young woman whacked me with the huge basket she carried. She mumbled an apology and hurried off.

Jarka looked over his shoulder. "What work does that woman do?"

"Do you have to do this all the time?"

"Do you want to be a good fake or not?"

An excellent question.

"Her hands were red and chapped. A kitchen maid?"

"Smell?" Jarka prompted.

"Soap. She's a laundress."

"Good," Jarka said. "You'll be great today."

The white-haired bookseller allowed us a friendly nod but also issued the same warning he always gave. "Don't put your filthy paws on anything. I'll open the book for you. *The Book of the Wys*?"

"Yes, please," Jarka said. Living with him had taught me that folks in Rin got advice by opening *The Book of the Wys* and reading the first passage their eyes lit on. Jarka stopped here every morning to find out what the day would bring. I'd been surprised the first time I saw Jarka read, but he shrugged and said his ma taught him.

I shifted the strap of my carry bag higher on my right shoulder. It felt awkward there. I usually carried my bag on the left so as to leave my right hand free, but I couldn't handle the bag on the left at all just now because that hand was curled out of sight in a pocket at the end of my sleeve. A fake Powers' mark. And didn't that make me proud?

The bookseller opened the book at random and set it in front of Jarka. I looked over his shoulder. The marks on the page looked like a chicken had stepped in tar and tromped all over the paper.

"You want me to read it out loud, Doniver?" Jarka asked.

I backed away. "Writing is useless. What good are words when no one's here to stand behind them?"

"Uplanders! Writing makes the words last, so you can study them and add to them. They don't blow away on the wind." Head still down, Jarka grinned.

Joking about the wind and breath and speech made me cringe, which Jarka knew. "Writing is as dead as the brain of anyone who thinks otherwise."

The bookseller scowled and reached to take the book back. "Watch your mouth. Some things are sacred."

"Me?" I jerked my thumb toward Jarka. "What about him?"

Jarka's hand hovered protectively over the page. "You have to make allowances," he told the bookseller. "He's from the Uplands."

The man jabbed his finger at me. "Keep that cat hissing at a king disrespect in your mountains where it belongs."

"If I could I would."

Face sour, the bookseller stomped to the other side of his booth. I noticed he still watched us though, like we were thieves or something. In truth, every merchant in this market looked at us in the same way if we lingered by their stalls.

"*Wysmen and Wyswomen arise in every generation*," Jarka read. "*The faithful know them by their courage and wisdom, and by their selfless care for the weak and the needy.*" He barked a laugh. "Well, even you can be right once in a while, Doniver. No one stands much behind those words. Rin's short on folks running around taking care of the needy."

I leaned against the table, then jerked erect when it

27

wobbled. A baker was hawking a batch of sweet cakes I could smell from ten yards away. A broad-hipped matron was complaining about a price which I'd have paid in a flash if I had it. A slim girl in a red gown waited at the matron's side, her mouth sulky with boredom. She caught me watching her and turned her back. My face grew warm. I couldn't blame her for shunning me in my current state. I looked away and daydreamed about how nice girls smelled when they leaned close.

Jarka nodded his thanks to the bookseller, and we headed for the stairs leading from the market to the wide walkway atop the city wall. I felt sicker with every step we took. A knot of people were already waiting, folks from the docks mostly, with a few better-dressed travelers and merchants mixed in. Jarka used this spot often, and people knew it. They mostly gathered to watch, though, looking for free entertainment. Jarka set his bag down on top of the wall and slid his wind box out.

I moved off a little way to watch one last time before I tried to fake a fortune on my own, but I couldn't stand to look. Instead I lifted my head to the rain-scented breeze and curled my toes inside my too-tight boots. Below the wall, gulls cawed and wheeled over the river. They could go anywhere they liked. What had gone wrong in their tiny brains that they stayed here?

When I made myself turn back, Jarka was busy with a chubby man in a wide-brimmed hat that probably meant he was a landowner from the Basket. I felt the tension in my stomach ease at how I'd figured that out without prompting. Maybe I was ready to fake fortunes after all.

The Powers save me. I'd just thought of being a fake wind reader as a good thing. I tried not to picture the disgusted look Da would have given me. Stone it all, anyway.

The round-bellied man blew into Jarka's wind box. Jarka's paper bits always settled into patterns that made him a convincing wind reader, even though he wasn't an Uplander. Of course, Jarka had lots of practice. He'd been pretending to tell fortunes ever since his cousin sent him out to earn his keep. A few months ago, Jarka'd had some sort of fight with the cousin's new husband and stopped going home. I hadn't asked him about it. Every street kid I'd talked to was close-mouthed about some part of what had dumped them in the gutter. If you were friends, you left them alone about it because that was the stuff that broke their hearts. That was what they hid in a place so dark they could keep themselves from thinking about it. I couldn't imagine choosing to live in the streets, but then, it was possible Jarka had no choice. Even in the Uplands, kids were sometimes better off leaving home. Not to grub for coins in the city streets, though.

"You had a rough voyage to Rin," Jarka told the man in the wide-brimmed hat, "but your trip home will be smoother."

"Good," the man said. "I was sick all the way here. What about my estate? I left my wife in charge. Is she managing well?"

Jarka peered into the box. "She's managing well, all right." He rubbed his mouth. "Your grain is flourishing. You'll have a rich harvest."

"Excellent." The man swept his arm toward the onlookers. "You hear that? Tebryn of the Basket will be a rich man come autumn." A patter of applause echoed off the stone walkway and walls, while Tebryn fished a tiny gull coin from his pouch and tossed it into Jarka's palm.

Tucking it away, Jarka tipped his head to shoo me toward the spot we'd chosen for me the day before. I hauled myself upright and walked toward the castle-end of the wall which, just as we'd expected, was buzzing with rich people. I set my wind box up on the wall. At least the walkway was clean here. Someone must sweep it so nothing would foul the spotless leather slippers of the equally clean people chatting and strolling past.

"Well, well," a man in a silk shirt said, "a wind reader. What's my future going to be?"

Now was the moment. Was I going to thumb my nose at the sacred voice of the wind? Well, how much did I want to eat? How much did I need to survive to get home?

I handed the man the wooden cup full of paper bits. "Toss the paper into the box, and we'll see what the wind tells us."

Chapter 3.

Fortunes

B Y LATE AFTERNOON, I'd almost grown used to being a fake. Almost. Behind me, half a dozen folks chatted about the glorious fortune I'd just predicted for a smirking dolt of a lordling. Sadly, none of the chatters looked ready to pry a purse open and hear about their own future. I scraped paper bits from the box and dropped them into the wooden cup.

My head ached like someone had tied a leather strap around it and twisted the ends. Not much longer, and I could go find Jarka and Dilly, count up our supply of coin, and buy something—anything!—to eat.

The crowd shifted, making room for a man with a nose shaped like a potato. At the sight of my wind box, he halted and drew in his chin. I pretended not to see him. Just a day into being a fake, I could tell he was such a pigeon that he nearly cooed. Given a moment to settle in, he'd swagger toward me, looking for good news. And, the Powers help me, I'd deliver it. *I have to*, I pleaded inside my throbbing head. *I'll be dead in a gutter if I don't.*

"The boy's a diviner?" Potato-nose asked. "A missing hand for the Powers' mark?"

"Aye," answered a wrinkle-faced woman with a pinched mouth. "An Uplander. Probably calling goblins, water sprites, spirits of the dead, and who knows what else."

Stone the woman. She was going to spook the man off.

"You hear what happened up there last month?" Potato-nose asked.

"Savages."

What were they talking about?

"No wonder Mother Earth struck them down with Mountain Fever," Pinch-mouth said.

I whirled to face her. "Plenty of folks have the Fever all along the Winding River, not just in the Uplands." Spots of color burst out on her cheeks, but she clamped her mouth shut. I turned back to the box, clutching the edge of the wall to stop my hand from trembling. *Get hold of yourself, fool.*

Shuffling feet announced the arrival of more people. Given the way the crowd made room, the newcomers were either powerful lords or dangerous criminals. Probably both at once, this being Rin. I snuck a look, then froze, hunched over the wind box. In a respectful circle of empty space, stood a young man in a scarlet doublet, the Tower of Rinland embroidered in glittering silver on his chest. He was laughing at something the girl touching his arm had said. Behind him, two guards scanned the crowd, the wall, and me.

My heart quickened. Beran, Prince of Rinland, King Thien's heir. I'd seen him riding through the streets, but I'd have figured him for someone powerful anyway because of the way he ignored the bystanders as if they were scenery. His guards let folks be, though, which at least made him less of a bully than a lord who'd walked past an hour ago, knocking people out of his way.

"Look!" the girl said. "A wind reader."

She was pretty, tall and slim, with dark hair so shiny it reflected the sunlight. If the rumors I'd heard all day were true, she had to be Lord Grimuld's daughter, Lineth. The thought of Grimuld made me want to spit. I'd heard city folks say Thien was a good king, but Thien was the one who'd set Lord Grimuld over the Uplands, and that was hard to forgive.

My stomach gave a loud rumble that said, *Feed me, stone you!* I bowed to the pair, face growing hot because I was fawning on Thien's and Grimuld's spawn. But it had been a long day, and the vagueness in my head meant I was too hungry to be choosy. "Would you like to know your future, sir? Or perhaps the lady's?"

"Presumptuous boy!" the pinch-mouthed woman cried. "His Highness wants nothing to do with calling up the Evil One."

I threw her a look that would have knocked her off the walkway if I really did have the Evil One at my disposal.

Prince Beran acted like he didn't hear Pinch-mouth. He had the same stunned look one of my friends at home had when he looked at the girl from the farm next to ours. You couldn't talk to him at all when she was around. "Would you like it, Lineth?"

"You're not worried he'll tell me about some mischief you've done?" Lineth asked.

Beran winked at me like we were cronies, the Powers save me. "Not a chance. We men stick together or we'd never survive."

Lineth drew her hand from Beran's arm and flitted to my side. Her face shifted a little when she came close enough to smell me, but she didn't back off the way some folks had been doing. I'd crushed the last handful of paper bits in my fist so I had to scrape them off on the edge of the cup I handed her.

Then I raised my arms, which did make her lean away a little. "The Powers move in the wind," I intoned. "Wind sweeps between Earth and Sky. It whispers of where it's been and where it goes. We humbly beg you, Mother Earth, Father Sky. Use the white of the North Wind—"

I paused while Lineth flung some of the paper bits into the box.

"—the blue of the East Wind—"

She threw a second handful of paper.

"—the red of the South Wind, the green of the West Wind."

Lineth tossed a third and then a final handful of the colored paper.

"Tell us what lies ahead for your child—" I waited.

"Lineth, daughter of Grimuld." She set the empty cup on the wall.

"Lineth, daughter of Grimuld," I said. Lineth's brows lowered. Had she heard the tightness in my voice when I repeated Lord Grimuld's name? Too bad. In the Uplands, she'd hear that tone everywhere if she set foot outside her father's manor. I waved toward the box. She blew at the paper, sending it swirling. As I bent over the tangle of colors, I watched her from the corner of my eye.

"Your question, lady?" I asked.

"I'm worried about something," she said. "Can you tell me how to settle my worry?"

The onlookers crept closer to hear what fortune I might tell for the girl the prince was courting. Prince Beran edged protectively between them and Lineth, and the older guard shouldered his way to stand like a shield between them and Beran. Pinch-mouth had to crane her neck to see around the guard's broad back.

To my surprised gratitude, the breeze gusted as if summoned by a real wind reader. The crowd let out a soft *ooh*.

When Lineth raised a hand to brush her blowing hair back from her face, I glimpsed a stripe of skin all around her wrist, paler than her hand or the arm above it. "You've recently lost something," I tried.

Her eyes widened. "I have. Just this morning. Where is it?"

So far, so good. I groped for an answer that would save me from a lie yet be convincing. Where could Grimuld's daughter have left whatever she usually wore around that wrist? She'd have searched the most likely spots. That pale stripe reminded me of something. I fished in my memory and came up with the stripe on my oldest sister's wrist the time she lost the leather bracelet Da had worked for her. She'd found it caught in the sleeve of her too-small jacket.

"Search the clothes you wore yesterday," I said and watched her consider the idea, her eyes darting from side to side, studying some scene in her head.

"Thank you! I'll do that."

I stole a glance at Beran and found him regarding Lineth with the soft-faced look of a man drunk on happiness. An idea was trying to nudge itself into my head, a dangerous idea. The Uplands used to have one of its own as lord, but he died with no heir, so Thien named Grimuld to rule. The thieving weasel was making the most of his chances and growing rich at our expense. He jailed people and seized their land at the least excuse. Da had always said that Grimuld borrowed his power from King Thien, and if we could present our grievances to Thien, he might take it back. But what would happen if Thien's heir married Lord Grimuld's daughter? Wouldn't Thien want to keep his son's wife happy? Grimuld would be in charge forever if that happened. I made my face as earnest as I could and peered into the box. Bits of colored paper blinked back at me.

"I see you have another worry, lady," I said.

She'd shifted as if ready to return to the prince, but now she faced me again with an uncertain smile. "What do you mean?"

"There's a man you're fond of," I said slowly, "but there'll be problems if you marry him."

Lineth's smile faded. "What problems?"

"He should marry someone else," I said. It was the right thing to say, a true thing even, but I was dizzy at my own daring.

"That's enough." Beran's voice cut like a whip. "I don't know what game you're playing, but it's done now."

My heart punched against my ribs, but I ignored it. I was a fake wind reader, but here was a chance to maybe make up for it by keeping Grimuld in check. "If you and this friend keep on as you're going, I see unhappiness and danger."

"Danger? What danger?" Beran loomed over me, slanted brows drew together over his nose. "Are you talking about the threat to the king? What do you know about that business?"

An excited murmur rippled through the crowd. Sweet Powers. What was this about?

The older guard pushed forward and grabbed my arm

in a vise. He bent close enough that I saw thin creases fanning out from the corners of his narrowed eyes. "Answer His Highness!"

"The king?" I choked out. "I'm not talking about the king. I'm just saying there'll be trouble if the lady marries her friend."

"Fair day, Your Highness." Lineth dropped a stiff-backed curtsy and hastened off along the walkway, gaze straight ahead, mouth pressed in a thin line. I knew that look. Back home, Jona had marched away from me like that after I admitted I'd danced with the girl from the inn even after I told her it meant nothing.

Beran had maybe seen that look before too because he groaned. "See that she comes to no harm, Jem," he said to the younger guard, who hurried after the girl.

The older guard tugged on my arm. "I'll divine a future for you, street trash. You're about to tell the Tower Guards everything you know."

I dug my boot heels into a crack between the stones of the walkway. "Wait! Wait! I wasn't threatening the king. I wouldn't threaten anyone. Do I look threatening to you?"

Beran's eyes flicked down, then up again. He gave a wry smile.

Fighting an urge to punch someone, I kept my head erect. I knew what I looked like, but I'd be beaten bloody if I'd hang my head in front of Thien's heir. I was cat hissing at a stoning king. Or a future king, anyway.

"Let go of him, Carl," Beran told the guard. Carl

opened his fingers but stayed close enough to knot them around my throat if he were allowed.

"What's your name?" Beran asked.

"Doniver."

"Where do you live?"

For a moment, my hazy mind drifted. *Where the air smells of pine, and my sisters argue, and Ma cooks porridge every morning and drags me out of a warm bed.*

Carl slapped the back of my head. "His Highness asked you a question."

I jerked alert, brain rattling inside my skull. "I *live* on a farm in the Uplands, but until the quarantine's over, I sleep on the streets of Rin."

Beran snorted. "There's that Upland nerve I remember so well." He pursed his lips, then nodded to the guard. "Leave him."

My knees nearly gave way.

"But, sir—" Carl began.

"Leave him. He has no idea what he's talking about."

Well, that was true enough.

Beran pulled a tower from his belt pouch and held it out. Ignoring the dismissal in his voice, I snatched the coin. It had barely left his fingers before he strode after Lineth. I looked at it lying on my filthy palm. It was the first tower I'd seen today, worth ten times the gull I'd been charging.

Carl leaned close. "I'm reporting you to the Tower, street trash. We'll be watching you." He rapped his knuckles against my chest, sending me staggering back against the wall. He hurried after Beran. The spot he hit felt like a mule had kicked it.

I collapsed the wind box, scattering paper bits all over the wall. Time to be gone. The gray clouds rolling overhead told me it would rain soon anyway. The place between my shoulder blades twitched under the gaze of the crowd.

"Uplanders," Pinch-mouth said. "The king should let Lord Grimuld teach them a lesson."

Clumsy because I was one handed, I jammed the box and the cup into my bag, flung it over my shoulder, and hurried along the walkway in the opposite direction from the one Beran took. I'd done the right thing for the Uplands, a thing that maybe made up some for pretending to read the wind. But while Beran had let me go, I knew what Jarka would say about trusting the powerful. The prince could change his mind because he had indigestion after supper. He could crack me like a walnut under his new leather shoes.

Chapter 4.

Back to the Shambles

I KEPT GLANCING over my shoulder as I strode along the wall at a pace just short of a run. Running would attract attention, which was not something I wanted more of. I slowed only when I spotted Jarka in the same place I'd left him. A few folks were still around, but no one was having their future read. As soon as he saw me, Jarka shoved all his gear in his bag and heaved it over his shoulder.

We descended the steps to the East Market. As always here, Jarka kept his eyes cast down, watching where he set the tip of his crutch because the steps were solid stone, but narrow and old enough to be hollowed in the middle. I itched at our slow pace. I'd feel better if we were out of sight completely for a while. Besides, now that supper was close enough to make my mouth flood, I was half-crazed to get it. Did you still call it supper if it was your day's only meal? I curled my fingers against the urge to take Jarka's elbow and hurry him along while making sure he didn't fall. Jarka would just shake me off and tell me where to put my hand.

"All I have is eighteen gulls," Jarka said. "How did you do?"

"All right." I picked over the coins in my hand, twenty tiny gulls and the prince's tower. "With what you have, enough for bowls of pottage and some small beer for us and Dilly." I tried not to show I was pleased with myself. This was the first time I had the most money.

"You shut your mouth and listened like I told you to?"

I hesitated only an instant. "I listened."

"If you watch pigeons and listen to them, they'll give you all you need to know to tell them what they want to hear."

I decided Jarka didn't need to know about my encounter with the king's son. "We should trade places tomorrow so you can work closer to the castle."

"No. The fine folks are tired of me. Besides, they know reading the wind is an Uplands trick. As soon as I open my mouth, they can tell I'm not one of you foul mountain magicians."

"Very funny. You might as well take the space by the castle though. I want to work down by the docks tomorrow. That way I can also find out if the king's lifted the quarantine so boats can go north again."

"Sailors don't have any money, Doniver. Not for long

at least. And last I heard folks in the Uplands were still down with the Fever, so the king won't be allowing anyone to travel in or out."

"I'll try anyway."

Jarka scowled. "Suit yourself. Don't blame me if we go hungry." He swung to the next step, slipped, and caught himself, swearing.

As we neared the bottom, I scanned the square for Dilly, who'd gone off with Tuc that morning to look for work as a messenger. Even though the market was about to close, she wasn't there. The permanent stalls were mostly empty, the old clothes dealers, ironmongers, and egg sellers having gone. My eye caught on a notice pasted on the pillar between two stalls.

"Jarka, look!" I hustled across the market to stand in front of the notice. A jagged line slanted across it in an unmistakable symbol for mountains that I recognized.

Jarka's crutch scraped up behind me, and his finger came over my shoulder to point at two words scrawled under the symbol. "*Wind Dancers.* What are Wind Dancers?"

"Uplander acrobats. The best you'll ever see. More than that, really, because they tell a story, like a puppet show does." I found myself smiling. "When I was six, I tried to run away and join them." My brain shook off its stupor and came alert with possibilities. "They must be going to perform here. If they've come from the Uplands, maybe the river is open again. And if they're going back, maybe they'll take me with them."

After a moment, Jarka said, "Yes, well that'd be nice for you, wouldn't it?"

Surprised by his flat tone, I turned. "I have to go home," I said. "You know that."

"Of course I do," Jarka snapped. "I'll cheer when it happens. One less farm boy to look after."

"Jarka, you know you'd miss him," Dilly said. I looked past Jarka to find her grinning at us, Tuc at her heels. "How did it go?" she asked me.

"Well enough." Despite her cheery tone, something wasn't right about her. Her shoulders curved in as if she were protecting herself, and one side of her skirt was smeared with fresh mud. "You run into a problem?"

"Nothing I couldn't manage," she said. "I couldn't find the house I was supposed to take some flowers to, so a gentleman helped me, but then he wanted to help himself *to* me. I had to hide in an alley that was dirtier than I thought. He paid for his nastiness, though." She fished a man's linen handkerchief out of her pocket and gave a tight-lipped smile. "I'll sell this tomorrow."

My breath hitched, and beside me, Jarka stiffened. Dilly didn't talk much about what happened when she was alone on the streets every day, but Jarka and I had heard and seen her in the middle of nightmares.

I pretended nothing was wrong. "Thieving will get you in trouble."

Jarka pretended too. "Like I said, farm boy, folks like

us can't afford honesty. Were you honest up on the wall today?"

"I didn't lie," I said sharply. "I was just careful what I said. If the person listening isn't clever enough to understand, that's not my problem. My father says—used to say a man has to be truthful, but he also has to use the wits the Powers gave him."

"Well, I'm using the wits the Powers gave my fingers," Dilly said. "I'll be hanged if I let you or Jarka pay for all of us every single day. Besides, that pig shouldn't get away free." She tucked the handkerchief into her bodice, where the lacing strained over her high breasts.

Warmth spread from my belly to my face. Hastily I looked away. *She trusts you*, I reminded myself, and she didn't trust many men. I wasn't going to risk fouling that up. The gown was filthy and ragged. Dilly'd been wearing the same one since her mother died in the spring, leaving Dilly alone. The man who'd brought Dilly and her mother to Rin had already been long gone by then.

"Let's go," I said. *Tower Guards, yes. That's what I should be thinking about.* Also, I was hungry, but I didn't need to remind myself to think of that.

As if sensing my hurry, Tuc ran ahead, almost tripping a young man near a big house that had stood empty all the while I'd been in Rin. Now its windows yawned wide and servants in blue livery ferried goods from a cart to the back door. Jarka stopped.

"Come on," I urged.

Scowling, Jarka drew close to whisper. "I'm going to say this just one more time. Never pass up a chance to get news for divining." While I jigged from foot to foot, Jarka raised his voice and spoke to a red-haired servant. "Hey there, friend. Who's taken the house?"

"I'm not your friend," the servant drawled, "and it's none of your business."

Dilly gasped and pushed between me and Jarka. "You're from Lac's Holding!"

When the young man's gaze fell on her, his face broadened into what he probably thought was a charming smile. "You too, if I'm not mistaken."

If a boy had looked at my oldest sister like that, she'd have blushed and fluttered her eyelashes, but Dilly frowned and took a step back. I didn't know the full story, because that was what Dilly kept tucked in her dark place, but clearly life had taught her to be cautious in a way I hoped my sister never had to be. "What are you doing here?" Dilly asked.

The young man leaned an arm on the cart. "Since it's you who asks, sweetheart, I'll say Lord Suryan's ambassador is arriving tomorrow, assuming his ship stays out of storms."

"Why's he coming?" Dilly asked.

The young man shrugged. "You think anyone lets me in on stuff like that? Tell you what. Come inside and make friends with a fellow Lac's Holder. Send these two away."

This man sounded way too much like strangers on the

street who coaxed kids into their grasp, which Dilly knew too, but she was saved the trouble of telling him off when an older man came out from the alley behind the house. "On your way, you three. Don't be hanging about here. And you, Huryn, get back to work."

With his face growing as red as his hair, the young man turned away. I jogged off with Jarka hobbling after me. "Come on, Dilly," I called.

To my relief, she followed, though she looked back at the house until the young man disappeared behind it. "If the ambassador's coming, maybe Lord Suryan will come too, maybe even Lady Elenia."

"Who?" I asked.

"Elenia. Lord Suryan's daughter." Dilly's mouth curved, and her gaze shifted to the space between Jarka and me, seeing something better than the streets of Rin. "She's beautiful, but not just beautiful. She runs a shipping business, so she hardly ever leaves Lac's Holding. She must have decided she wants to see Rin." Dilly tilted her head back and looked down her nose at us. "In Lac's Holding, women do what they like."

"No one does what they like anywhere," Jarka said, "not unless they're rich. Your mother wasn't doing what *she* liked in that house where you lived when I first met you."

Dilly's mouth tightened. "She was sick. She couldn't help it. And I'm not my mother." She marched ahead, with Tuc running after her, looking worried.

I could guess what her ma had been doing, but *couldn't help it* was more or less what I thought about being a fake wind reader too, so my sympathies were with Dilly's ma. Dilly had left with Jarka the moment her ma was dead, which told me all I needed to know.

"Ah, Dilly," Jarka called. "We're sorry."

"We?" I said. "I didn't say anything."

"For once," Jarka said.

Dilly slowed her step and let us catch up. "Maybe I should have been more friendly. If Lac's Holding people come, maybe I can work for them. Maybe they'll take me home."

Jarka puffed out his cheeks. "Why not? Doniver's going home. Why not you too? My life would be a lot easier without you two to look after."

"We should all go to Lac's Holding." Dilly took Jarka's arm. "I'd tell them you were my brothers."

"Doniver's too homely for that," Jarka said, "but they'd be sure to believe it about me and you because we look so much alike." Despite his sharp tone, he smiled, his dark head bent to her red-gold one.

Yeah, he wasn't as far gone as Prince Beran, but he definitely had a soft spot. The miller's daughter at home had made it clear to me that I was no expert on girls, but I didn't think Dilly felt the same way he did. When she said *brothers*, that's what she meant. Romance wasn't high on her list of helpful things to do. I felt bad for Jarka. Sometimes it seemed like life on the streets was one big unfulfilled wish.

At last, we turned onto Fishbelly Lane and arrived in the Shambles. Fishbelly Lane stretched wide where it first left Kings Way, but within a few yards, it narrowed enough that a carriage would never be able to scrape through. I didn't imagine anyone owning a carriage would want to come to the Shambles anyway. Houses tilted like drunken uncles, and the thatched roofs were slimy with age. I pulled my left hand out of its hiding place, glad to work out the kinks that had dug into it during the day, but also ready for any trouble hiding in the shadows. At least there'd be no Tower Guards here. They didn't care what happened in the Shambles. It was a world in itself, separate from the rest of the city. Some people eked out a living, raised decent kids, and helped their neighbors when they could afford to, and some people would cut you for a farthing. There were good and bad and strong and weak people in the Uplands too, but something about being crowded close together in the Shambles made it easier to be tense and mean.

"Let's go to Min's place," I said. "Her pottage is good, and maybe she'll have news of the Wind Dancers."

"Can't we go somewhere better?" Dilly asked. "That Uplands food has no taste at all. And what's a Wind Dancer?"

"Min's is cheap," Jarka said. "Wind Dancers are Doniver's new favorite people. We're just folks he used to live with." Jarka's voice was light, but his face was grim.

Even though he knew Dilly and I both wanted to leave Rin, he could be funny about us doing things without him.

The biting smell of onions set my stomach rumbling as we rounded the last corner toward Min's shop and the tinkle of wind chimes. Her counter was still lowered across the window, but Min wasn't leaning on it the way she usually did. Instead, she'd drawn back and stood stiffly, barely in sight. She was talking to two soldiers. Not Tower Guards though. Instead, it was a pair of Lord Grimuld's Ringmen, their loyalty to Grimuld marked by the rings all of them wore. The nasty metal things extended halfway down their right forefingers, jointed like armor and marked with Grimuld's raven sigil. With that ring behind it, a punch from one of them would break your jaw. A shiver snaked down my spine. Ringmen were supposed to keep the law in the Uplands, but most of them came to Rin with Lord Grimuld when he fled from the Fever. As far as I could see, they never kept law in the first place, but just did what Grimuld said, which wasn't the same thing. I had no more desire to run into them than the prince's Tower Guards.

I backed up to peer cautiously around the corner of the public privy.

Jarka and Dilly had kept going. They both halted and turned to look at me.

"What's the matter?" Dilly asked.

"Ringmen," I said low enough that Grimuld's soldiers wouldn't hear.

"You afraid of them?" Jarka raised an amused eyebrow.

"Of course not. I'm just being careful."

"Oh yeah, that's you all the way." Jarka leaned against the wall just around the corner from me. Dilly crouched to pet Tuc.

"It was murder plain and simple," one of the Ringmen said to Min. "Lord Grimuld's magistrate and the Ringman with him. Killed and robbed, both of them. The word is the killer headed for Rin to murder King Thien next."

My breath stuck in my throat. This must be what folks on the wall had been talking about when they said Uplanders were savages. No wonder Prince Beran and his guard had looked so grim. An Uplander predicting danger to the royal family—what must that have sounded like to them?

"If the killer comes here," the second Ringman said, "he threatens us all, not just the king, because he breaks quarantine and brings Fever into town. If you've heard anything, tell us now."

"It happened in the Uplands, thirty leagues away," Min said. "How would I know anything about it?"

"You people all stick together," the Ringman said. "For all I know, bats carry messages back and forth."

"If any bats bring me news, you'll be the first to know," Min said.

"Tell us, mind you," the Ringman said, "not the city Watch and not Thien's Tower Guards. This is Lord

Grimuld's business." He and his partner came up the lane toward where we hovered.

"Uplands witch," one of them muttered, looking over his shoulder at Min.

The other was busy eyeing Dilly with his tongue hanging out. "Aren't you a pretty little thing?" He crooked a finger at her. "How about a kiss?"

Blood pounding in my ears, I jumped between her and the Ringman. "Shut your mouth," I snarled. The alley spun, and I lay jammed flat on my stomach on the street, my cheek grinding into the gritty stone. Hard hands twisted my head, and stones dug deeper into my cheek. I clenched my teeth around any sound that might leak out.

The Ringman not crushing me grabbed his companion's arm. "Let him be," he said, choking on what luckily for me was a laugh. "Come on. We have more people to question before that first mug of ale."

The man gave my neck a final wrench and released me. The two of them walked away, the head twister muttering to himself, while his friend continued to chortle. They vanished around a corner.

Dilly sprang to my side. "You didn't have to do that! Are you all right?"

I struggled to my feet, brushing away a pebble stuck to my throbbing jaw. I scooped up my bag and settled it on my shoulder. "I'm fine," I said with what I hoped was dignity.

Jarka glared at me. "Could you for once shut it? What

was that supposed to do? I've told you and told you, we have to keep our heads down so nobody notices us. It's the only way to keep safe."

"Would you have let him make Dilly kiss him?" My voice shook. "A man takes care of the folks who depend on him."

Jarka drew back like I'd slapped him.

"He was just talking," Dilly snapped. "And I don't need a man to take care of me. Not Jarka and not you."

"She's smarter than you are about this stuff." Jarka spat into the dirt. "You begged for trouble none of us needs." He clumped down the alley, his crutch thumping with each step like a series of sharp words. Dilly shook her head and marched after him.

I drew a deep breath. It was probably a good thing Dilly didn't depend on me. Jarka was right. I was too stoning big-mouthed to stay out of trouble even in the Shambles. I followed Jarka and Dilly to Min's window.

"Fair evening, you three," Min said.

I laid my gulls and the prince's tower on the counter and waited while Jarka and Dilly added their earnings. "Three bowls of pottage and small beers for each," I said. My voice had steadied, I was happy to note.

"Is there enough for bread too?" Dilly asked.

Min counted the coins and gave me back three gulls. "Sorry, no. Flour's grown so dear in the last two weeks that I have to ask more for the bread. They say there's not enough grain despite those big granaries the prince has been building."

Dilly made a face but was quick to take one of the bowls and mugs Min shoved across the counter.

I squatted next to Dilly, my back against the shop front. Jarka lowered himself awkwardly to the ground on the lane's other side. Between us, Tuc pretended to lie down, darting looks from bowl to bowl. I scooped up a quick spoonful of the boiled barley and onion. The taste of the hot food sent a shudder right through me.

We ate with silent concentration. When I'd scraped up the last speck, I put my empty bowl down for Tuc and stood to return my mug to Min. "I saw a Wind Dancers poster in the East Market. Does that mean travel north is allowed again?"

"No," Min said. "The carter talked to one of them who said they were in the Basket when the Fever struck."

I kicked at an unidentifiable bit of trash, then regretted it when it smeared across the toe of my boot. "I'm just going around to the alley for a moment," I told Jarka and Dilly.

"Hurry up." Jarka still sounded annoyed. "It's about to rain."

I WENT BACK to the corner, turned, jogged a dozen yards, and turned again down a passage so narrow my shoulders nearly brushed the sooty walls. A short way down it lay the yard behind Min's shop. Fence posts marked with green streamers stood at either side, but Min had torn the fence down so the Uplanders who lived in this part of the Shambles could get to the shrine she'd made. There were half a dozen shrines hidden away along the nearest three or four streets, but Min's was the one I liked best because it reminded me of the one near my family's farm.

In the gathering dark, I approached the yard. It was hard to honor the Powers right in the city, but Min had piled rocks to cradle a bowl of water that reflected an early star. She'd also planted mountain laurel all around, and, though it grew only scraggily, it still smelled of home. In the rocks, Min had wedged a pinwheel. The wind seldom managed to push its way this far down inside the city walls, so the pinwheel was still.

I blew on it, sending it whirling. "Carry my words home," I prayed. "Tell them I'm all right and will be there soon." The pinwheel slowed and stopped. "I'm sorry, Ma," I whispered, like I did every time I came here. "I'm so sorry." My family was still there, right? A hollow in my chest that had nothing to do with food ached with emptiness.

Chapter 5.

Street Trash

A S I ROUNDED the corner, Dilly grabbed the bowl Tuc had been licking and handed it to Min. Min pulled the counter up across the window to close for the night. A fat raindrop splashed into the dirt in the lane. Another tapped on my head.

"Shall we head for the Rat Hole?" Jarka asked.

Dilly walked off with Tuc at her side, which told me she was still annoyed at my thinking she couldn't be safely out on her own. I checked my pace to stay next to Jarka. The lane would be slick once it was wet.

"Go on." A muscle jumped in Jarka's jaw.

"Rain's not getting down between the walls much anyway." I shrugged. "Even the rain hates coming into Rin." Water already trickled through the gutter in the street's center, though, enough to have started washing trash down from the higher parts of the city. A limp cabbage leaf swept past my foot. At home, when it rained, waterfalls sprang to life, white ribbons in the distance.

Dilly ducked into the stinking alley where we lived at the moment. By the time we turned into it, she was disappearing through a doorway. The alley slanted down to a dead end against the city wall, and the gutter spilled into a tunnel running through the wall, dumping filth of all sorts into the river beyond it.

Jarka hauled himself through the doorway, and I went after him into the dark single room of what had once been a tailor's shop. The old tailor had died a month ago. Since then the furniture and goods in the shop had vanished, though now that Dilly had found it for us, more people lived here than when the tailor was alive.

"Fair evening," quavered the old woman in the corner, her accent unmistakably Uplands.

"Fair evening, Tava," I said. From the edge of her filthy headscarf, Tava's gray hair emerged in a tangle. Her skin was dark with dirt. Da had once made my smallest sister a doll with a dried apple for a head. Tava reminded me of that doll. If you trusted what she said, she'd arrived from the Uplands only the week before. How she slipped past the quarantine, I had no idea. Tava didn't seem to have one either, and I'd asked every which way I could, hoping to find a way home. But then, from what I could tell, Tava had few clear ideas about anything. She didn't go out much, so in her favor, she guarded our place for us so no one else could claim it. In trade, we'd once or twice brought her some of our food. Usually, though, we didn't have enough. An empty pocket robbed you in ways you didn't think about ahead of time, which was maybe why it was called being *broke*.

Jarka skirted the room to where Dilly sat scratching Tuc's ear, as far away from Tava as she could get. Given the reek coming from the canvas bag at Tava's side, I didn't blame either of them. Jarka sent me a narrow-eyed look that meant, *She's an Uplander. Take care of this.*

"Tava," I said, edging back to the doorway where garbage made the only stink, "I don't mean to hurt your feelings, but that bag—" She was an old lady, so I settled for the nicest word I could think of. "It smells like dung."

Tava smiled and hugged herself. "It's terrible, isn't it?"

"What is it?" Jarka asked.

"Didn't you hear Doniver?" Tava said. "It's—" she gave the ghost of a smile—"dung."

"Do you have to keep it in here?" Jarka asked.

Tava cackled. "Just for now."

Tuc lunged from under Dilly's hand into a black corner. Claws scrabbled, and something briefly squealed. The dog emerged with a rat hanging limp in his mouth.

I shut the door, and for the first time since Carl the Tower Guard threatened me, I felt safe. I'd have been happier if the brackets meant to hold a bar weren't broken, but we were out of the weather and out of sight, which was as good as it got for a street kid. I groped a path across the room to drop down on Dilly's other side, while Jarka dragged out the torn bits of sailcloth we used for bedding. Dilly freed her hair and thrust the fancy leather clasp deep into her pocket. It had been her ma's and was the only thing Dilly still had from what she took with her when she joined Jarka. She'd sold all the extra clothes during a hungry stretch.

Getting my tight boots off felt so good, I moaned. My right big toe stuck out through a hole in the stocking. That was new. I pulled the stockings off too and rubbed the toes that had been jammed against the end of the boot all day.

"Her bag's almost bad enough to cover the smell of your feet," Jarka whispered.

"Shut it." I set my wind box aside and tucked my bag under my head for a pillow. My shoulders itched under my rain-damp shirt.

"Are you going to let her keep it in here?" Jarka asked.

"She's old," I said, "and not right in the head. Leave her alone."

Jarka flopped down, muttering under his breath. Dilly and Tava, too, stretched out to sleep. Tuc finished crunching the rat and curled up next to Dilly, smelling of blood and raw flesh. "Good dog," Dilly murmured and wriggled closer to me to make room for him. When her warmth touched me, my body responded. Suppressing a groan, I rolled over. I was going home, so nothing was ever going to happen between me and Dilly, even apart from how much Jarka liked her.

A roof-rattling snore erupted from Tava's corner of the room.

Jarka lifted his head. "Tava! Roll over."

Without really waking, the old woman obeyed. "Not right," she muttered. "Thieves."

Rain thrummed on the thatched roof and rushed through the gutter into the drain outside. I closed my eyes. *All the trash gets washed down here.* I drifted into uneasy dreams in which I ran after Da, crying in painful gasps. *Don't trust me. Don't listen to me. I talk too much. I changed my mind. I don't want to go to Marketon after all.*

A crash sent my heart thumping. I swam far enough up from sleep to think, *Thunder.* Then Dilly screamed, and solid hands grabbed my arms and yanked me to my feet. I looked wildly around. Pale morning light slid through the open door.

Carl the Tower Guard shook me the way Tuc shook rats. "Wake up, street trash. Prince Beran wants to see you."

Air refused to be sucked into my paralyzed chest. My heart pounded: *Get out! Get out!* But Carl had a good, hard grip. Besides, Jem, the other Tower Guard who'd been with Prince Beran the previous day, blocked the doorway, his hand resting on the hilt of his sword. It was sheathed, but still sharp, I'd bet.

I realized my left hand hung from my sleeve, and my knees nearly gave way. I jammed it into its pocket, but the Tower Guards didn't seem to notice because they were both watching Dilly and Jarka, who crouched, backs to the wall, feet drawn up under them, gazes sliding from man to man. Dilly had one arm wrapped around Tuc's neck. Tava was nowhere in sight, thank the Powers. I'd never yet seen Tava's presence improve anyone's temper. The smell of her bag must have still been shut in with us though because Jem wrinkled his nose and said, "Sweet Powers, what a stench."

Carl wound his hand in my collar and dragged me toward the door, my bare toes scuttling to grip the floor and my windpipe cinched tight.

"What are you doing?" Dilly sprang to block our path, her hair in a wild red tangle around her face. "Leave him alone."

"Dilly!" Jarka said.

Jem grabbed her by the upper arms and tried to hold her off while she clawed at his face. A gray blur streaked across the floor, and Tuc sank his teeth into Jem's calf. He shouted, let go of Dilly, and reached for his sword, but she snatched up Jarka's crutch and jammed it between his feet. Arms whirling, Jem crashed to the floor. Tuc scuttled backward, barking.

"Jem, you fool, get up." Carl leaned to help the cursing, red-faced Jem, and his grip on my collar eased.

I tore loose and was out the door before I knew I'd decided to do it. Filthy water from the gutter splashed under my bare feet. Footsteps thundering behind me, I rounded the corner, ran a few yards, and leaped sideways into a tiny alley. Stones bit into my soles. The alley forked, and I took the left-hand path. I ran around the curve, up two steps, and through the yard behind the poulterer's shop, dodging geese tethered to rings in the wall and squishing something vile between my toes. The geese honked loudly enough to tell every guard in the city where I was. I squeezed between the poulterer's and the butcher's and came out in Burden Lane.

I hesitated, breathing hard. *Which way?*

"Here!" shouted a voice.

I looked right, saw Carl, and took off in the other direction. Jem rounded the corner, heading me off. I rocked to a halt and was looking frantically for an escape route when Carl's arms closed around me from behind, tight enough to lift me, and leave me kicking air.

"I've orders not to hurt you." Carl breathed heat down my neck. "But accidents happen."

I heaved against his grip one more time, then looked into the flushed face of Jem, who had run up in front of me. Jem's jaw moved as if he were grinding his teeth. Trapped between them, I let the fight go out of me. Carl held me for a moment, then eased his grip enough for my feet to touch the ground. "Jem here will be right behind us. If you so much as twitch, he'll knock you down and beat you like a drum."

Jem braced one hand against the wall of a pastry shop and bent his leg to show me his torn trousers. Blood spotted the edge of the tear. "I'm begging you to try to run again."

I flicked my gaze from the bloody trousers to Jem's scowling face, then looked straight ahead. Now would not be a clever time to see what an elbow in Carl's stomach could do for me.

Carl started up the street, shoving me along ahead. Shops were opening, and curious faces peered from doorways and windows. My cheeks burned. I'd once been in the village at home when the Watchman passed towing a man who'd been caught stealing a length of wool cloth. I remembered the way the neighbors had clucked their tongues, the scorn I'd felt too. Now I wanted to protest, to cry out that I wasn't a criminal. This was a mistake. Everything that had happened to me since I left home was just a string of mistakes leading to Da's death and my living in filth with hunger gnawing my body to bones.

Chapter 6.

Prince Beran

CARL HAULED ME through New Square and up Kings Way toward the castle, visible against the sky at the city's highest point. Jem followed so closely behind that his shadow overlapped mine. I couldn't fight free of them both, but maybe I could talk my way loose before we got to the castle and I was at the mercy of Thien's son.

"Carl, listen," I said. "You got the wrong idea yesterday. I'd never hurt the king. How could I? I'm just street trash."

"Shut it." Carl yanked my arm hard enough to make me gasp.

"Let me explain," I started again.

"One more word, and I'll gag you," Carl said.

So much for talking my way out of trouble. I was apparently only good at talking my way into it.

The street grew steeper, and the castle walls loomed higher and higher. At its gate, two guards in gold tabards kept watch, but we walked past them without a word. The lingering dark under the gate slid cool over my skin, and we emerged into the pale dawn light of a stone-walled courtyard. The walls were impossibly far away and at the same time rushing toward me, penning me in. Jem limped off somewhere, probably to whine about his leg. Carl dragged me toward a jumble of stone buildings, all connected, with the tower emblem on a raised shield over a wide doorway. He didn't take me through that doorway, though. Instead, he hustled me through a smaller one, past two more guards, and up a flight of stone steps. At the top was a wide corridor lined with doors. Carl paused outside one on the left.

"Let's be clear on one thing," he said. "If you harm His Highness in any way, I'll rip your good hand off and feed it to you."

"I swear I'm harmless!"

"And I swear that's what will happen." Carl knocked.

"Enter," a voice called.

Carl pushed the door open and shoved me into the room. In a cushioned chair near the fireplace sat Prince Beran, wearing a stone face that made him look about fifty years older than the laughing young man I'd seen on the wall. On a bench across from him was a woman I didn't know, but at that moment, I didn't care because on the low table between her and the prince lay a tray holding a half-finished meat pie. I had to swallow to keep from drooling.

Carl bowed, yanking on my arm so I wound up bent over too. I straightened to find Prince Beran regarding me with flinty eyes, and my stomach curled into a tight knot where even a tiny bite of pie would never fit. I lowered my gaze. The stuff I'd stepped in was oozing from my toes onto the thick rug.

"Look at me." Beran's voice was cold.

The whip snap of his voice made me jerk my eyes toward him. He cocked his head, watching me like I watched pigeons. Maybe a ruler had to be good at judging people too, though I wouldn't have thought they'd have much practice with street kids. I stopped breathing. Carl's grip on my arm tightened.

"Wait outside, Carl," Beran finally said.

"With all respect, sir, I think not. You and I have an agreement."

I glanced at Carl to see his jaw set and the hand not on me knotted around his sword hilt, quivering like Tuc did when he was guarding Dilly.

Beran sighed. "At least let him go. He's of no use to me if you're scaring him to silence." Carl gave my bicep one more squeeze before releasing it. Shaking my aching arm, I watched him back away to stand near the door, eyes still on me in case I twitched toward his precious prince.

For an endless time, no one said anything. I glanced at the woman sitting across from Beran and flinched. Her reddish brown hair was scraped back so tightly that her face would probably crack if she tried to smile. Her arms were folded across her chest, hiding most of the pendant she wore on a thick chain around her neck, but they couldn't hide the rapid rise and fall of her breath. Anger rolled off her like waves of heat from a bonfire. Anger at me? I'd never laid eyes on this woman before. How could I already have made her so mad?

"How did you know?" Beran said.

"Know?" I repeated stupidly. "Know what?"

"Know that I was about to be betrothed to someone other than Lady Lineth." Beran slapped the arm of his chair. "Even I didn't know that, so how did you?"

The Powers help me. Well no, they wouldn't. This was my punishment for pretending to have their gift of wind reading. I tightened my left fist in its secret pocket. I'd be lucky if the Powers were the only ones meting out punishment. "I read it in the wind box." The lie leaped out before I could stop it.

"Nonsense." The word exploded out of the angry woman on the bench. She unfolded her arms and leaned toward me, neck chain swinging, breathing such fury that I hopped a step backward. "I saw not even a hint of the marriage in *The Book of the Wys*," she said, "so it's not possible this boy did in a box."

I barely heard. Instead, I was staring at her pendant, which I could see was shaped like a book, namely *The Book of the Wys*. I knew who the woman was now: Adrya,

King Thien's Wyswoman, the woman who told folks what to do based on what she read in *The Book of the Wys*. I nearly choked. I didn't know if Wyswomen really had pull with the Powers, but finding out was likely to be painful.

"The boy knew about it yesterday," Beran insisted.

"You said you'd let me test him," Wyswoman Adrya said. So that was why she was here, the trouble-making old biddy. My legs trembled. "I don't believe he can read the wind," Adrya said, "and I, for one, want to know his real source of information."

Beran kept me pinned with his arrow sharp gaze. "Believe me, Adrya, no one wants to know that more than I do."

"A test with a so-called wind box should at least rule that out as his source," she said.

"I don't have my box," I managed to squeeze out.

"There's an old one in the library," Beran said. "Send for it, please, Carl." Carl opened the door and spoke to someone in the hall, then resumed his place, scowling at me.

"I can't do it in here," I said. "I need to be on the wall where the wind is strongest." Once outside, maybe I could bolt for the Shambles.

"We'll go up on the castle wall," Beran said.

Inside the castle walls was no good. "I need to be where you found me yesterday. That's where the winds speak to me most clearly." Which was true since it didn't speak more clearly anywhere else.

Beran raised an eyebrow. "You wouldn't be planning on running, would you?"

If Beran could tell what people were thinking, I didn't see why he needed a wind reader at all.

"It's Doniver, isn't it?" Beran said. I nodded. "I lived in the Uplands for a while as a boy," Beran said.

"I told His Majesty it was a bad idea to send you away so much," Adrya put in, though no one asked for her opinion. "You'd have been better off at home, studying among civilized people."

"For the mountain people I knew, spoken words were sacred," Beran said, ignoring her, "a pledged word most of all. Is that true for you too?"

I chose my answer carefully. "My words are good." *Not counting that one lie I just told you.*

"And do you pledge your word not to run?" Beran asked.

Once, at a fair, I saw a tinker use a lodestone to pull iron filings. I could no more have looked away from Beran's gray eyes than the iron filings could have skittered sideways off the tinker's table. If I'd been able to think of a slippery answer, I'd have given it, but then, if I had wings, I'd fly out the window. "I promise."

Someone knocked, and Carl opened the door to reveal a servant boy holding a velvet-wrapped square, about a foot long and half as high. A wind box, I guessed. The velvet bag dangling from the boy's wrist probably held the paper bits. I took one last look at the leftover meat pie.

Beran had so much to eat that he didn't finish his breakfast. A bitter taste filled the empty space on my tongue.

As Beran led the way out, Adrya rose. She was tall for a woman and walked like she expected folks to get out of her way, but she gestured for me to go next, and I obeyed, her eyes poking holes in my back. The servant boy wrinkled his oversized nose as I passed. What a little weasel. If I could smell like flowers, I would. Maybe a snoot that size sucked in more stink.

Making things even better, Carl slipped beside me and took my arm. With gentle care, I tested his grip. I couldn't possibly answer whatever questions Beran planned on asking. They'd all know I was a fake, and it wouldn't take them long to learn I had two good hands. Shamming a mark of the Powers was blasphemy, but I couldn't let them lock me up. Ma needed me at home if she and the girls weren't to join me in starving. I'd pledged my word, but maybe I *should* run anyway.

Da's voice sounded inside my head. "People have to be able to trust a man's word. He has to live by it or he's lost." *Lost* was the right word for how I felt as my thoughts twisted. When they finally stopped twisting, though, I knew what I had to do. I'd formally given my word. That wasn't something you wormed your way out of with clever speech or a quick dash into hiding. It wasn't even a single lie that surprised you when it spilled out of your mouth. It was honor.

Beran led us down some stairs and out into the courtyard, where we crossed to the gate with everyone around us bowing. The avalanche of attention flattened me out so hard that for a moment I forgot to be afraid. What must it feel like to be Beran and be watched this way all the time? To me, his lot in life didn't look much different than being dragged up Kings Way under arrest. Allowing for the better clothes, soft bed, plentiful food, and absence of fleas, lice, and rats, of course.

Beran went through the gate with Carl hustling me along after him. The streets stretched wide and quiet in this part of town, but in the shadow of a garden wall opposite, something moved. My heart leaped. Jarka and Dilly drifted along, their eyes on me, their movements slow enough to look casual and unthreatening. Even Tuc trotted like a good dog at Dilly's side.

Carl's grip tightened. "If you think I don't see your friends over there, you've a lot to learn. I was dealing with street trash when you were messing your diapers. You have as much chance of fooling me as of flying."

"I pledged my word not to run."

"Solid as stone, no doubt," Carl said.

Fury burned through me, tightening every muscle. I hadn't asked to be here in Rin. In my head, I told Carl what I thought of him. *You're a pimple on a rat's rear, Carl. You're a heap of stinking donkey dung.* Once I failed this test, I'd say all that out loud. What difference would it make then? Jarka and Dilly weren't going to be able to save me. Truthfully, I was surprised they'd shown up at all given how often Jarka said street kids had to keep their heads down.

"You talking to yourself?" Carl asked.

I realized I'd been muttering my thoughts because I. Could. Not. Shut. It. "I like a smart listener."

"Smart mouth, you mean," Carl said.

Beran bounded up a flight of stairs, and Carl and I followed, the stone steps hard beneath my bruised feet. Behind us, I heard Adrya's brisk step and the servant boy's lighter one. And behind them, came the drag of Jarka's crutch, Dilly's soft slide, and the clatter of Tuc's claws. At the top of the steps, the walkway lay empty. It was too early for rich folks to be idling there yet, though the lower part of the wall would be busy. The wind smelled of grass and water and freedom. It lifted the strands of my greasy hair and dropped them again as if disgusted.

Beran stopped at a flat length of wall and raised an eyebrow. "All right?"

I licked my lips and nodded.

Carl whacked me on the back of the head hard enough to rattle my teeth. "Yes, Your Highness."

"Yes, Your Highness," I repeated. *Donkey dung, Carl.*

The servant boy set his burden on the wall and slid the velvet bag off, revealing a box made of glass strips with gold edging the rim. For a reverent moment, my danger didn't matter. The wind box glittered in the low morning sunlight streaking across the river. I could picture the

Powers swirling their breath through this box, pleased with the space their people had made.

Prince Beran nodded at Carl, who released my arm, and the spell of the box broke. The servant boy held the velvet bag out but yanked it away when I reached for it.

"Your hands are filthy," the boy said.

"Hush," Adrya said, surprising me. "Behavior like that is why I don't want you as an apprentice any more."

The boy flushed but still handed the little bag to the prince rather than me. As Beran wiggled his fingers to loosen the bag's drawstring, Jarka, Dilly, and Tuc slipped into place behind him, and a scowling Carl moved between them and Beran.

"On your way, you two," Carl said. "Take the mutt."

When Wyswoman Adrya glanced over her shoulder to see what worried Carl, her gaze and Jarka's caught. For two heartbeats, they stared at one another. Then Jarka looked away over the wall. "Let them stay," Adrya said. "The boy has a Powers' mark."

"Keep your distance," Carl snarled.

"Enough," Beran said. "Begin, Doniver."

Adrya turned, tight-lipped, to glare at me. What was her problem?

In as strong a voice as I could muster, I recited the invocation. I didn't watch Beran fling the paper. Instead, I watched the river far below. An ore boat was wallowing into dock, though given the quarantine, its decks were stacked with timber, not iron. Some of the water sweeping south had washed down from the mountains, had run past home. All I wanted was to get back there and leave these city folks to swim in their privies for all I cared. Leaving didn't seem likely now. Not in time to do my family any good.

The prince blew at the paper in the wind box. The bits swirled like colored snow and settled into bright heaps.

"Your questions, Your Highness?" I flinched at the way my voice shook.

"An important stranger is on his way to Rin to negotiate with the king," Beran said. "Can you see him on the road? Can you tell me who he is?"

Heart pounding, I looked into the wind box. Strangers must arrive in Rin every day. Beran couldn't mean the person I was thinking of. I pretended to study the paper, then drew a deep breath. "The ambassador of Lord Suryan of Lac's Holding. Only I think he's coming by ship, not road."

The weasely servant boy inhaled sharply, and Wyswoman Adrya stifled an exclamation. "People are probably talking about the ambassador's arrival, Your Highness," she said. "The boy must have heard rumors. He can't possible divine more of the future than I do. Let me ask him something else."

My knees nearly gave way. Behind Carl, Dilly and Jarka were grinning. I grinned back, then caught sight of Beran's thoughtful face and swallowed my smile.

"Go ahead," Beran said. "Another question or two

should settle matters."

"The breeze is falling, Your Highness," I said quickly. "I'm not sure I can still read it."

"It's strong enough," Adrya said. "Here's my question."

"No," I interrupted. "His Highness flung the paper. He has to ask the questions." It occurred to me that the Wyswoman might be angry because she saw me as a rival diviner. If I got out of this fix in one piece, I might find that funny one day. A day in the far, far future.

Adrya eyed me like a snake about to strike. "Let me suggest a question, Your Highness. Then you can ask it."

"Very well." Beran shrugged. "As long as I know the answer, I don't see that it matters."

While Adrya whispered in Beran's ear, I looked to Jarka for encouragement, but he shifted his gaze to the glass wind box. Even Dilly didn't look my way, but rather crouched to grab Tuc, who had stiffened, his eyes on a hole where the wall met the walkway. Adrya stepped back, looking pleased with herself.

"To provide for the city's needs, I've been building new granaries," Beran said, "but a blight's affecting the grain. What's the nature of the blight?"

I braced my good hand on the wall. I'd seen a dozen different blights on grain at home. I'd never be able to guess the right one.

Jarka clutched Dilly's arm to draw her back out of trouble's way. My throat swelled at being abandoned, though in all fairness, I could hardly blame them. As Jarka tugged at Dilly, Tuc seized his chance to slip from her grasp and lunge at the hole he'd been watching. The dog was behind Beran, Adrya, and Carl, and they all glanced over their shoulders at the scrabble of his claws, but they turned quickly back to me, so I was the only one who saw Tuc clutching a dead rat in his jaws.

When Jarka's eyes met mine, he nodded toward Tuc.

I tensed. Maybe one of Jarka's pigeons had told him something. I grabbed at the faint hope. "Rats. Rats are eating the grain."

Wyswoman Adrya looked as if I'd spit on her shoes.

"That's right?" I squeaked. "I mean, that's right, isn't it?"

"It is," Beran said. "How would you like to live in the castle, Doniver?"

Behind Beran, Jarka shook his head, and Dilly's eyes grew huge.

"Live in the castle?" I repeated.

"Yes, for a while anyway. The king has need of you…of your talent."

In a voice a lot like Jarka's, one part of my mind said, *This must have to do with danger to the king. I don't know anything about that. And how could I live in the castle and keep my hand hidden?* But most of my mind filled with a vision of meat pies so plentiful that some were left over. My stomach cramped with longing. "I'd like that," I said. "I'd like that just fine."

Dilly's face crumpled as if she were about to cry. Jarka thumped his crutch once, then elbowed her toward the steps, with Tuc scrambling ahead of them. I watched their backs as they went down into the city, leaving me alone.

Chapter 7.

Plots

TO MY RELIEF, Wyswoman Adrya stomped away as soon as we returned to the castle, taking the snooty servant boy with her. My feet kept surprising me by moving freely as if my head knew I wasn't being dragged off to jail but my body hadn't gotten the message yet. When I followed Beran into his sitting room, my eyes went straight to the table, then skittered frantically over its surface only to have to admit the truth I'd seen at first glance. The meat pie was gone. I took a step but ran smack into Beran's back. "Sorry," I mumbled.

Beran shrugged me off as if I didn't exist. He'd halted two paces into his room, his eyes on a man in the room's best chair, the one Beran had been in earlier.

The man rose and bowed. He was shorter than Beran, but broad-chested with muscular shoulders and a military bearing that said he'd kick you forward and back if you crossed him. A small scar slanted upward from the corner of his left eye, a ten-year-old souvenir of the Battle of Lac's Holding. I'd seen the man ride through the village at home, so I didn't need the jointed ring on his forefinger to know who he was.

Grimuld, Lord of the Uplands, Thien's chief councilor and one-time war leader, father to Lady Lineth, Beran's girl. Grimuld should have been seeing to the welfare of folks in the Uplands, but of course, he'd taken his daughter and most of his Ringmen and fled to Rin as soon as the Fever broke out. My muscles tightened the way they did when a rat scurried close to my head at night.

"Welcome to my quarters, Grimuld," Beran said. "Make yourself at home."

At Beran's snotty tone, glee took a quick jog through my chest.

Lord Grimuld bowed with a sweep of his hand as if to invite Beran to sit in his own chair. "Forgive me, Your Highness. I couldn't resist. I've been waiting to talk to you about what Wyswoman Adrya read in *The Book of the Wys* this morning." Grimuld ran his gaze over me, his scarred eye making him turn his head more to the left than most people did, like a one-eyed horse my family had once owned. "I heard you were dealing with one of my people claiming to be a wind reader. Is this the one?"

"He is," Beran said.

Lord Grimuld frowned. "No one is more concerned

for the king's safety than I am, sir, but are you sure this is wise?"

"I know you think wind reading draws on the forces of evil rather than on the Powers, Grimuld, but I'm willing to try anything that might help us ward off a would-be assassin."

Despite the way Grimuld was glaring at me, my eyes went back to the empty table all on their own.

"Have you eaten yet this morning, Doniver?" Beran asked.

I jumped. "No," I said faintly. Hope fluttered alive as the hint of food outweighed the realization that Beran had his way-too-perceptive eye on me.

"Carl," Beran said, "send someone to the kitchens to fetch bread and meat for Doniver. Ask for a washbasin too."

I tucked my filthy hand behind my back.

"Then see if the king can receive me," Beran went on to Carl.

"I'd like to be there if he can." Lord Grimuld flexed his forefinger, making the jointed ring squeak. "The boy is answerable to me, and I'd like to keep an eye on him."

It was true that the people in each area of Rinland answered to their own lord, while the lords answered to Thien, but I'd hang before I thought of myself as accountable to Grimuld.

Carl glanced at Grimuld as if assuring himself someone was there to smother me if I so much as sneezed in Beran's direction. Then he vanished. Beran seated himself in the chair, while Grimuld sidled around the table to the bench where Wyswoman Adrya sat the last time I was in here. When Beran pointed to the other end of the bench, it took me an instant to realize he wanted me to sit next to the thieving Grimuld. The idea of being that close made my skin crawl, but Grimuld frowned, no happier than I was at the idea of being side by side, and that was irresistible. I plopped onto the bench, careful to sit up straight. The bench was wooden so no matter how filthy I was, I was unlikely to do it much damage, but looking as I did now, Ma would have made me strip and wash on the doorstep before she let me in the house, and I didn't want to look like I didn't know any better.

Grimuld slid to the bench's far end, his face paling, just like the face of the pinched-mouthed woman on the city wall. His body tensed in the same way hers had, too. Wyswoman Adrya might believe wind reading was fake, but like his daughter, Lineth, Lord Grimuld believed it was real. Da used to say folks feared what was strange, and non-Uplander that Grimuld was, wind reading must look strange to him because despite his years as a soldier, he was afraid. I fought off the temptation to make a hex sign. Instead, I watched the door. How far away were the kitchens and how long would the food take to arrive?

"How do you come to be in Rin, Doniver?" Beran asked. "Is your family here?"

I swiveled around to face him. His steady gaze

suggested interest, maybe even sympathy. I cleared my throat. "My mother and my sisters are at home. We have a farm about a league outside of Merinoic."

"Then how do you come to be here?" Beran asked. "Did you run away?"

"Of course not!" I heard the sharpness in my voice and briefly pressed my mouth shut. "I was on a trip with my father." I stopped, misery swelling like a toad in my chest.

"Go on," Beran said.

I drew a breath deep enough to drive the toad back into its hole. "We were on a boat." *Because I nagged Da into it*, I thought but didn't say. Even Jarka and Dilly didn't know that. "Everyone came down with Fever. I was the only one who lived, and now I'm stuck here." I blinked. I'd rather be beaten til I bled than cry in front of Lord Grimuld. "I want to go home, but of course, no boats are going."

"Have you looked for honest work?" Grimuld asked.

"I've had work. Not steadily though. It's scarce with all the sailors idle. Also, you'll never believe it, I know, but they won't hire me for more than day labor when I say I'm leaving for the Uplands as soon as I can."

"Watch your tone of voice," Grimuld snapped. "I'm your lord."

A knock sounded before I could give an answer that even I knew would be stupid. At Prince Beran's invitation, a servant woman entered with a steaming basin and towels over her arm. A wispy-haired girl followed, straining to hold a tray laden with two loaves of bread, a hunk of cheese, cold roast pork, and a mug of ale. I hadn't seen that much food at one time since I woke up from the Fever. The girl set the tray on the table, then left when the woman pointed to the door.

I stretched a hand toward the food, but the woman nudged it out of my reach. I made a noise that sounded horribly like a whimper.

"It's for him?" the woman asked Beran.

"It is indeed," Beran said.

She set the basin down, dipped a towel, and handed it to me.

"You'll be fed once you're clean." The faint lines around her mouth grew deeper.

"I've always found it wisest to obey Maras," Beran said.

Eyes still on the tray, I swiped the wet cloth over my face. I couldn't wipe my lone right hand, so I plunged it in the basin, careless of the water being wicked up my sleeve. Maras matter-of-factly dried the hand for me.

"That's better." She cut up some of the pork and sliced the cheese and bread, making me feel like my littlest sister. Finally, she pushed the tray toward me, then turned to Beran. "By your leave, Your Highness?" When he nodded, she left.

I shoved pork and cheese onto a slab of bread and bit into it, only just managing to keep the bite small enough that crumbs didn't dribble out of my mouth. Ma would have scolded my ear off, but I couldn't help myself. I hadn't had meat in over a month.

Carl appeared in the doorway. "The king says he can't see you until after today's council meeting, sir."

"We'll have to wait then," Beran said.

"Perhaps we should question the boy now," Grimuld said. "We wouldn't want to wait and have the king come to grief in the meantime, and if wind reading's to be used, better it be out of His Majesty's presence."

I paused, bread laden with pork halfway to my mouth. What could I say about an assassin? If I said there was no danger and there was, Thien could be harmed, and I could see right now that Grimuld was ready to blame this plot on Uplanders. The best thing might be to keep my mouth shut, something Da had occasionally told me I should try to do more often.

It was funny. I'd spent the last year ignoring what Da said, but fool that I was, since he died, I'd clutched onto those things, like maybe that would keep him from slipping away.

"I can't divine right now," I said. "The wind's gone."

"We'll wait until we've spoken to my father," Beran said. "I want him convinced of the usefulness of Doniver's divination before it happens. Like Wyswoman Adrya, His Majesty is skeptical about wind boxes."

"He tolerates them though," Lord Grimuld said.

"He sees them as harmless entertainment." Beran's sober voice suggested he might disagree, given what had happened with Lineth the previous day.

Grimuld pushed to his feet. "Lineth and I will sup in the castle tonight. Shall we plan on seeing you afterwards?" He flexed his ring again, making that same irritating squeak. "She was upset last night. I hope you two haven't quarreled."

So no one had told Lord Grimuld that I "predicted" the breakup of Beran and Lineth's romance. Thank the Powers for small favors.

Beran stilled in his chair. "I'm sorry, but I expect to be busy."

"Very well. I'll see you at the council meeting. By your leave?" When Beran nodded, Grimuld left the room, brushing Carl out of the way as he passed. Carl frowned and flicked at the spot where Grimuld had grazed his sleeve. I decided that in different circumstances—those in which Carl didn't seize me, drag me through the streets, and threaten me—I might like him. I looked away in time to catch Beran grinning as if he thought Carl was funny. Maybe if you lived long enough with Carl breathing down your neck, that's what happened to your sense of humor.

I bit into a hunk of bread, thinking furiously. What I needed was advice from Jarka. He'd been exceedingly clever about the rats.

Beran rose. "You can wait here, Doniver."

I scrambled to my feet. "Please, I need to tell my friends where I am. They'll worry if they don't know."

"*Please, Your Highness*," Carl said, "or *Please, sir*."

"Please, sir," I said.

"Those two on the walkway this morning?" Beran asked.

I hadn't been sure Beran would remember Jarka and Dilly. Most powerful folks acted as if street kids were invisible. Jarka said they had to do that to get through the day without hating themselves. "Yes. And would you mind, maybe, if I don't eat all this, I'd like to take them some. I swear I'll come back."

Beran snorted. "If you didn't, you'd regret it."

"I gave my word not to run," I said, "and I won't."

Beran twisted his own ring, which had the merit of being silent. "Why not?" he finally said. "I've had friends who were my temporary family when I was away from home. Mind, if you run, I'll send Carl to retrieve you, and you can't hide from him. The king named him my keeper when I was only a bit older than you, so I speak with the voice of sad experience." He tossed two tower coins onto the tray. "Take your friends the coins and whatever's left here. Be back by the sixth hour. Carl will show you out when you're ready." He patted my shoulder and strode from the room.

I stared from the towers to Beran's disappearing back, twitching the shoulder he'd patted. Who could have guessed that Thien's son would be so generous?

Carl leaned against the doorframe, wearing a look sour enough to curdle milk. I set about cramming food in my mouth. Jarka and Dilly would be excited by the food and coins, and we all needed to plan if I was going to survive in the castle. A lump of cheese stuck in my throat. "*If* is a weak horse, Doniver," Da used to say, "one likely to dump you on your backside." Well, I'd already been dumped about as hard as a body could be. It was time to take a chance.

Chapter 8.

Friends

I WENT BACK out into the city and reached the Shambles still thinking hard about how to live in the castle so Jarka, Dilly, and I got what we needed, while I stayed safe. Stones biting into my bare feet, I hurried along the center of our alley, well out of reach of anyone who might lurk in a side lane. It had taken me a while to catch on to the way danger and ordinary life sat side by side in the Shambles. Even now, shabby women sat on their doorsteps gossiping and sewing, and two grubby toddlers splashed in puddles left by last night's rain, but dark corners could hide someone desperate enough to steal the sweaty shirt off my back.

I saw no sign of Jarka or Dilly, but then I hadn't expected to. The South Market was today so Jarka would be there, and Dilly had probably gone to the messengers' post in New Square. I'd find them as soon as I'd retrieved my stuff.

I ducked into the Rat Hole and immediately ducked out again. Tava wasn't in the old tailor's shop, but she'd been back long enough to leave her bag of dung. I sucked in a chestful of clean air and slid back into the stinking room. Her bag lay in one corner, with my bag, boots, and stockings still opposite. I yanked on my stockings, then gritted my teeth and jammed my battered feet into the boots. Stuffing my wind box and the sack of food into my bag, I took a step toward the doorway and stopped. Maybe I should get rid of Tava's bag. I wasn't going to sleep here tonight, but Jarka and Dilly probably would. I held my breath and reached for it.

"Get away, thief!"

I jumped at the sound of Tava's voice, then scrambled out the door to find her struggling with a man in a deerskin jacket like that worn by half the Uplands men who lived in this part of Rin. He must have been new in town though, because I didn't recognize him.

"He was going into our house, Doniver!" Tava said. "He was going to rob us! Grimuld must have sent him!"

The man gave a single, wordless cry, shoved Tava to the ground, and ran.

I dashed to her side and helped her to her feet. "Are you hurt?"

"That thieving rat's rear end couldn't hurt me." Her voice quavered. "He was following you, Doniver."

Sweet Powers. She was off on another crazy brain ride. The poor man had probably been asking the way to the nearest well.

"He was going to steal from us, just like they did at home. But I showed them, and I showed him, too." Tava sniffled. A tear ran down her hollow cheek.

I brushed rotting straw from her bony hip, then wiped my hand on my shirt. "It's all right, Tava. He's gone now."

She looked over her shoulder to where the man had vanished. "He won't come back. He's afraid of me now."

"Absolutely," I said.

She gave a sharp nod. "I'll just stay inside for a while and keep guard though."

"You do that."

She marched into the house and shoved the door closed.

With the door shut, the house would really reek by nighttime. I'd warn Jarka and Dilly when I found them. I set off. When I turned into the street running past Min's, she was talking to a slim, blond man I didn't know.

"Doniver!" Min cried. "Jarka said Prince Beran was keeping you in the castle. Are you all right?"

"I'm better than all right." I patted my stomach. "I'm full of roast pork."

"You talked them out of food?" Min laughed. "I should have known not to worry. That tongue of yours is a gift from the Powers."

"You live in the castle?" the stranger asked. He had the

thickest Uplands accent I'd heard since landing in Rin.

"This is Tel, Doniver," Min said. "Show him what you can do, Tel."

Tel gave a sweeping bow, then leaped toward the building opposite Min's. Clinging only with his fingertips and toes, he bounded up the wall, arched his back, pushed with his legs, and flipped over backwards to bounce his feet off Min's wall and somersault back to earth. He gave another elaborate bow.

If Min had handed me a pot of gold, I'd have been less thrilled. "You're a Wind Dancer."

"That I am," Tel said.

"Can I join you?" I blurted, asking the question I'd been burning to ask when I was six, though then I wanted the Wind Dancers to take me away on adventures, not home.

Tel raised an eyebrow. "You an acrobat?"

"No, but I'd work, I swear it. Just take me back to the Uplands when you go."

"We don't need anyone right now," Tel said.

"But I'd work really hard," I said.

"As I said, we don't need anyone." Tel's voice took on the same edge Da's used to right before he told me to stop arguing with him.

"Listen now, Doniver." Min must have heard the edge too. "You can still help them."

I swallowed the words still trembling on my tongue. "How?"

"The king hasn't granted them permission to perform yet." Min held up a fistful of posters like the one I'd seen in the East Market. "What we can do is make sure folks know about them and want to see their show. That way, the king will have to allow it whether he wants to or not. So tell everyone you see how wonderful they are."

"I can do that." I'd make myself useful to the troupe. They'd see I wouldn't be a drag on them. They'd be glad to let me join and go home when they eventually left for the Uplands.

"What did Prince Beran want anyway?" Min asked. "Not just to feed you."

"He thinks there's some danger to the king and wants me to read the wind for him."

Min looked at my two good hands and snorted. She'd been the one to sew the pocket into the end of my left sleeve. She'd frowned at the idea of my pretending to read the wind, but when I'd pulled off my shirt and held it out to her, saying, "Please," she'd eyed my bony ribs, taken the shirt, and told me to steer clear of lies.

"Why does he think there's danger to the king?" Tel asked.

"It sounds to me like the castle Wyswoman read something in *The Book of the Wys*," I said. "And I guess they think whoever killed Grimuld's magistrate is after the king, too."

"Tower Guards *and* Ringmen have been all over the Shambles since noon." Min's hand tightened on the edge of her counter. "Surely the prince doesn't think Uplanders are the danger?"

"He might," I said.

"If he does," Min said, "you have to talk him out of it. If they manage to pin treason on the Uplands, we'll all be in trouble."

"Don't worry. I'll keep them away from us." I glanced at Tel to make sure he was taking in how useful I was. "Was Jarka going to the South Market?"

"I think so, but he didn't say."

"If he or Dilly comes back here, tell them I'm looking for them and I'll meet them at the Rat Hole before the sixth hour. Actually, tell them I'll meet them *outside* the Rat Hole." I gave Tel a comradely nod and went on my way to the market just inside the city's South Gate.

I HEARD THE hubbub of voices echoing between the houses and shops long before I came near the market. The city was never quiet, but the human noise was worst around the markets. I felt a sudden longing for the sighing of wind in pine trees, a longing so strong that my stomach ached, despite the food I'd stuffed into it. I kept a shield of buildings between me and the noise until the last moment. Jarka would be near the gate anyway, where he could catch travelers before they'd spent all their money.

It was risky to have my hand out of its pocket once I

left the Shambles, so I slid it in as I turned a corner, emerging into the marketplace between an apothecary displaying pricey quack cures and a cutler. The polished surfaces of the cutler's knives gleamed blue in the sunlight.

Jarka was right across from me, his wind box set up on a stone ledge in front of a glass seller's. Jarka always divined the glass seller's future for free in trade for the use of the ledge. At the moment, he was divining for a tall young man in a tunic the same rusty red as his hair. I waited, shifting from foot to foot. Two women lingered outside the apothecary's, chattering. Judging by their talk, one of them kept an inn.

"I tell you," the innkeeper said to her friend, "he got the message, turned white, and packed up. He was on his way back to the Basket before I could get anything more out of him."

"His wife truly ran away? Who with?" asked the friend.

"I don't know. Tebryn didn't say, and I didn't want to press."

"You mean you didn't have a chance," the friend said.

The innkeeper laughed. "Truth enough in that."

Wasn't Tebryn of the Basket the man Jarka had divined for the previous day? The man had asked if his wife was managing all right, and Jarka said she was. I smothered a grin. Jarka had spoken more truly than he knew.

Jarka finished with his current pigeon, and the young

man strode away, so preoccupied with whatever Jarka had told him that he nearly ran into me. "Beg pardon," he drawled and went on his way.

I frowned after him for a moment. The man had Lac's Holding red hair and the accent too. You didn't see Lac's Holders in Rin much, and this one wasn't wearing the livery of the ambassador's house, so he wasn't with them. I shrugged and crossed the street toward Jarka, who was still bent over his box, gathering paper bits. Jarka said a wind reader needed to look cheerful because no one wanted to hear gloomy predictions, but his dark brows were drawn down and his mouth drooped. What had gotten into him?

When he caught sight of me, he straightened. "What are you doing here? I figured we'd seen the last of you."

"Don't be stupid. Street trash sticks together, right? I told the prince I had to see you and Dilly. And look! He gave me this." I lifted the flap of my bag and turned so Jarka could see the bread, cheese, and pork. "Where's Dilly?"

Jarka dragged his gaze away from the food. "She went to see if anyone was hiring messengers. Then she was going to the Lac's Holding house. She had some notion of getting work there. Said you'd had good luck, and she needed it too if she was ever getting out of Rin." Looking much more cheerful, he shook a handful of paper bits into their little sack and pulled the string to collapse his wind box. "Let's see if we can find her." He folded the box and shoved it into the bag resting against the wall near his feet.

"Was your pigeon from the Lac's Holding house?" I asked.

"No. He's a sailor on an ore boat. He had one of those chunks of iron ore they all wear hanging from his belt." He snitched a hunk of bread from my bag and took a bite.

"But no one's shipping ore now, not with the quarantine."

"Some other cargo then," Jarka said around a half-chewed mouthful. "Come on."

If Jarka hadn't pried out everything there was to know about the sailor, his head really had been gloomed up. Because he'd thought I was gone for good? I was torn between guilt because I did mean to leave and warmth at being missed. Dilly had spoken truly that first day on the docks when she said the city was a hard place to be on your own. I'd just never realized that was true even for Jarka, who acted so tough most of the time.

We wove our way up the street, dodging between shoppers and hawkers. I wriggled between a couple with an arm's length of space between them—Married, my Jarka-trained brain catalogued—and dodged another couple glued to one another's sides—Courting. As we went, I told Jarka what Beran wanted from me.

"I don't know, Doniver. I've found it's best to keep out of the lords' sight. My grandfather told the tale of a diviner in the Vale who made a prediction a rich man didn't like and died after the man hit him with a stick. They can crush you with a flick of their finger and not even know they're doing it."

I recognized his fear. It was what I'd felt as Carl dragged me up Kings Way to the castle. Carl was a guard, so he likely wasn't rich, but he worked for the prince, and he looked at Beran the way Da looked at me and my sisters. He'd throw me in jail without an instant's hesitation if he thought I was a danger to Beran.

"A real diviner would lie low to keep rich folks from squeezing every drop of use out of him," Jarka went on. "You shouldn't go back. Dilly and I can hide you till they forget about you."

For an instant, I was tempted. Staying with Jarka and Dilly sounded homey and safe compared to living in the castle. There was just that one nagging fact. I might be a fake wind reader, but there was a line I hadn't yet crossed and didn't mean to. "I gave Prince Beran my word I'd go back."

Jarka snorted. "So you said a word out loud and now it's your *honor*?"

"Don't make fun of it," I said sharply. "If you don't care about that, think about the food I can get for us—for all of us! Thing is, it's going to be tricky. That's why I want your help. I don't want them blaming Uplanders for whatever happens to Thien, but I don't want to get anyone else in trouble by saying they're the ones plotting against the king unless they really are."

"That's a lot of things you don't want to happen, and at least one of them probably will. I'm more worried about you getting into trouble when they discover you're having them on about the Powers' mark. They tossed a man into jail for that last year. He was lucky they didn't mark him for real."

"I have to go back," I said, trying to keep the regret from my voice.

After a silent moment, Jarka sighed. "You'll have to keep your readings vague." He drew his crutch in closer to avoid tripping a middle-aged woman hawking ribbons from a tray hung around her neck. "And do what you did today. Tell them you can only work at that particular place on the city wall, and then only at the second hour. That way, Dilly and I can be there to help."

"Good idea." The tightness in my shoulders eased. "In the meantime, you keep an ear out for anything about a plot against Thien. How did you know about the rats eating the grain?"

Jarka fluffed the question off with a wave of his hand. "I saw Tuc with one, and it seemed likely given all the little buggers we've seen."

"I'll also tell Beran I have to be able to see you and Dilly during the day. I'll tell him you're like my family. He was decent enough once he decided I wasn't going to hurt his da. I'll bet I can get food and maybe other stuff to pass along to you."

Slowly, Jarka's mouth bent into a grin. I grinned back. Looking at Jarka now, you'd never guess he'd looked so doom struck only a few moments ago. We walked on, looking for Dilly so the three of us could plan and celebrate together. Maybe this would work out all right after all.

Chapter 9.

Trips Home

THE MOST LIKELY place to find Dilly was by the fountain in New Square where would-be messengers waited for customers. "What's Thien's Wyswoman like?" Jarka asked as we headed that way.

"Ticked off, mostly."

"I saw that up on the wall," Jarka said. "So it's you, not me, she was mad at?"

"She doesn't like me, which makes sense I guess. When you think about it, Beran wants me only because he doesn't think Adrya can do the job."

"What about Beran? Is he likely to let you go when you've done what he wants?"

"I think so. He seemed really worried about his da, which I understand." In the back of my mind, a boat burned.

"Move!" boomed a deep voice.

I skipped out of the path of a tall man carrying a firkin of ale on his shoulder. "Beran gave me towers for you and Dilly without my asking." I realized Beran had trusted me to pass the coins along rather than growling about street thieves. "Does he give food and stuff away often?"

"He hasn't been around much. He was with the army, I heard, and before that the king sent him to live in other places."

I recalled Beran saying he'd lived in the Uplands. "Why? Don't they get on?"

Jarka shrugged. "They didn't confide in me."

"My parents would never have done that. They couldn't really. They need us all to work on the farm." I smothered the panic that bubbled in my gut at the thought of Ma and the girls trying to survive without me and Da. The farm always needed every pair of hands we had. "But they wouldn't have wanted us away all the time even if they *could* spare us," I said with certainty.

"Yes, well, some of us aren't as lucky." Jarka's mouth twisted. I followed street kid rules and didn't ask what he meant. If he wanted me to know, he'd tell me.

We turned into New Square. It didn't look very new to me, but it was newer than the smaller Old Square up near the castle. It was lined with rich people's houses, including Lord Grimuld's, which you could spot by the Ringmen standing guard. I usually walked on the square's other side, even when it was the long way around.

"Do you see Dilly?" I asked. The only folks near the fountain were two women filling buckets with water to tote home.

"She's probably off delivering a message." Jarka lowered himself carefully onto the sun-warmed lip of the fountain's lowest pool and thrust both hands into the water. A cloud of dirt danced away. He wiped his hands on his thighs and dove into my bag to grab another chunk of bread and some meat and cheese. He stuffed it in his mouth and snatched up more.

I recognized the signs of hunger so sharp it hurt. All the way here, Jarka must have been fighting the urge to grab for the food. All it had taken was one good meal for me to forget that, which maybe explained why well-fed folks could walk right by hungry ones. I fished in my belt pouch for one of the towers Beran gave me and held it out.

Jarka shoved a last fragment of meat into his mouth and took the coin. He was silent, chewing and turning the tower over in his fingers.

In the shadows along the square's edge, someone moved. It looked like the deerskin-clad man who had shoved Tava. For an instant, the man's eyes met mine. Then he jerked his gaze the other way. The hair on the back of my neck rose. He looked more threatening lurking here than he had running away while Tava babbled. Lots of people ran away from Tava.

Jarka shoved the coin in his belt pouch and reached for his crutch. "I have to go see someone. Where will you be?"

"I'll come with you." I felt a horrible urge to approach the man and ask what he was after and why he'd pushed an old lady. Going with Jarka seemed like a non-stupid alternative.

"No need," Jarka said, voice clipped.

When I turned to face him, he was looking at the deerskin-clad man.

"Something wrong?" he asked.

"I don't know. Probably not."

Jarka chewed one corner of his mouth. "I guess you should come with me." He led the way to a street running west from New Square, away from the Shambles and into an area where small tradesmen lived over their shops. I looked back, but no one followed, and my neck hair flattened out.

"Where are we going?" I asked.

"My cousin's."

"The one you lived with?" I was ready to back off, maybe leave if he told me to shut up, but he nodded without looking at me. I realized he was letting me into his private place because he was worried the man in the square might be after me. I felt unspeakably touched that his concern outweighed his usual prickly guardedness.

Jarka rounded a corner and stopped. On both sides of the street, signs showing needle and thread hung over shop doors. A tailors' street, then. Not many people were around since it was a market day, but near a shop on the right, a little girl crouched, arranging pebbles in a long line. When she reached to brush her dark hair from her eyes, she spotted us, jumped to her feet, and raced toward us.

"Jarka!" she cried.

Jarka patted the air with his hand. "Shh. How are you, small fry?"

"I'm growing, see?" She eyed me. "Who are you?"

I smothered a pang of loss. She looked to be about four, the same age as my littlest sister, with the same round cheeks and bouncy energy. "I'm Jarka's friend, Doniver."

"Does Jarka live with you now?"

I cut my eyes toward Jarka. "Sort of."

Jarka's mouth twisted. "I used to anyway. Is your ma home?" he asked the girl. She nodded. "Can you tell her I'm here? Don't tell Clovyan though, all right? Doniver and I will be just around the corner back there."

She scampered off, and Jarka led me back the way we'd come.

"Clovyan is your cousin's new husband?" I asked.

Jarka nodded and leaned against the wall, his emotionless face a clear message that we'd reached a boundary, and he didn't want to talk about Clovyan. I leaned next to him to wait, but it was only a few moments before a stout woman in a russet gown hurried around the corner.

"How good to see you!" She flung her arms around

Jarka's shoulders and kissed his cheek. She backed away, still holding his shoulders. Her face set in anxious lines. "You're so thin! How are you?"

"I'm fine. I have something for you." Jarka lifted her hands away and pulled Beran's tower from his belt pouch. He pressed the coin into his cousin's palm.

She caught her lower lip in her teeth. "Are you sure you can spare it?"

"Yes. Promise me you won't give it to Clovyan, though. It's for you, so you'll have an easier time leaving."

She closed her fingers around the coin. "Clovyan isn't so bad, you know. You could still come back and live with us. I'm sure I could talk him into it."

Jarka shook his head. "He's worse when I'm around. But even without me, if you stay, he'll hurt you."

"You're not still upset over that beating he gave you, are you?" the woman said. "You're too stubborn, Jarka. Me and Izabeth need him. I'll trade a little slap for a roof over my head and hers. Yours too, for that matter."

"It won't be just a little slap," Jarka said.

"You and I both know you didn't read that on the wind. You made it up because you were angry." She gave me a trembling smile. "You must be the friend. You probably already know how stubborn this boy is."

Jarka lifted his crutch and set it back down with a sharp thump. "Listen to me!"

"Woman!" a man's raised voice called.

"I have to get back to the shop." She tucked the coin

away. "Thank you, Jarka. Take care. Come and see us more often." She whirled and disappeared around the corner.

"Wait!" Jarka hitched his way along in her wake, but he'd gone only a yard when his crutch caught on a cobblestone. He pitched sideways, shooting his hand out to brace himself against a wall. With a curse, he heaved himself upright and hurried to the corner.

I peered around his shoulder. His cousin had already vanished, presumably into the shop. The only sign of the little girl was the line of pebbles.

"You want to go after her?" I asked.

Jarka's face was white. "I'd only cause trouble. Come on. Let's go see if Dilly's back yet." He limped back toward New Square, and after a heartbeat, I followed. I already had enough problems on my plate without taking on one that couldn't be solved.

In New Square, Dilly was still nowhere in sight, and thank the Powers, neither was the stranger in the deerskin jacket. I must have been mistaken about him nosing after me. "She should be back by now. Maybe we missed her and she's already gone to the Lac's Holding house." I strode in that direction.

No one was in the street in front of the house, but in the alley behind it, Tuc lay outside the closed back door. The dog scrambled to his feet and trotted to me. Scratching his ears, I studied the door. Maybe I was overly suspicious because of what I'd just seen with Jarka's cousin, but shutting Tuc out struck me as a bad sign.

Jarka hobbled up. "Where is she?"

"I don't know, but if Tuc's here, she's not far away." I walked to the house's back door and laid my ear against it. For a moment, I heard nothing. Then a burst of male laughter made me stiffen. I knocked.

"She's in there?" Jarka asked.

"We'll see." I banged on the door so hard that I had to shake my stinging fist.

The door sprang open to show the young man who'd been carrying goods into the house the previous day. Huryn, that was his name. "What do you want?" he said. Behind him stretched a short hallway, ending in what was evidently the kitchen because I could see the end of a table and shelves filled with crockery. Tuc wriggled past us and pattered into the kitchen, tail wagging.

"Is Dilly here?" I craned my neck to see around Huryn.

Dilly appeared at the end of the hall, Tuc at her heels. "Doniver! Aren't you going to stay in the castle? And Jarka. Is something the matter?" She took two steps toward us.

Huryn blocked her way out with his arm. "Nothing's the matter. They're just looking for you. Tell them you're fine, and send them on their way."

"Are you keeping her from leaving?" I tried to shove Huryn aside, but he braced his palms on my chest and pushed me.

"What are you doing?" Dilly cried. "Stop it!" She rushed forward and grabbed Huryn's arm. "Stop it, Doniver. Huryn means to help me get work with Lord Suryan."

Yanking my left hand from its pocket, I jammed my right forearm against Huryn's neck. Tuc growled and darted in to nip at his heels. "If that's all he means, he should let you come with Jarka and me. I have coin and food. You don't need him for a thing."

"I need work, and I need to go home, just like you." Dilly's face was red with fury. "You have both those things. Why shouldn't I?"

"She's here because she prefers me to you two." Huryn smirked. "I don't reek."

I hooked my foot around Huryn's heel, sending him sprawling, then shoved past him to grab Dilly's wrist. "You hear him, Dilly? He thinks you're after *him*, not work."

"He doesn't, and he's from home," she cried. "You of all people know how good the right accent sounds."

"What's going on here?" Behind Dilly loomed the older man who'd chased us away and sent Huryn back to work the day before.

A red-faced Huryn scrambled up to face the older man, all the while trying to shake a growling Tuc off his left boot. "He shoved his way in, sir. I couldn't stop him. And the one with a crutch is outside."

The older man turned toward the interior of the house and shouted. "Help! Come quickly! Intruders!"

I jumped out the doorway, dragging Dilly with me, and slammed the door behind me. That wouldn't stop them, but at least they wouldn't see which way we went.

"Let me go!" She pried at my fingers. "You've ruined everything. Let me go!"

"Come on!" Jarka was already moving back the way we'd come.

A blur swept toward me, and Dilly's punch landed in my gut. I gasped and doubled over. She slipped her wrist free and shoved me so hard that I stumbled backward and landed on my rear in a puddle next to a rain barrel. Bread meant for Dilly spilled from my bag and splashed into the water. She whirled as if to go back into the house, but when Jarka's crutch slipped, she groaned, seized his arm, and helped him speed on his way. Tuc raced after them.

So much for the three of us sticking together.

I'd just struggled to my feet when a shadow flickered against the back of the house. Some instinct honed in the Shambles made me jerk aside. A knife sliced across where my throat had been but caught on the skin at my hairline, just below my ear. For an instant, all I felt was pressure. Then pain leapt to life.

I flung my elbow up to ward off the attacker and grabbed his forearm. We grappled, both of us focused on the knife, but I glimpsed enough of him to recognize the Uplander who'd been outside the Rat Hole and then in New Square.

The door of the house burst open, and Huryn and two

other men charged through it, clubs in hand.

"Help!" I cried.

They turned toward us, but my attacker was already running. Huryn took a step toward me, brandishing his club. I skittered back, my hand pressed to the cut in my scalp.

"Where are they?" Huryn demanded.

My hand came away sticky. I felt warm blood running down the side of my neck. "I don't know."

He swung the club, catching me on the shoulder and knocking me into the house wall. I slid back into the puddle. "Uplands criminals," he spat. He and the other two ran in the direction my attacker had gone.

Heart thundering, I staggered upright again and braced my back against the house. I cursed myself for letting down my guard, assuming that since I was out of the Shambles, I was safe. But then, unlike what happened in the Shambles, this wasn't a random attack. The Uplander was after me personally. And the only thing that might mark me as a target was that I'd been taken into the castle to be the royal diviner. Not many people knew that yet, but some did because Beran had asked me in public on the wall. Uplanders took wind reading seriously. If this attack was connected, then the only reason that made sense was that my mugger was trying to stop me from identifying an Uplands assassin.

The thought stopped me where I was. Obviously I wasn't able to identify anyone, not unless I did it by accident. But how did I feel about one of my countrymen assassinating King Thien? I hated Grimuld and Thien had named him Uplands lord, but did that justify creeping up on Thien and killing him?

The bells in the New Square tower chimed the sixth hour. I was going to be late getting back to the castle. Maybe Jarka was right and I shouldn't go. But how could I stay away? Beran would just send Carl to sniff me out and drag me back. He'd had no trouble finding me in the Rat Hole. My brain settled on a vision of meat and bread. I gave what I meant to be a laugh, but it came out sounding more like a moan. Of course I was going back. Anyone who said they wouldn't had never been hungry enough.

Besides, I'd given my word. *Stone it, stone it, stone it.*

I scooped up my bag and stumbled in the opposite direction from the one Huryn had gone. Blood still dripped from the cut which throbbed along with my heartbeat. At the end of the alley, I hid my left hand and set off for the castle. A vision of Dilly's furious face flashed into my mind, and righteous anger flared in my chest. Couldn't she see Huryn wanted her as a pretty girl, not a fellow worker? She was usually so quick. What was wrong with her? She'd been deliberately dense. She'd been… I heard again her tone of voice. What she'd been was in despair.

My own desire to go home had driven caution right out of me. Maybe Dilly's had too.

Chapter 10.

A Change of Appearance

I N THE COURTYARD outside the castle gates, I slowed my steps, letting my heart and breath settle. Whoever had hit me was gone, and I needed all my wits if I was to look out for myself, my friends, and maybe King Thien. The guards both lowered their pikes at my approach, but before they could challenge me, Carl emerged from the gate tunnel. "You're late. If you were a guard recruit, I'd send you to muck out the stables." His gaze locked on the blood on my neck. "Have you been brawling?"

"Not by my choice. A man jumped me." I adjusted my carry bag on my shoulder and realized my hand was shaking.

He shoved my hair out of the way and took a good look, sending hot breath down my neck. "There's a loose flap of skin, but the cut's shallow. You'll live." He flicked a look at my hand. "Head wounds always bleed a lot," he said gruffly. He pulled a handkerchief from his pocket. "Press that against it. Why did someone attack you?"

I shrugged. "You know what the Shambles is like." It was the truth and all he needed to know. If he thought someone was after me, he might decide I was no use to Beran if I were dead and keep me from leaving the castle. I wouldn't be able to take food to Jarka and Dilly.

Jerking his head for me to follow, Carl strode back into the courtyard, so annoyingly sure I'd obey that he never even peeked over his shoulder. I walked after him, scanning a space I'd barely seen when dragged through it earlier. At the far side, horses were being led into the stables. A trio of Tower Guards entered a long wooden building that was probably their barracks. A woman sat shelling peas in front of a building that was evidently the kitchens. The tops of apple trees showed over the kitchens' roof, the first trees I'd seen inside the city. The whole thing oddly resembled the village back home.

"Get a move on," Carl called.

I reminded myself that this wasn't the village. This was tricky territory, and someone had just tried to kill me. I hurried to catch up. Carl led me through the same doorway we'd used that morning and bounded up the steps.

"His Highness says you're to bed down in his wardrobe," Carl said, "so we can keep an eye on you."

"I'm sleeping by myself?" Concealing my hand would

be much easier if that were the case.

"Don't get any ideas about helping yourself to the prince's silk shirts." Carl strode down the upstairs hallway. "If I'm not around, another guard will be."

"I'm not a thief."

Carl snorted. "Honest as a daisy, no doubt."

Shut it, Carl. Shut it a lot. I darted looks left and right. Woven hangings covered the stone walls. One showed a red-headed man standing on a ship's deck, pointing a sword toward small, square-sailed pirate ships. Lac, undoubtedly, back when he was a hero for driving off the pirates, before he turned into a villain and led his people into rebellion. Suryan, their present lord, was Lac's grandson and rumored to be the same kind of liar, though I'd never say that to Dilly. Not that she seemed likely to listen to me at the moment.

Carl hurried me down the hall and into Beran's room. A fire burned in the hearth, and the bench, chair, and table had been moved aside to make room for a wooden tub with wheels on the bottom. Maras stood over it, directing the snooty servant boy to add a bucket of water to what already steamed in the tub.

"Is that for me?" I could hardly keep from diving in, clothes and all.

Maras's smile faded. "Are you hurt?"

"He's all right," Carl said. "I've seen worse injuries in training. Mag, lad?" He spoke to the servant boy. "Fetch some of the green salve from the guards' watch room. Ask for the stuff High Highness gets from his friend in the Westreach."

The scowling boy followed Maras out of the room, swinging an empty bucket that barely missed my groin.

With a jangle of brass rings, Carl pushed aside a leather curtain and motioned me into a tiny, windowless room lined with chests and boxes. A thick pallet and blankets lay atop one of the boxes. A towel and comb lay on another.

"You reek," Carl said. "Strip, get in that tub, and wash all the dirt off. All, or I'll be forced to do it for you, and neither of us wants that." His back to me, he pulled a small chest off a larger one, flung the larger one open, and rooted through the clothes packed away there. The room filled with the smell of cedar chips, sending my heart flying to a farm in the Uplands. Ma also used cedar chips to keep the moths away.

I laid Carl's bloodstained handkerchief and my bag down, picked up the comb, and plucked at one of the teeth with my thumbnail. If I dawdled long enough, maybe Carl would leave. Otherwise, my stay in the castle was going to end quickly and badly. I didn't need to remind myself that both feeding Jarka and Dilly and getting home to Ma and my sisters depended on how well I acted the part of a wind reader.

"What are you waiting for?" Carl held a shirt and trousers up in front of me, tossed them on the makeshift bed, and turned back to the chest. "His Highness has lived among enough different people that he's more sympathetic than most until it comes to threats against his family or Rinland. You make him wait too long, and I won't be the one dragging you."

"Beran's worried about his da?" Time to find out what I could, just as Jarka always told me to do.

"Adrya says what she read in *The Book of the Wys* shows danger to the king, but typical of you diviners, she's useless in saying who or what or when."

"I thought Adrya was a Wyswoman, not a diviner."

Carl shrugged. "Looks much the same to me."

I choked on a laugh. "Adrya would spit nails if she heard that."

"I've found that one man's superstition is another man's religion." Carl pushed more clothes aside.

My world tilted a little. "How about you, Carl? What do you think about wind reading?"

"I'm just a soldier. As long as people aren't trying to kill me, they can believe what they like."

I felt a surge of fury at how ambiguous the rules for goodness had become. At home, things had been simple and clear. I had a childish desire for them to be that way again and a terrible certainty they never would be.

Setting the comb down, I chose my words with care. "The king should be on his guard. You wouldn't want to take a chance."

Carl shot me a look from under lowered brows. "Never fear. We're taking all the care we can." He added linen underclothes to the pile on the bed and dropped boots at my feet. He glanced where my left hand should be. "You need help undressing?"

"No." I held my breath.

"I'm going to see if His Highness wants you yet. Be ready when I return. Wash your disgusting hair too. I'll hack it all off with a knife if it looks like that when I get back. Mag should be here soon with the salve. That'll close the wound and stop infection. Rub it on once the cut is clean."

I followed Carl back into Beran's sitting room. As Carl stepped out into the hall, the snooty serving boy—Mag?— arrived. Carl gestured him in and went on his way. Mag watched him go, then closed the door and lowered the bar.

Alarm surged up into my throat. "Are you barring me in?"

Mag pointed. "The bar's on the inside, stupid. Bars are meant to keep whatever's on the other side of the door from coming through. Unfortunately, you're already in here, but we can fumigate later." He set the jar he carried on a side table and faced me, his mouth twisted in a sneer.

I took a cautious step back. "You need something?"

"You think you're so smart. I know you. I used to be you."

"I don't know what you're talking about."

"It's your fault I'm being dismissed."

"If you're dismissed, why are you still here?"

"Oh, I can stay on at the castle." He moved toward me,

and I backed off. I didn't want to fight him one-handed. "But I'll never be a Wysman. I'll never replace Mistress Adrya."

I couldn't help feeling sorry for the pain in his voice. "On the wall, she said she didn't want you as her apprentice. That had nothing to do with me."

"You owe me," he insisted, voice rising.

"Look, what do you want from me? What is it you think I can do?"

"You can divine for me."

"What?"

"You knew rats were eating His Highness's grain. You have the gift." He went into the dressing room, came back with my carry bag, and thrust it into my hand.

"There's no wind in here." I felt helpless in front of his half-crazed determination.

He marched into the adjoining room, which was dominated by a huge, canopied bed. I hovered in the doorway and watched him open the window as far as it would go. "Do it," he said.

"Fine." I dumped my wind box out on the bed and yanked the cord that snapped it into shape. I wanted this over with, so I'd have time to wash and dress again before Carl came back. Besides, the bath water was getting cold. I handed him the cup of paper bits and invoked the winds as he tossed them into the box. "Ask your question."

When he did, his voice shook. "Should I do what my aunt wants?"

I frowned into the box. No telling what this boy's auntie wanted. It could be anything from polishing her shoes to marrying the girl next door. "You should do what makes you happy."

"Too late for that."

"Then what makes you—and thus the rest of us—less miserable," I said impatiently.

For a long moment, he looked at the paper bits and chewed on his lip. Then he headed back into the sitting room. At the doorway, he paused long enough to take a small, jeweled box from a table and tuck it into his pocket.

"Wait." I ran after him. "Put that back. They'll think *I* took it."

One corner of his mouth curled. "Yes, they will, and that will definitely make me less miserable."

I grabbed futilely with my one free hand while he unbarred the door and flung it open. Unable to stop him, I could only watch as he left with the stolen box. I freed my left hand and slammed the bar back down into its brackets. Carl would roar if he returned before I could unbar the door, but that was better than having him walk in while I had both hands out, splashing around in the water like a fish waiting to be speared. I shifted things around on the table where the box had been in an effort to make its absence less noticeable. Then I shoved my wind box back into its bag and stowed it away.

Finally, I yanked off my clothes, climbed into the tub, and lowered myself with a groan. Despite its sting on my cut scalp, the hot water felt better than a fire on a snowy day, better than the first taste of Ma's mutton stew, maybe even better than kissing Jona at the fair last spring. I slid down, letting the water close over my hair. I'd stay in this tub forever.

A vision of Carl popped into my head, and I sat up. A cloth and a jar of spicy-smelling soap sat on the floor next to the tub. I scooped up a palmful of the soap and set about scrubbing off layers of grime while the water grew murky. Black specks that were drowned bugs floated on the surface. I finished by rubbing a handful of soap as best I could through my tangled hair and sliding under the water again.

I surfaced to the sound of someone rattling the door. My heart burst into a gallop. "Carl? Wait! I'm coming!"

I hopped out of the tub to stand mother-naked and dripping on Beran's carpet. Door or clothes? I darted toward the leather curtain. Facing Carl naked was a horrifying idea. The noise stopped. No one was shouting. No one had *been* shouting, a distinctly un-Carl state of affairs. "Carl?"

No answer.

I inhaled and tried to calm myself. It must have been a servant, maybe come to clean or fetch something since Beran wasn't here. I squashed the picture in my head of a snarling enemy with a knife. In search of the forgotten towel, I hustled into the wardrobe, wiped myself dry, and pulled on the underclothes. As I started to fasten the trousers, I paused. The black wool was softer and finer than any I'd ever worn. I fingered the shirt, which still lay on the pallet. The unmistakable Tower of Rinland was embroidered over the left breast. Could these clothes once have belonged to Beran?

Through the bedroom's window drifted the raucous cawing of gulls, a sound that reminded me of nothing so much as mocking laughter. Well, the Powers knew there was probably a funny side to this. I'd look back and laugh some day. Maybe.

I didn't want to bleed all over the shirt, so I dabbed the salve on my cut. It burned, but it also seemed to stick the cut closed. At last, I shrugged into the shirt and pulled the left sleeve down as far as it would go. It covered my hand, but the pull dragged the neck crooked, and I couldn't be sure the sleeve or my hand wouldn't slip. What to do? Laces dangled from the ends of both sleeves. When I tugged at the left one, the sleeve's opening grew smaller. I yanked harder and the sleeve closed like a drawstring bag, leaving a finger-wide ruffle. My girly middle sister liked ruffles. Stone it. Who cared? I tore the shirt off, tied the lace tight, and examined the results. It should work, though I wouldn't want to bet on how long.

I pushed my way into the shirt again, leaving the lace on the right sleeve dangling. After all, a boy with no left hand wouldn't be able to tie it. I shoved my feet into the boots, wiggled my toes, and moaned at their freedom. The boots were a bit too big, but that was better than too small by a long bowshot. Clean skin, clean clothes, boots that didn't hurt, and a safe bed inside. Sort of safe, anyway. These were part of why I'd come back here, and at the moment, that felt like a good decision, one that would make it easier for me to survive long enough to get home.

In the sitting room, the bar clattered in the door's brackets. A fist pounded, and Carl shouted, "Open up! Don't make me dig you out of there, you little weasel."

I galloped to the door and lifted the bar. The door burst open, barely missing my nose, and Carl charged in, face red, eyes bulging. He looked quickly around the room, eyes sweeping past where the box had been. To my surprise, my hand twitched with the urge to point out where the box should be and tell him Mag had taken it. But he'd already called me a thief, and he knew Mag. Before I made up my mind, Carl strode into the bedroom and crossed to the window. My heart tripped. I'd forgotten to close it. "Why did you open this?" he demanded.

"I needed to feel the wind." I glared at him, daring him to deny me an imagined Uplands ritual.

He opened and shut his mouth, then settled on snarling. "You bar me out again, and wind won't be what you're feeling. His Highness wants you. You're going to meet with him and the king." He pushed aside my hair to examine the wound. "Good," he grunted, then hauled me into the wardrobe where he dragged the comb roughly through my hair.

"I can do that myself!" I grabbed the comb from him

and began working through the tangles while Carl stepped back to scan me head to toe. His brow puckered, and as if I were eight and he was Ma, he crouched to roll up the trouser legs and tied the lace on the shirts right sleeve and the one at the throat. Finally, he took the comb from me, tossed it onto my old clothes, heaped on the sitting room floor, and kicked the whole pile into a corner.

"I'll send someone to collect those and burn them. Come."

I went after him, so relieved to have at least escaped arrest for stealing that I barely had space to be afraid of having to bluff my way through a meeting with my king.

Chapter 11.

To Serve Rinland

C ARL LED ME to the opposite end of the hall, down a narrow staircase, and through a series of passages that turned for no apparent reason. Finally, we went down two shallow steps, turned left, and entered a wider hall ending in a door flanked by two Tower Guards. Carl pointed to a bench. "Sit." He plunked down next to me.

I slid my fingers gently around the wound on my neck. At least, my clean hair mostly hid it, which meant folks wouldn't be asking me about it or shying away from me as a street thug.

Footsteps tapped on the stone floor. Wyswoman Adrya arrived and scowled at me. She inclined her head toward the closed door. "The council is still meeting?" Carl nodded, and Adrya sat across from us.

Carl shifted on the bench. "Do you know this girl,

Adrya? Is she good-natured, kind?"

"I don't know. She was a child when I left Lac's Holding," Adrya said.

I heard the leftover traces of a drawl that I'd missed before. "Are you from Lac's Holding, Mistress?"

She tilted her head back and looked down her nose. "I used to be. Now I'm from the City of Rin."

She annoyed me. It wasn't my fault Beran didn't trust her to keep the king safe on her own. "I have a friend who's frantic to get home to Lac's Holding. She'd never leave if she could help it."

Adrya shrugged. "Then your friend doesn't care about learning or books."

"She has other things on her mind, like finding enough food. Aren't Wyswomen supposed to care about that? Doesn't *The Book of the Wys* say you care about the weak and the needy?"

Carl looked back and forth between us with his mouth twitching.

"I thought you couldn't read," she said.

"I can't. Another friend read it to me."

"You have a good memory, then. I've observed that in Uplanders before. I suppose you have to because you can't preserve wisdom in writing." She fiddled with her pendant. "The Wys serve all people best by insuring good rule. Clearly that means King Thien. Suryan is concerned only about his own province."

I glanced at the door guards. This wasn't the time or

place to say Thien chose badly when he made Grimuld lord.

The door opened, and a stream of men poured out. Carl snapped to attention, then dipped to yank me to my feet.

The men all looked as if they'd been born wearing their costly clothes. They didn't even glance at Carl or Adrya, much less at me. I spotted the tree insignia of the Westreach on one chest and the scarlet flower of the Vale on another. I felt like an arm had wrapped around my chest and squeezed. These were the lord rulers of Rinland's provinces, or the men they'd sent to represent them in advising King Thien.

A man in an ankle-length purple gown paused near us to wait for a second man in a gold-trimmed uniform distantly related to the one Carl wore. "Well, that's a surprise," muttered the man in the gown. "I wonder how long His Majesty has been planning that."

"Grimuld didn't like it. Did you notice he clearly already knew?" the man in the uniform said. "I'll wager he's been arguing about this since he first heard. Thien must be up to one of those schemes he hatches on his own."

"Thien has always been a good strategist," the man in the gown said. "But after leading the army at the Battle of Lac's Holding, Grimuld will never trust that Suryan isn't about to kill us all in our beds. Besides, he had his daughter in mind for that job."

"I fear Beran did too." The two men moved out of hearing, and no more men came out.

From inside the room, Lord Grimuld spoke. "Your Majesty, I beg you to reconsider. Suryan is not to be trusted. Marrying your heir to his daughter will not result in a lasting alliance."

"We thank you for your counsel, Grimuld," said a deep, in-charge voice that made my stomach drop even though I was all the way out in the hall. "You know how we've trusted you to keep Rinland safe, but a country can't battle its way out of every problem. The decision has been made. Beran, you have another matter for our attention?"

"Yes, sir. One moment." Beran appeared in the doorway, face pale enough that I thought he might be sick. He beckoned to us.

Carl moved close and spoke in a low voice. "I delivered your message."

"Thank you." Beran's speech was clipped. "Come in."

My throat worked, but there was no spit in my mouth to swallow. Like the cat, I was about to have a chance to hiss at my king, which no one had told me would be terrifying. Wyswoman Adrya swept into the chamber. Carl prodded my back, and I moved on unsteady legs, my new boots clattering like horseshoes on the stone floor. Carl shut the door, closing us into a windowless chamber lit by ornate lamps. The room smelled ripely of leftover sweat, which men in fancy clothes evidently produced too. Beran seated himself on one side of the table that dominated the room. Adrya settled on the other, next to Lord Grimuld, who'd stayed behind when the other lords left. Grimuld's face was flushed, but at least his temper wasn't aimed at me.

Then my eyes were drawn to the table's end, where, in a high-backed chair, sat King Thien. I'd seen him riding through town, surrounded by guards, bannermen, and lords, so I knew the king was dark, with the solid build of middle age laid over muscle. But I'd never before had his intent brown eyes boring into my own as if he could read all my secret thoughts. My insides shriveled into a tight little ball, and I wasn't the only one who was intimidated. Adrya and Grimuld both turned slightly toward Thien but sat back in their chairs as if to give him more space.

Evidently too subdued in Thien's presence to smack me on the head, Carl nudged my spine, and I gave a hasty bow.

Thien raised an eyebrow at Beran. "Yes?"

"My lord," Beran said, "this is Doniver of the Uplands. He has some talent as a reader of the wind, and with your permission, I intend to ask his help in uncovering the danger Adrya has seen in *The Book of the Wys*." The prince nodded respectfully to the sour-faced Wyswoman. I judged it would take more than that to sweeten her, although maybe she'd ease up for Beran when she wouldn't for me.

The king drummed his fingers on the arms of his chair. "A wind reader?" He lifted an eyebrow at Lord

Grimuld. "One of your people?"

"I've tried, but I can't keep the fools from indulging in every kind of evil practice." Grimuld thumped his ring on the table. "So of course, the Fever rages on."

"Really, Grimuld," Adrya said, "they're ignorant, not evil."

I couldn't decide if Grimuld or Adrya offended me more.

Thien lifted a single finger from the arm of his chair, and both Grimuld and Adrya clamped their mouths shut. I'd give a lot to be able to do that trick too. "The danger Adrya saw was vague, Beran, and over the years I've found it doesn't do to become obsessed about predictions of what might or might not happen. Adrya would be the first to tell you that *The Book* shows only the possible, not the inevitable."

I glanced at Beran. *Go ahead and argue*, I urged silently. *You need me to stay in the castle.*

"I understand, sir," Beran said, "but this concerns your safety." His voice was toneless, the words delivered evenly. "I think Doniver's talent is genuine, judging by something he told Lady Lineth yesterday." Lord Grimuld threw him a sharp-eyed look but held his tongue. For a moment, Beran clenched his teeth as if he hated to let the words escape. The pause lasted long enough that the king turned his head to study him, showing a nose like a hawk's beak. He and Beran were both dark, but they didn't look much alike.

"Well?" Thien said.

"Doniver told her she had a friend but the friendship wouldn't turn out the way she hoped. The boy said her friend should marry someone else because otherwise he foresaw danger." Beran gave his father a level look, and I changed my mind about their not looking alike, because Adrya and Grimuld were both leaving space for Beran too. When it suited them, father and son could both ignore everyone else and concentrate on their own concerns. I shivered. "Since the boy was right about the false hopes," Beran went on, "I think we need to take him seriously about the danger, and I'm concerned it might still loom despite the fact that I am indeed to marry someone other than Lineth."

Thien's face stiffened into a mask. The air in the room quivered with tension. "You've made promises without my permission? Without consideration for the consequences to Rinland?"

"No, sir; only hoped to. After all, Lineth would tie the Uplands to us in the same way Elenia ties Lac's Holding."

Grimuld crossed his arms over his chest but had the wits to stay out of the way. I felt like I was watching a battle between long-horned sheep. Was it between father and son or only king and prince?

"Lord Grimuld already ties the Uplands to us," Thien said.

For a moment, the room was silent, as he and Beran exchanged a long look. Carl squeezed my shoulder tightly enough to hurt, but I didn't think the guard even knew he was doing it. Then Beran put his hand over his heart and leaned forward in a seated bow. "I live to serve Rinland and her king."

Thien's flinch was so short lived, I almost missed it, but that look told me that a father hid under the kingly manner. Then he ran a palm over his face, cleaning it of emotion. Carl's soft sigh stirred my clean hair.

"At the moment," Beran said in an astonishingly steady voice, "the service I wish to provide is to insure your safety, sir. Adrya suspected Doniver might have been simply guessing in what he told Lineth, so I tested him further. I'm sure he can read the wind."

I shifted uneasily. If Beran ever found out I was faking, he was going to feel like a total fool. That could kick up a hornet's nest of trouble. But I couldn't afford to feel guilty about using Beran. I need him to convince Thien that the castle should keep feeding me and my friends.

"I must admit, I'm concerned," Lord Grimuld said. "If there's danger to you, Your Majesty, my magistrate's murder suggests that this boy's people are behind it. He may be cooperating with the assassin, worming his way in here to do you harm."

"I wouldn't!" I cried. "Beran, I mean Your Highness, I never would."

"Shh," Carl hissed.

"Your countrymen may be using you." Grimuld turned to me.

His scorn for Uplanders got under my skin like a chigger. I strained toward him, held back by Carl's hand on my shoulder. "I give you my word that I mean the king no harm. If you knew the Uplands at all, you'd know that was good enough." My wound throbbed. *I truly mean no harm*, I thought desperately. *But I can't be sure what that attack on me means about other Uplanders.*

"I also think the danger comes from the Uplands," Wyswoman Adrya said. "*The Book of the Wys* passage I read this morning spoke of a cold wind from the mountains."

Thien's keen gaze fixed on me, and I struggled to stand still under the inspection. "When he came home from a stay there," Thien said, "His Highness reported that Uplanders are more outspoken than wise people usually are, but they have the great virtue of holding a man's word sacred."

"They do." My hidden hand twitched inside the sleeve. My stomach's memory of hunger said I'd done only what I had to in order to survive and help my friends survive too. Maybe a word that saved a friend was sacred, even when it was a lie. If that was dishonorable, then the Powers shouldn't have left me on my own in Rin. "I give you my word I mean you no harm. Sir," I added.

Carl's fingers loosened by a hair.

"Lord Grimuld," Beran said, "I know you aren't happy that I want to use a diviner, but you want to know who killed your magistrate. Perhaps Doniver can tell us."

Help Grimuld find the Uplanders who'd killed his magistrate? Never! Then I remembered I couldn't divine anything anyway. Was that bad news? Good news? The Powers' little joke?

"I could find the killer myself," Grimuld said, "if His Majesty would allow me to treat these people with proper severity. A few public hangings and confiscations of the villains' property would teach the rest of them to behave."

I stopped breathing.

"Enough, Grimuld," King Thien said, and Grimuld snapped his mouth shut so fast I was surprised he didn't bite his tongue. "Adrya, I assume you are continuing to pray for insight?"

"I'll consult *The Book*, just as I always do, sir," Wyswoman Adrya said. "The boy is welcome to try to see more in a box." Her tone made it clear how unlikely she thought that was. Well, she and I thought alike on that one.

"Then we're agreed," Prince Beran said. "Doniver will help us find those who wish harm to the king or Lord Grimuld."

All eyes turned on me. A trickle of sweat ran down my back. "I'll do…what I can." I hesitated then spoke to Thien rather than Grimuld. "Sir, is the Fever still bad?"

"Yes," Thien said. "Lord Grimuld received a messenger bird this morning."

Grimuld shook his head sadly. "My men tell me they've found even more wind shrines than they expected.

The Fever will burn until they destroy them." Grimuld leaned toward Thien. "But Your Majesty, bad as the Uplanders are, the untrustworthy actions of Lac's Holding are worse. You must reconsider this marriage."

Beran stared at the tabletop, his jaw tight.

"Lord Grimuld, you know how I rely on your judgment, but you will not argue further." Thien glanced toward Beran's lowered head and, though his hands tightened on the arms of his chair, he went on anyway. "Rinland has been divided long enough. It's not good for my people's safety or well-being, and if I can mend the situation, then doing so is my duty."

I couldn't tell if he was arguing with Grimuld or Beran, but Grimuld took it to be himself. My chest swelled with savage satisfaction at the way his face reddened. In my head I heard Da say, *A man needs to recognize wrong when he sees it.* Grimuld was wrong about everything, and he needed to know it. "You're wrong about why the Fever's in the Uplands. It can't be the wind shrines. They're here in Rin, and there's no Fever here."

Grimuld's head turned sharply toward me. "That can't be true." His eyes were wide enough to show a border of white. He clenched his fists, bending the jointed armor of his ring with little bat squeaks.

"It is true." I smiled coldly.

"Enough, Grimuld," Thien said again, more sharply this time. "Very well, Beran. You may let your mountain diviner read the wind as best he can."

I sagged a little in Carl's grip. Good. All I had to do was watch my back and keep food coming long enough for the Fever to end in the Uplands. Oh, and stay out of jail for stealing a jeweled box. Then I could slip away and go home.

Wyswoman Adrya twitched, jingling her chain, but said nothing.

"You'll listen to any warning he gives?" Beran said.

"Assuming it's not too ridiculous, I'll listen."

"Thank you, sir." Beran jumped to his feet and bowed. "By your leave?"

"Go." Thien nodded to Adrya, who had also risen.

As Beran hastened out the door, I had a sudden memory of thanking Da for agreeing to the timber selling trip and of me rushing out of the room before he could change his mind. I suspected Beran might be doing the same thing. The Powers forbid Beran suffer the same loss I had because of the favor he'd begged. I was grateful that, as Carl said, they weren't relying only on me for the king's safety.

When Wyswoman Adrya jostled me on the way out, I caught an unexpected whiff of perfume sweeter than anything I'd expect from her. She vanished into a side hallway.

Behind us, Lord Grimuld said, "I'd like another word, if I may, sir. I swear it's not about the marriage." I glanced over my shoulder in time to see Grimuld close the door.

Face impassive, Beran paused in the corridor, waiting

for Carl and me.

"I'm sorry, Beran," Carl said in a low voice. "I thought the council might talk him out of it."

Beran gave a painful smile. "Lord Grimuld tried."

Carl awkwardly patted his shoulder.

"See that Doniver gets to supper," Beran said. "Then tuck him up in my quarters. I want him rested. He and I will be on the wall right after prayers tomorrow to see what he can tell me. Right now, I need to bash someone with a sword." He strode away, closed in with whatever was on his mind. I felt sorry for him. It was good for the Uplands that Lord Grimuld's daughter wasn't marrying Thien's heir, but Beran seemed fond of Lineth, so this must be hard for him. I had problems, the Powers only knew, but at the moment, I was glad I was only wearing a prince's clothes.

Chapter 12.

Fathers and Sons

J AW TIGHT, CARL watched Beran until he vanished around a corner.

"He was the only decent person around that table," I said. "No one else cared who they hurt as long as they kept power."

Carl sighed. "That was about love as much as power."

"Beran and Lineth."

Carl shook himself like he was surprised to find it was me he was talking to. "Among others. What am I supposed to do with you until supper?" he demanded, as if I was the one who'd said we should hang about together.

"I could just look around," I offered. I wanted to find Mag and make him give the jeweled box back.

Carl snorted. "Not likely. You come with me." He charged off along the hall, leaving me scrambling to keep up. We twisted our way through more irrationally turning corridors until Carl shoved a door open and we emerged into the courtyard, squinting into the westering sun.

A man shouted, and the clang of steel rang from near the barracks. Through a screen of soldierly backs, I glimpsed two Tower Guards sparring while a gray-haired man barked criticism. Beran wasn't among them yet, of course, but would be soon. I wouldn't mind seeing the prince swing a sword. I took a step in the men's direction, but Carl waved his hand toward the courtyard's opposite side. "This way."

Head still turned to watch the soldiers, I trailed Carl toward the kitchens. The smell of roasting meat snapped me to attention. Maybe Carl meant to feed me even before supper.

With his usual ability to strangle my hopes, Carl led me past the kitchens and opened a gate. Reluctantly, I followed him through and found myself looking at rows of apple trees. For a moment, I felt as if I'd been lifted out of the city and moved thirty leagues north to the Uplands. The stone wall and the rustling leaves muffled the sounds from the courtyard. I could almost pretend I was in the orchard behind my family's farmhouse. Longing to be there for real rose so strongly in my throat, I thought I might choke.

Farther along the row before us, a man stood on a stool, wielding wicked-looking shears on a tree branch. He stopped as we approached. "He's back there, Carl," he said, pointing with the shears.

"How is he?" Carl asked.

The man shrugged. "He doesn't complain."

Wrinkles appeared between Carl's brows. He walked another dozen yards to where the far wall showed through the gnarled branches. A short way to our right, an old man sat on a bench, eyes closed, face raised to the westering sun. Carl tromped on a thick twig, and the old man jumped and blinked. He glared at Carl. "I wasn't asleep."

Carl grinned. "Of course not." He dropped onto the bench. "How are you, Da?"

I blinked, then reminded myself that obviously Carl had parents, though picturing him as a little boy staggered me.

"Fine." The old man inspected me with Carl's keen eyes nested in wrinkled folds. "Who's this? You taking on another boy to cluck over now that your charge is old enough to tell you to mind your own business?"

Cluck over me? I pictured Carl crouching to roll up my trouser legs like he was Ma. I choked back a laugh. Maybe the old man was right.

"Beran's taken him in, not me," Carl said. "Or maybe been taken in by him." He narrowed his gaze at me. "I'm thinking he might be low enough to take advantage of a young man's fear for his father."

I froze. Carl's suspicion was too close to reality. I clenched my teeth. Why shouldn't I think of my family before Beran's?

The old man cocked his head. "Speak up, lad. What's your name?"

"Doniver of the Uplands, sir."

"Call me Grandda. Everyone does." He pointed a gnarled finger at the trees behind me. "You're from the Uplands? What kind of apples do you think these are?"

I eyed the nearest tree. "They look sort of like the Robin Reds we have at home, but they're too big for the time of year."

"Clever lad!" Grandda heaved himself to his feet and tottered toward me, wobbly enough that I rushed to take his elbow.

Carl got to the other elbow first. "Get away," he snapped at me.

"Oh, shush." Grandda shook him off. "The boy's not going to drop me." He leaned against my hold. Carl inched backward to perch on the edge of the bench, watching every twitch the old man made. "The shoots came from the Uplands," Grandda said. "Robin Reds, they were. Hardy, which is what I wanted, but too tart, you have to admit."

"They make good cider," I said.

"Strong enough to knock you on your rear, I hear," Grandda said, sounding approving. "When you graft the shoots onto southern sweetness, though, you get fruit the Powers could eat for a treat."

"What do you mean, *graft*?" I staggered a little under his weight as he tipped sideways. Carl lifted his rear off the bench, then settled down again.

Grandda launched into an enthusiastic explanation. I slitted my eyes, trying to picture what the old man was describing while holding him up with my one good hand. Finally, I ran out of questions and lowered him back on the bench. Carl leaned back and let his shoulders sag.

"Tongues are wagging," Grandda told him. "They say your boy is about to be betrothed to some foreign woman."

"Not foreign," Carl said. "It's Lady Elenia, Suryan's daughter from Lac's Holding. That's part of Rinland now."

"Might as well be foreign." Grandda sniffed. "I hear Suryan won't set foot in Rin."

"True enough. The king hopes this marriage will turn Suryan into a better subject. He needs Suryan's port, just as he needs Grimuld's iron, but he'd rather get them by sweet talk than swords."

"How's the boy taking it?"

Carl grimaced. "At least he's saved from having Lord Grimuld as a father-by-marriage."

"Many's the lover who mislikes his girl's father." Grandda cackled. "The old man gets in the way after all. I expect the boy would have learned to put up with Grimuld if he had to."

The old man was right about that. Da hadn't gotten on with Ma's father either, but for Ma's sake, they'd been civil when we were at big family gatherings. Pain twinged in my chest.

"Grimuld's genuinely concerned for the good of Rinland," Carl said. "I'll give him that. And he was a wily war leader. He thinks this marriage is wrong, and he won't give up easily. He's probably at home plotting right now, so Beran may wind up with Lineth after all." He nodded along to his own words and perked up a little.

"I don't see how you can know what Grimuld will do," I said, making Carl scowl again. "He was spinning like a top in there, trying to decide if he hated Lac's Holding or the Uplands more. This is our Uplands *lord*, mind you."

"Both places make trouble," Carl said. "Thien hoped to calm you wild Uplanders by putting his war leader in charge, and he hopes Beran will take care of Lac's Holding for him."

"Doesn't Beran's da care what Beran wants?" I asked. "Mine would have." The hollow place inside me twinged again.

"Things are complicated between fathers and sons." Carl rubbed his hand over his face. "You want him to be happy, but you also want him to be honorable, strong, self-sacrificing if he has to be. It doesn't always work out well."

I pushed away the thought of Da groaning but letting me help care for the sick on The *Rose of Rin*. Something in Carl's voice made me think he wasn't talking only about Thien and Beran. Grandda patted his knee, and Carl gave him a half smile.

"And of course Thien has the weight of a country on his shoulders," Carl said, "a weight he'll pass on to Beran.

He always has to think of Rinland. Always."

Somewhere off to our left, a man said, "Leave me." My heart sped up. I knew that power-steeped voice. As if we'd called him by talking about him, Thien was in the orchard. I glimpsed him at the end of a row of trees as a Tower Guard turned away. I held very still. I had no desire to have Thien's hawk-sharp eyes measure me a second time.

"What's he doing here?" I whispered.

"I expect he's come to sit by his tree," Grandda said in a lower voice. "He does that sometimes."

"Aren't they all his?"

"Yes, but the day his son was born, he came in here and asked to plant a tree. His wife was Forest born, you see, and he did it to please her, which shows he's a smart man." Grandda cackled again. "Did the work himself with me telling him how. Talked to me more than he'd done since he was a tiny lad. *The boy is a wonder*, he said."

"They all are," Carl murmured. He looked off along the rows of trees, with his mouth drooping as if he were peering into some dark space of his own.

We waited without moving. Eventually, Thien passed the end of an aisle of trees and left the orchard, taking his guards with him. For another long moment, we sat in silence. I tried to match the king I'd seen talking to Beran in the council chamber with a young father who saw his new son as a *wonder*. Had Da thought of me like that? I'd seen him look at my newborn sister as if she were magical.

"Thien should take a good look at Beran," Carl said.

"He needs to find out how fortunate a father he is before it's too late to mend matters."

Too late, echoed in my head.

"All fathers make mistakes," Grandda said.

Mine surely did, I thought. *He followed me onto that boat.*

"The boy'll be fine," Grandda said gruffly. "He's lucky to have you."

When a horn sounded in the courtyard, Carl rose. "We have to be on our way, Da. Will you come to the Hall for supper?"

The old man shook his head. "Not tonight. Maras will see I'm fed."

"Shall I take you to your room?" Carl asked.

"Not yet," his father said.

Carl bent to kiss his withered cheek and beckoned to me. We started toward the gate.

"Come see me when you can, lad," Grandda called. "I'll show you how to graft."

"I will," I said over my shoulder. "Thank you."

"You gave him a chance to deliver one his favorite lectures," Carl said as we went through the gate.

When I turned toward him, he was smiling, apparently at me, but the look disappeared so quickly I decided I must have been mistaken. "I never thought I'd find a farmer in Rin." I cleared my throat. "My da would have been interested in what he was saying." He'd have been interested in a lot of things that weren't ever going to interest him now.

Chapter 13.

Filling Empty Spaces

C ARL STEERED ME into the castle and along crooked hallways toward the sound of male voices until he halted in a wide space at the end of a corridor. Men and boys already milled around troughs along the walls. A buzz of conversation spilled through a nearby doorway.

A cheery looking man in a padded doublet spoke to Carl. "The Hall's crowded tonight."

Carl grunted and stepped up to an empty trough. A basin was set in the stone with a bronze knob and spout jutting above it.

The man in the doublet glanced my way. "His Highness's diviner?"

Carl nodded. He turned the knob, and to my surprised fascination, water gushed into the basin.

"Where's the water coming from?" I asked.

"Cisterns on the roof." Carl scooped a fingerful of soap from a little dish and began washing his hands.

The man in the doublet seemed about to say more but stopped when Carl turned his back. The man pulled a cork from his basin, and the water drained away. A servant boy hastened to offer him a towel. He dried his hands and went through the doorway into what was presumably Thien's Great Hall.

"We're eating in there?" My stomach fluttered with something besides hunger. The more people I had to fool, the more chances I had to foul up.

"If you wash your hands—hand, we are." Carl's cheeks turned faintly pink. "Sorry," he growled.

Ducking my head to hide any guilty looks, I shoved my right hand into the water, and splashed it around, though since I'd just had a bath, it was cleaner than it had been in a long time. My fingers curled to cling to my left sleeve, securely out of Carl's sight. Like Beran, Carl would feel like an idiot if he ever found out I wasn't maimed, which might mean my unmaimed state would end. The boy appeared with a towel that I swiped at before following Carl into the Hall.

Heat washed over me, spiked with smoke from the oil lamps. I was battered by the roar of talk from men and women sitting along the outer edges of two long tables or milling about finding their places. Through a doorway directly across from us, women and girls drifted into the room.

Carl paused to run his gaze along the tables. "Where shall we put you?"

I scanned the tables too. Better-dressed folks sat at the far ends, closest to a third table spanning the space between them. That third table held several of the men who had emerged from Thien's council chamber that afternoon, along with women who looked like polished treasure in gowns of blue, yellow, and green. Lord Grimuld sat next to Lineth, who was looking down at the tabletop and toying with a spoon. Her father patted her hand, and she gave him a weak smile. Guilt took a jab at my heart.

Back off. I did the right thing.

"I can just sit with you," I said. Sweet Powers, I was clinging to Carl. I must feel even more out of place than I'd realised.

"I have business elsewhere." Carl eyed three boys seated nearby.

I put my Jarka-trained divining skills to work. The boys wore simple gold tunics with leather belts. Flecks of hay lurked in one head of dark hair, and a second boy bore a hastily cleaned smear down his front. Horse slobber, I identified from experience. Stable boys, then. I could manage them. I'd ask them to share their superior wisdom, and maybe they'd tell me something I could use in divining. At least they weren't likely to arrest me. "I can sit with them if you want."

"You won't smart off to them?" Carl sounded

doubtful.

"I'll just keep my mouth shut."

One of the boys caught me watching them and said something to the others. All three of them spit on their left hands, warding off its loss, no doubt.

"That's right," I muttered. "Spit your tiny brains out."

"Not there." Carl's face creased in a smile. "I know. Your fellow diviner dismissed her apprentice yesterday. You can have his place." He strode down the length of the room to where Adrya sat, not far from the head table.

"No!" I tried to catch Carl's sleeve but was too late. I could follow Carl or stay by myself. I followed.

Carl indicated the empty space on the bench next to Adrya. "Here you are, Adrya. Doniver's at your service."

Adrya's eyes narrowed. "Carl!" she called to the guard's retreating back.

I shared her outrage. "It's all right, Adrya," I said loudly. "Carl says we're both diviners anyway."

"What!"

Carl's shoulders hunched, but he kept going and vanished in the crowd.

"Is this your new apprentice, Adrya?" asked the man on Adrya's other side.

"Of course not," Adrya snapped. "Oh, sit down, boy. It won't hurt you to serve your betters." She brightened. "It fact, it's symbolically appropriate—old superstition serving true Faith."

What a load of codswallop. We all worshipped the

same Powers. Still, barging in on my own elsewhere struck me as even less appealing than eating with Adrya. I lowered myself onto the bench.

"Mag was your apprentice, right?" I said. "You didn't dismiss him on account of me, did you?"

"Carl apparently pried him loose from the city Watch and dragged him into the library one day, saying he was bright." Adrya said. "And he is, but he's only interested in being respected as a Wysman, not in the learning that justifies the respect."

I winced. Mag would have a secure life in the castle, but he'd hate being one of the servants.

A man in a gold tabard rapped the butt of a pike on the floor. "His Majesty, Thien, King of Rinland," the man declaimed.

Feet shuffled over the stone floor, and everyone rose, so I did too. *Don't do anything that makes you stand out,* I told myself. *Blend in.* Thien strode the length of the room and circled behind the head table. When the room grew silent, Thien looked toward me and nodded. I froze like a hunted rabbit before realizing he was nodding to Adrya.

Adrya closed her hands around her book pendant. "The Powers bless us with meat and drink. We thank them for their mercy and goodness. We aim to be worthy of their gifts."

My chest squeezed. Da used to speak the same blessing. I wondered what Adrya would say to that, but since I didn't want to talk to her about Da, I was unlikely to find out.

Thien sat, and everyone resumed their seats. The chair to Thien's right was empty. I didn't see Beran anywhere, so it was probably his.

A hand reached for the cup at my place, and I looked up to find Mag. He poured wine into the cup and set it down with a superior smile, keeping his hand on it. "Perhaps you'd rather have ale, like the stable boys drink?" He pointed his honker of a nose down the table, where folks were indeed being served ale instead of wine.

At home, I drank good mountain water every day and cider to celebrate holidays. In Rin, though, the water gave me the squits, so I'd been drinking weak ale. But this joker meant to insult me by offering it, and I'd be hanged if I'd let him do it. I tugged the cup from his grasp. "Not at all. Keep that wine coming." I took a big swallow, then struggled to control my face as my tongue curled away in alarm from the unfamiliar drink.

Mag reddened and stalked off along the table.

I took a more cautious second drink. The wine felt thick in my mouth. It was probably stronger than ale, so I needed to be careful. From the corner of my eye, I peeked at the woman on my left. She and the woman she sat with were gossiping about Beran's betrothal to Suryan's daughter, planning new gowns for the wedding, mostly. They'd expect no conversation from me on that topic, but they were also unlikely to tell me anything useful.

My stomach leaped to attention as another servant set

two shallow wooden bowls between me and Adrya. One bowl held chunks of what looked like venison in thin gravy. The other was heaped with frumenty. I reached for the serving spoon and was ferrying a chunk of venison toward my plate when Adrya spoke sharply. "Serve me before you serve yourself."

All up and down the tables, bowls sat between pairs of people, and in each case, one of them was serving the other. My stomach growled at the delay, but I flung the meat into Adrya's plate and added a glob of frumenty. Once again, I reached for my own food.

"Salt, please," Adrya said.

I paused with my hand hovering longingly over the bowl of venison. "I don't see it."

"There." Adrya pointed to a dish with four hollows, each filled with different colored crystals.

"People put that on their food? What kind of salt is that?" I asked.

"Dyed," Adrya said dryly.

I pulled the dish closer, hesitated over the choice, and then used a tiny spoon to sprinkle blue salt on Adrya's supper. It looked so bizarre I had to stifle a laugh. Adrya was satisfied though, because she started to eat.

Finally, I served myself a chunk of venison and a big scoop of frumenty. Feeling daring, I was dipping the little spoon in the red salt when an arm descended from nowhere and whacked mine. My hand nicked the edge of the silver salt dish, dumping it and sending white, green, red, and blue salt spilling out across the cloth. The woman on my left raised an eyebrow.

I glared at the descending arm's owner—Mag, who had returned to refill my wine cup. "I'm so sorry." He smiled smugly. "How could that have happened?"

I blew at the salt. It skittered rather than swirling like the paper in a wind box, but the effect was much the same. "Let's see how the winds answer your question. Oh look. They say your nose made you lose your balance."

Mag slammed the wine jug down on the table.

"Here," Adrya said hastily. "Is that how you behave in the king's Hall?"

"He's a thief, you know, Mistress," Mag said. "You should be careful." He gathered up his jug and stomped away.

"That was unkind and irreverent by your own standards," Adrya said. Her forehead puckered. "What does he know about you that His Highness and Carl don't?"

My pulse was racing. "Nothing. I never saw him before this morning." When she kept frowning, I added, "He thinks I'm going to replace him." She popped her lips scornfully and returned to her supper.

Wine trembled on the rim of my cup, so I drank two fingers' worth, then pinched salt off the cloth, sprinkled it over my food, and set about filling my stomach around the knot Mag's accusation had left. It glowed with gratitude at the presence of meat, and the wine seemed to be warming me, too. The frumenty was good, full of eggs and milk, but I missed the raspberry sauce most people at home spread over it. I served myself more venison, abiding by the street kid rule that you ate and drank all you could when you could. For all I knew, I'd be in jail with only a crust of bread and a cup of water tomorrow.

"Lord Grimuld is upset," said the man on Adrya's other side.

I looked up from stuffing myself in time to catch Grimuld leaning across Beran's empty chair and speaking quickly to Thien, Grimuld's head turned just that little extra bit his scarred left eye made necessary. Thien shook his head and resumed speaking to the woman on his other side. Lord Grimuld retreated and took a drink of wine. Next to him, Lineth poked listlessly at her food. I felt another twinge of guilty pity. She'd been gracious to me when she asked to have her fortune told.

"Lord Grimuld believes this marriage is a bad idea," Adrya said. "He believes Lord Suryan will be a treacherous ally. And of course, he's worried about his daughter."

The man speared a hunk of venison on his knife. "Grimuld thinks like the war leader he used to be, and he's been right a good many times."

"A ruler needs subtlety," Adrya said. "Grimuld would be a better lord if he didn't believe he could accomplish everything by force."

"I thought you'd approve of how hard he is on wind superstition in the Uplands," the man said.

"He'd do better to build schools," Adrya said. "They can't even read up there. How can they appreciate *The Book of the Wys?*"

Ma would have liked that part about schooling. I emptied my wine cup, but as soon as I set it down, Mag came along and refilled it. "That's enough," I said.

"I'll be glad to get you ale," the boy said. "Not every man, or rather, boy can hold his wine."

I scowled. "It's not that. And aren't you supposed to be off doing something for your aunt?"

He topped off the cup. "That box is worth more coin than you'll see in a lifetime." He vanished down the table with Adrya's gaze shifting from him to me.

"Mistress," I said, "if you suspect me of thieving, have Carl search my belongings, such as they are. He won't find anything." *Not unless Mag planted it*, a voice whispered in my head. And Carl was the one who brought Mag to the castle. Which one of us would he believe? A drop of sweat ran down my back.

More servants arrived to clear away the bowls of venison and frumenty. Good. I'd be out of Adrya's suspicious sight soon. But no. Platters of beef marrow pastries and chunks of eel in a hot sauce appeared in front of me. Apparently, the venison was just a starter. And this was only supper, I marveled. These were the leftovers of what would have been an even more sumptuous midday dinner. If folks in the Shambles saw this, they'd riot, and I for one wouldn't blame them. I started shoveling it in.

The meal dragged on, a blur of food spicy enough that I had to wash away the burn of it with wine. The next time I looked toward the head table, Lineth's chair was empty. Maybe she'd found the heat in the Hall too much for her. I was certainly hot enough and a little dizzy too. I tried to loosen the lace Carl had tied at my throat, but my left hand seemed to be tangled in my sleeve. I wriggled my fingers inside the ruffle some fool had attached there. Oops! I was supposed to keep that hand out of sight. I snickered. That would have set the fox among the chickens. Wait. That would make me one of the chickens, and I was really much more like a fox. Look how cleverly I'd remembered to keep my hand hidden.

I was forking up the last hunk of eel when my stomach lurched. Carefully, I lowered the spoon. Maybe I'd eaten enough. More on target, maybe I'd drunk enough. Maybe more than enough. Luckily, the meal seemed to be drawing to its close.

A hand reached over my shoulder and set a small bowl of frumenty in front of me. I blinked. It was topped by a red smear.

"What is that?" Adrya sounded as if she were gagging. The woman on my left wrinkled her nose.

I prodded the quivering lump. Was someone actually trying to make me feel at home? "It's raspberry sauce, I think."

Adrya averted her eyes.

I was stuffed, but I'd hurt through too many hungry

days and nights to pass up food, especially food that felt homey. I shoved a spoonful of it into my mouth, then had to pinch my lips together to keep from spitting it out. The red stuff was raspberry sauce, more or less, but the taste was off. These city folks didn't know how to make it right. No one but Ma did, really. I sniffed another spoonful. The smell of it pinched in my nose, reminding me of something nasty and maybe dangerous that I couldn't quite name. My stomach fluttered and rose tentatively toward my throat. A slick of sweat broke out on my forehead.

Mag appeared to refill my wine cup. "You're not wine sick, are you?" he asked sweetly. "I thought you wanted me to keep it coming."

I scrambled to my feet and tried to climb over the bench, but my too-big boot caught and I fell. I popped upright again. I had to get out of the Hall before I puked into some lady's lap. Faces turned toward me, but I didn't care. I stumbled out to the room with the wash troughs and looked wildly around. Which way had Carl shown me to the privy? I staggered down the corridor, then took a chance on a short passage. Yes! Two leather curtains closed off alcoves set in the thick castle wall.

I yanked a curtain aside, startling a man who sat with his trousers down around his ankles. I lunged for the other curtain, flung myself to my knees before the hole, and sent my supper hurtling down the long chute to the river. Behind me, I was vaguely aware of the fleeing man's footsteps. Again, my stomach sent wine-soaked vomit shooting out my mouth and nose. Sweet Powers, how could there still be anything to puke up? I clung to the edges of the privy seat while the street kid in me noted with horror that I was wasting food.

At last, my stomach seemed to have cleaned itself out to its own satisfaction, which made sense, given that my navel must be touching my spine by now. I wiped my mouth on a handful of hay from the box and flung it into the chute. One hand on the wall, I made my way back to the room with the basins, stuck my head under a spout, and rinsed out my mouth. On shaky legs, I set off to find Beran's quarters where I might be able to sleep off the wine and gather my wits.

Chapter 14.

Twisty Passages

I TURNED YET another corner to find yet another unfamiliar hallway. I pressed my forehead against the cool stone wall and fought a wave of queasiness. This castle had been laid out by a madman. I drew a deep breath, pushed myself erect, and stumbled on. At a crossing corridor, I heard a familiar voice, and my hope rose. Was that Beran? If it was, he sounded odd. I peered around an open doorway to find Beran and Lineth, standing in the shadows on the opposite edges of a pool of lamplight. Lineth was swiping at her eyes. Beran swayed toward her, but stayed where he was.

"I know this is right," she said. "You don't have to explain. I know you have to do it."

"I have no choice, Lineth. I am who I am, and this is my duty. I'm honor bound to do it."

"I know. I told you, I know!"

A hand clamped around the back of my neck just as another clapped over my mouth, muffling my shout. I twisted to look into Carl's face. He dragged me back to the crossing hallway, his thumb pressed painfully against the wound at my hairline. "Eavesdropping's not nice."

"I wasn't eavesdropping. I'm lost."

Carl sniffed. "Sick too, it smells like. No head for wine?"

"No stomach. I never want to even see it again."

"Come." Carl set off along the hall, me trailing. We spiraled through hallways and up some steps. A Tower Guard leaned against the wall, and I had no time to realize what that meant before Carl opened the door to Beran's quarters, took a single step, and bowed deeply. "Your Majesty."

I peered around Carl's back to see the king in the chair by the fireplace. Carl reached back to snatch my arm and pull me, too, into a bow. It didn't matter. Thien never flicked an eye in my direction.

"Fair evening, Carl," he said. "Where's Beran?"

"I'll fetch him for you, sir." Carl shoved me past the table where the stolen box had been and into the wardrobe. "Go to bed," he ordered and closed the curtain. He opened it again. "Drink water from the pitcher." He pointed. "You'll feel better in the morning if you do. Don't leave this room until I come for you tomorrow. There's a chamber pot there." With a jangle of brass rings, he slid the curtain shut again.

Uneasily aware of the king a few yards away, I sat on the makeshift bed. Under the stand holding the pitcher, a brown mouse lay on its side next to the small dish of white powder. I had a moment to appreciate that, like my family's house in autumn, the castle had mice they poisoned with what looked like the same stuff Ma had me put out. The understanding flared to life white hot. The sharp scent of the raspberry sauce on the frumenty was the smell of mouse poison.

My stomach spasmed, and I flopped onto the pallet, drawing deep breaths. Was I sick from the frumenty? No, I'd been queasy before it was set in front of me. No denying it. I'd eaten and drunk too much on a stomach used to a bowl of pottage a day. But getting sick was lucky, as it turned out, because something was sure enough wrong with the frumenty. Who had brought it? I couldn't remember. I thought about the man who cut me in the alley behind the Lac's Holding house, and about the way someone other than Carl had rattled the door while I was in the bath. I swallowed bile. I'd been in the castle for only one day, and already someone had tried to cut my throat and poison me. I needed to get out of here, but unless I also left the city, running wouldn't do me much good. Carl had found me in the Rat Hole within hours. I squeezed my eyes closed like maybe that would shut out my worries.

The door of the sitting room opened and closed, and the king's voice spoke low, answered by Beran's. I heard

Thien say "your magician." The curtain's rings jingled as it opened and closed again, and Beran said, "He's asleep." Snatches of conversation danced in and out of my head, as the room spun slowly around me.

"I'd allow the match if I could, Beran, but duty and honor mean I'm not free and neither are you."

"You owe me no explanation, sir. I do it for Rinland."

"I know," Thien said. "No prince could serve his people more faithfully."

After a long moment, Beran said, "Thank you." He sounded startled.

I frowned. Pain and what sounded like love mingled in those two voices. My mind ran around in paths as twisty as the castle hallways. Beran was relying on me to keep Thien safe, and I liked Beran, who was willing to feed Jarka and Dilly as well as me. If Beran loved his father, then he'd asked for my help for reasons that went beyond duty. A vision of a charred boat drifted into my head. I swallowed hard, despairingly certain that no matter how much I ate, there was a place inside me that would always stay empty.

"Still," Beran said, "you could have told me. I feel like a piece on a game board, moved around with no explanation."

You and me both, I thought.

"The negotiations have been delicate. Suryan is pressing for every advantage he can get. Until his ambassador actually took ship, I feared it might all collapse. And then," Thien added slowly, "I suppose I'm not used to having you here as an adult, ready to understand."

What if harm came to Thien because Beran trusted me? As I'd thought before, with Jarka and Dilly, and with Da, sometimes being trusted was a pain. I'd boasted of how good my word was, yet here I was in a situation that, in the privacy of the dark, I had to admit felt wrong.

"I knew you spent time in her company of course," Thien said.

"Of course you did," Beran said in a voice edged with bitterness. "You've always had efficient spies."

"I hadn't realized you let yourself fall in love," Thien said more sharply.

"I didn't *let* myself love her. It just happened."

Silence stretched like a wall. Then Thien said, "You can still have love, Beran. Your mother and I grew to love one another only after we married."

I shouldn't be listening to this. It was too private, too full of what might be Beran's and Thien's dark places. I staggered erect long enough to dump the dead mouse into the chamber pot and slam the lid closed. If I couldn't see it, maybe it was a wine-sick dream. I dropped my shirt, trousers, and boots in a heap next to the bed and lay back down, pulling the warm blanket up to my chin. I considered following Carl's order to drink water, but I didn't want to get up again. The pallet rustled with straw that felt soft as goose down. I turned over onto my unwounded side and flexed my left hand, still stiff from being bent into my sleeve all day. Living here, I wasn't going to be able to hide it forever, but I couldn't see what to do about it. I closed my eyes in an invitation to sleep that took its own time coming, as Beran's and Thien's voices murmured on into the night.

Chapter 15.

Warnings

I STOOD AT Carl's side, grateful for the dimness of the morning light in the Hall. I held myself very still, afraid that if I moved too suddenly, the hammer pounding at the inside of my head would slide to one side, bash clear through my temple, and clatter to the floor. On second thought, that might be an improvement. My stomach was happier since my careful breakfast of bread and mint tea in Beran's wardrobe, but I still would never drink wine again without someone holding my nose and pouring it down my throat. Ah well, as Da had told me after too much cider at the spring fair, I'd been stupid enough to earn a hangover, so it was undignified to whine about it.

I flexed my fingers inside the sleeve of the same shirt I'd worn the day before. Thank the Powers I didn't puke on it because the sleeve hid my hand well. Carl had muttered something about finding me more clothes. I'd deal with that when the time came. No point planning too far ahead. If I failed to manage this morning's wind reading, I wouldn't have to worry about it. At least, Carl hadn't said anything about the stolen box, so neither he nor Beran had noticed its absence, and Adrya hadn't told him what Mag said.

The Hall felt bigger this morning, with only the sleepy castle household gathered for what Carl said would be morning prayers. No councilors and their ladies, no Grimuld and his Ringmen. The boards that had formed the previous night's tables were hung on the walls, the trestles stacked in a corner. I scanned the crowd as well as I could without moving my sore head. Someone had tried to poison me last night. Someone had tried to kill me. Again. It wasn't like I'd never had someone angry at me before, but angry enough to kill me? My heart tripped at the thought. Was someone worried about what I might divine in the wind box? If Mag fussed with the frumenty in the kitchen, was he working for that person or being homicidal on his own? Maybe I was mistaken anyway. If the castle had mice, there'd be mouse poison put out. Maybe the frumenty had been fine. Yeah, and maybe I was about to be named Lord of the Uplands.

A shadow moved on Carl's other side. I cut my eyes toward it and saw Maras and Carl exchange a brief smile. Carl's arms were full of the velvet-draped wind box, which turned out to be some sort of priceless relic, meaning I wasn't allowed to touch it. But Maras's hands were free, and she laid her fingers on Carl's arm before folding her hands in front of her. I squirreled the affectionate gesture away in case Maras or Carl ever asked me to divine for them. Or Grandda, for that matter. I bet Grandda would be interested in what his boy was up to. How old was Carl anyway? Maybe Da's age? His hair was flecked with gray, but as I had reason to know, he was still plenty strong. "Old enough to marry, young enough to want to," Ma sometimes said. And then Da would say, "Lucky man," and laugh and put his arms around her. I swallowed away the swelling in my throat.

A stir in the front of the room told me things were getting underway. Thien and Beran entered through a side door and took up places at the front of the crowd. I only glimpsed their faces before they turned to face the front, but neither one looked as if he'd been up half the night talking. Drinking too. When Carl allowed me out of my cubbyhole, two empty pitchers sat on the table, reeking of wine. Maybe Beran's da had given him the same speech mine gave me about hangovers, stupidity, and whining.

Adrya followed them in, her gown covered by a plain white overtunic, a large book cradled in her arms. She set the book on a carved wooden stand facing the people in the Hall, then stood with her hands resting on it, her eyes closed. Silence spread through the room. She waited until it was total, then opened the book, clutched her pendant, and read in a clear voice. "*He who rises high shall plummet like a stone, but first he shall send winged death seeking its mark. Be wary, be wary, for the powerful can work much harm."*

Hair lifted on the back of my neck. What did that mean? Along with everyone else, I stared at the tense shoulder blades on Thien and Beran, the most powerful people in the room. I half expected them to stumble forward under the press of so many eyes.

Adrya cleared her throat. "The words of the Wys are not always easy to interpret."

No fooling. Which only went to show why it was dimwitted to rely on writing rather than a person, whose neck you could squeeze until they spit out an explanation. I shifted from foot to foot, silently willing Adrya to get on with whatever further silliness she was going to mouth. Not that I was eager to fake divining again. My chest tightened. I was going to have to take this risk every day until...Until everyone decided without my help that the danger was passed? That could take forever, and how many times could I pull off a convincing act up on the wall? Until someone killed Beran's da? That couldn't be right. Yet again, I saw no good way out of the fix I was in.

Adrya licked her lips. "While we cannot know exactly what *The Book* means, we can certainly accept that power brings responsibility, all power, even the most minor." Her gaze landed on me, knocking me back to step on the toes of the man behind me. He muffled a grunt and shoved me off. "So it behooves us all to be careful," Adrya went on.

"Lest we do harm even as we try to do good." She shut the book with a sound like a slap.

My stomach twisted. *It was only a book. Nothing to be afraid of. Only a book.*

I CLIMBED THE last few steps to the town wall, lifting my feet carefully so I wouldn't trip in my loose boots. We'd had to wait while Adrya shed her white overtunic, and a number of folks who had been in the Great Hall had mobbed up onto the walkway. They turned alert faces toward me, stopping me dead. They wanted entertainment and I was likely to provide it whether I named an assassin or jumped off the wall to escape arrest.

My headache eased when I found Jarka, leaning against the wall twenty yards away. After yesterday's scramble behind the Lac's Holding house, I hadn't been sure he'd turn up. I searched beyond him, but Dilly wasn't there, so she must still be angry, but at least Jarka would give me what help he could.

From the step below, Carl poked me with a corner of the wind box. "You're keeping your betters waiting."

I forced my feet to carry me to where I'd have a clear view of Jarka over Beran's shoulder and waited, trying to settle my breathing. At the tap of Jarka's crutch moving closer, Beran glanced back, and Jarka froze, looking out over the wall at the ripening morning light. The sky on the other side of the river glowed golden near the flat fields, then darkened to murky blue overhead. I'd seen it before, and it always felt upside down. In the mountains, the light washed over the highest points first before sliding down into the valley and washing over my family's farm.

On the river below, a boat was being rowed away from the dock. I recognized it as the ore boat I'd seen docking the day before, its deck covered with timber. The timber had been offloaded, but the boat still rode as low in the water as the *Rose of Rin* had. It turned south, and sailors scrambled over the deck, ready to raise the sails. I studied it like Jarka too was doing. Once you start noticing oddities, it was hard to stop even when you were a fake diviner talking to a prince about assassination.

Carl brushed past and set the wind box on the wall. He pulled off the velvet cover, gave Beran the little bag of paper bits, and stepped back to stand just behind the prince, hand on the hilt of his sword. He scanned the crowd, the steps, the streets of the city below. His gaze caught on Jarka for an instant, then evidently dismissed him and moved on.

Adrya, on the other hand, nosed right up next to Jarka. When he edged away, she closed in again. "What's your name, boy?"

Jarka tilted his head and opened his mouth, letting drool run down his cheek. "Morka the Idiot. Gimme a gull, pretty lady." He stuck out his hand.

With a disgusted click of her tongue, Adrya turned to

watch me. Behind her, Jarka swiped the drool off and flicked it toward her back. Despite the tension I felt in every muscle, I had to smother a smile.

Beran had been rubbing his temple, suggesting maybe princes felt the effect of too much wine after all. Now he dropped his hands to his sides. "Ready?"

"And honored to serve you, Your Highness." I invoked the winds as he flung the paper bits into the box. I eyed the pile of colored paper and tried to look knowing.

"Do you see the source of danger to the king?" Beran asked.

What I saw was a pile of colored paper. I tightened my muscles to stop the nervous jiggling of my right foot. "Maybe."

I glanced up to see Jarka frantically shaking his head. *Shut it*, he silently mouthed.

Beran stiffened. "Who?"

My throat closed, trying to hold back the words that were tempting me. I forced it open again. If my suspicions were right, I'd have earned more of Beran's trust, which I had to believe was a good thing. "There's someone who's not exactly an enemy of the king but isn't exactly a friend either."

"Who?" Beran took a step closer, his question more urgent this time.

"This person is taking some of the iron ore from the Uplands right out through the quarantine. That could mean they want to make weapons, couldn't it?"

"Who is it?" Beran's voice was sharp. Time to produce what answer I could.

I pointed at the ore boat on the river, heading south toward Lac's Holding. "Send someone to inspect the cargo on that boat."

Beran shot a look at Carl. "Tell the Guard captain to send a squad to the next port and hail that ship." He started for the stairs, then turned back. He'd been carrying a roll of paper under his arm. Now he took it out and hastily unfurled it. "What about these acrobats? Do they pose a danger?"

I was still trying to breathe again, but I recognized the Wind Dancers poster. Thank the Powers. Here was my chance to be useful so the Wind Dancers would owe me a favor. "There's no danger there, sir. I see a good show happening in New Square."

Jarka flinched. He probably thought I was pushing my luck. Too bad.

Rolling up the poster, Beran said, "Good work, Doniver. If we find smuggled ore, you may have identified the danger Adrya saw." He moved toward the stairs again but stopped at the sound of running footsteps. Carl tensed, then relaxed when Lord Grimuld climbed into sight. Grimuld bowed to Beran, his back military straight.

"Your Highness. I hope you don't mind if I join you. I'd like to ask the boy about my magistrate."

"Of course. He's been very helpful today." Beran waved toward the wind box. "Doniver, do you see anything about who killed Lord Grimuld's magistrate?"

I made a show of peering into the box. "No, sir." That was probably the wisest thing to say, and the Powers knew it was truthful. I wondered if Beran would tell Grimuld about the ore going to Lac's Holding—assuming I'd guessed right, of course. I certainly had no intention of telling Grimuld anything so likely to make him happy about a spoiled alliance and betrothal.

"Be on your way with your friend." Beran nodded toward Jarka and then winced as if wishing he'd kept his head still. "Be back by evening." He clattered down the stairs with Adrya on his tail in a swish of skirts.

Carl scrambled to cover the wind box, but he took the time to say, "Stay away from cutthroats today," before hurrying after Beran.

The other folks from the castle drifted down the stairs, buzzing over what might be found on the boat. Lord Grimuld turned his head sharply to listen. Ah well. News as exciting as Suryan smuggling ore would never stay secret for long.

Grimuld blocked my path toward Jarka. "Did you tell His Highness that Lac's Holding was the source of the danger?"

"Not really." I considered adding "sir" but decided not to. "Just that they might be taking iron ore."

"My iron ore?"

"Uplands iron ore."

Grimuld didn't seem to hear the correction. "Perhaps

you can be useful after all." He wheeled and disappeared down the steps.

Another test passed. Another day to eat and sleep while I waited to go home, assuming no one poisoned or stabbed me.

Chapter 16.

Slipping Out of Control

THE MORNING CROWD on the wall had mostly melted away. Fumbling in my carry bag for the package of bread and cheese Maras had given me when she brought my breakfast, I wove my way between lingering gawkers to Jarka. "I'm glad to see you. You got away from those Lac's Holding fools, then?"

"Dilly shoved me into a doorway and pointed them on a wild goose chase." A faint flush rose in his face. Usually he ignored the way his crutch made him slow, and he expected me and Dilly to pretend we didn't notice. It would have taken a chunk out of his pride to have Dilly save him. He balanced cheese on a slab of bread and took an enormous bite, cupping his other hand under his chin to catch the crumbs.

"Some of that's for Dilly. Where is she?"

"She went to the docks. The Lac's Holding ambassador is arriving this morning."

"She doesn't still think Huryn will get her work with them, does she? Why didn't you stop her?"

"It's not up to me, Doniver. You know what she always says. Women from Lac's Holding do what they like. Besides, you're trying to go back to your pile-of-rocks mountains. Why shouldn't Dilly get what help she can to go home?" Jarka chewed fiercely, as if the food had somehow offended him.

"And you say I'm fresh off the farm! You're not daft enough to think Huryn will help her because he's such a sweetheart, are you? He's blowing smoke."

Jarka snorted. "You're one to talk." He jerked his head toward the wall where the wind box had rested.

"With Carl ready to hunt me down, I don't have much choice. I just hope I was right about the boat. Why didn't you want me to point it out?"

"That wasn't what I expected you to say. You were sharp to see how low it rode. You'll be a wind reader yet, more or less." Jarka crammed the last of his bread and cheese into his mouth, and licked the crumbs from his palm. He opened his bag to shove Dilly's share inside.

I frowned at the waxed cloth package. "I think a servant boy named Mag tried to poison me last night."

"What?" Jarka eyed his wet palm and hastily wiped it on his trousers. As if what I'd said only just penetrated, his head snapped toward me. "Wait. Mag? The one whose family fences half the stolen goods in the city?"

"I don't know. He was Adrya's apprentice, and he blames me because she dismissed him."

"Yeah, him. He was killed last night."

I sucked in air. "Someone must have put him up to poisoning me and then wanted to be rid of him."

"No," Jarka said. "His aunt killed him. He stole something from the castle and she was furious. When the Watch came to arrest her for murder, she told them he was too stupid to live. She was drunk, not surprisingly." Jarka thumped his crutch on the walkway.

I felt the way I had when Dilly punched me in the stomach. "Sweet Powers. I pretended to divine for him. He asked what he should do about his aunt, and then at supper I told him to go see her."

"His family was always a nightmare. You can't be responsible for everyone."

I wanted to believe that because then I'd be free to be relieved that I wouldn't be accused of stealing the jeweled box. But the chances were good Mag wouldn't have gone back to his aunt if I hadn't pushed him. Besides, I'd seen how Jarka felt responsible for his own violent family.

"What happened to your neck?" he asked, as if happy to change the subject.

I smoothed my hair over the cut. "That Uplander we saw in New Square attacked me outside the Lac's Holding house after you and Dilly left."

"Curse it anyway. I knew he was after you! But why?"

"I thought he might be afraid of what I'd divine for Beran and Thien."

"I told you it was a mistake to get mixed up with powerful people. Let them fight their own turf battles."

"Give it a rest, Jarka. Stop wasting time telling me what to do." I felt an irrational urge to be away from this spot, as if I could run from my guilt over Mag's death. "We need to find Dilly and make sure she's all right."

"Which I'm sure isn't the same thing at all as my telling you what to do." Despite his words, Jarka was quick to pull his crutch under him, ready to go.

We made our way slowly down the stairs, through the broad, clean streets of Tower Hill, and down River Lane, the street slanting nearest the wall. The man who tried to knife me was out here somewhere, but I still breathed more easily out of the castle. *Too bad Mag's not breathing at all*, whispered a voice in my head. I shoved it into my dark space.

Servants and housewives were walking in the same direction as us, probably on their way to the East Market, which lay just inside the gate to the docks. As the street descended, the houses grew smaller, and shop fronts sprouted among them. Near the bottom of the street, I heard marching feet and glanced over my shoulder to see a squad of men wearing Lord Grimuld's green tabard.

"Out of the way," bawled the officer in the front.

Along with everyone else, we pressed up against a shop wall to let the soldiers pass. An elderly man failed to move fast enough, and a Ringman shouldered past him without pausing. The man stayed on his feet only because the young woman with him caught him under the arm.

"Pigs," Jarka said to the soldiers' departing backs. He spoke without heat though. I'd noticed before that while he didn't like the way the powerful could push people around, he seemed to accept it as normal. As I saw it, if that was normal, it was yet another reason to get out of this city. "I wonder where they're going," Jarka added.

"Now or when the Powers judge them?" I asked. Jarka laughed. I pushed away from the wall, and we followed the Ringmen down the street, although since we went at Jarka's pace, the soldiers were soon out of sight. We went out through the River Gate, and were met by the reek of fish and wet wood.

Men crowded the narrow quay, unloading and selling the catch from two fishing boats already back from their morning run. At the last dock, three or four men watched a large ship that had furled its sails and was being rowed into a berth. A man with fish scales in his beard stood in front of what turned out to be a Wind Dancers poster pasted on the city wall. I stopped next to him. "I hear they put on a good show," I said.

"Aye," he said. "So everyone tells me."

I ran to catch up with Jarka, who'd apparently just spotted Dilly and Tuc. Tuc had his nose in the air, quivering in hopes of a fish jumping out of the boxes being passed from boat to dock. Dilly was so intent on the arriving ship that she must not have noticed the big man in a fisherman's flat cap who sidled up next to her. He put an arm around her waist. Instantly, she spun away from him, one hand brushing across his hip. I smothered a groan at the way she'd just picked his pocket.

"Shut it, farm boy," Jarka murmured. "You know why she does it."

Over his shoulder, I spotted carts, horses, and men in blue pouring through the gate. They crowded the swearing fishermen closer to the river. I grabbed Jarka's arm and pulled him into a space behind a web of fishing nets hung up to dry. He scowled and opened his mouth to protest.

"Shh," I whispered. "The Lac's Holding folks. The ambassador must be on that ship."

Jarka snapped his mouth shut and peered around the nets. It was a good thing we were out of sight because Huryn walked at the side of the older man from the kitchen. When Dilly approached them, Huryn slowed, and I felt Jarka tense. Huryn bent to hear what Dilly said. The older man called sharply to him, and he winked at Dilly and went to talk to him.

"Let's get her out of here while they're busy," I said.

We slipped up behind Dilly. When I touched her shoulder, she jumped. "Oh, it's you."

"Yes, me. Come on."

She scowled. "No. Huryn's talking to the steward about getting me work with them."

"Dilly, what are you thinking?" I asked. "He tried to

keep you from leaving yesterday. You say you won't depend on a man, which I figure is because of what happened to your ma, but Huryn means for you to do just that. Then he'll collect what he thinks you owe him. How can you be so stupid that you don't see that?"

Her face had gone pale as I talked, but at this last, her eyes narrowed and her color flooded back. "Stupid?"

Jarka hopped between us. "We need to get out of here."

A fishmonger backed toward us, turning his cart to take it through the gate. As he pivoted, the cart tilted, and fish slid toward the edge. Tuc seized his chance, leaped from his crouch, and snatched a fat trout. His frantic pawing sent more sliding to the quay, their scales glittering.

"Hey!" the fishmonger yelled. Tuc tore off into the crowd, the fish flopping between his jaws.

We were scrambling to get out of the way of the fishmonger's wildly swerving cart, when the point of Jarka's crutch came down on a fish and slid out from under him. He lurched into a nearby fisherman, the one who'd touched Dilly, and grabbed the man's shirt to stay on his feet. Face scarlet, he yanked his crutch back under him and struggled upright.

The fisherman slapped at his pockets. "My pocketknife! You thief! Watchman! Someone call the Watch!" He seized Jarka's collar in one hand and delivered a back-handed slap with the other, snapping Jarka's head to the side.

I started toward them but saw Dilly charging and swiveled to grab her arm instead. Given that the man's knife was undoubtedly in Dilly's pocket, she needed to keep well away from the furor.

She yanked free of my grip, swooped toward the fishy surface of the docks as if picking something up, and darted into the excited crowd around Jarka and the fisherman. "Here!" she cried. "Is this it? It was on the ground." She flashed the fisherman a dazzling smile.

He blinked at her and slowly released his hold on Jarka. "That's it," he said gruffly, taking the knife. "I'm sorry, boy. I must have dropped it."

Without answering, Jarka hitched away from the gathered watchers, catching Dilly's arm as he went. I drew back behind the drying nets again to wait for them.

The moment he had Dilly out of sight, Jarka turned on her. "Why did you do that? I didn't have his knife, and he would have found that out, but it wouldn't have taken much for him to guess you were the one who took it. You should have cleared out."

"He was going to rough you up." Dilly pushed on Jarka's chest, barely containing her anger. "Anyone could see that coming. And you and Doniver are my friends, even when you both act like idiots."

"I don't need your pity," Jarka said. "I take care of myself, and that's what you should do too."

"So you say," Dilly said. "But then why are you here

nagging at me?" She leaned to peer around him and skipped out from behind the nets. "Here I am!" she called brightly.

I edged out to see Huryn approaching, smiling like his teeth had been greased. Head raised to listen, Dilly walked away with him.

"Nightmare take the pox-faced son of a snake," Jarka muttered savagely. Oh yeah. Looking weak in front of Dilly hurt him way more than the fisherman's slap. He swung around to glare at me. "Why did you call her stupid? It's your fault she's mad. For someone who believes in the power of words, you're mighty clumsy with them."

"I spoke the truth. She's trusting someone who's likely to hurt her."

"And you're not? Are you going back to the castle?"

"Are we going to do another round of this? I already told you, I'd rather not, but Carl will just hunt me down if I don't."

"You brought this on yourself by getting mixed up with them. The Powers save me from saddling myself with fools. You'd think I'd have learned."

"Fools?" I clenched my fists.

"It's sort of like stupid. What I don't understand is why you and Dilly are both so hot to leave Rin. What's so great about the mountains or Lady Elenia?"

"It's home." I didn't know how to explain it any better.

"Dilly doesn't even have a family, and you—" Jarka

clamped his mouth shut, evidently thinking better of what he'd been going to say.

"My family is still there." I thrust my face into his, daring him to tell me they weren't.

But he drew a deep breath and settled his bag higher on his shoulder. "I have to get going before shoppers at the market have spent all their coin. Come with me. Given that someone tried to knife you, you shouldn't wander around alone."

"You don't think we should go after Dilly?" I asked.

"Why? She doesn't have a lot of choices, and this is a bad one, but she gets to make it herself."

I felt sick, and I didn't think it was from my hangover. I shot one more look at where Dilly had vanished among the crowd of Lac's Holding blue livery. There was nothing we could do. "I'll go see Min. Maybe she'll have gossip about the Fever or something else I can feed them when I go back."

"I'll go along," Jarka said.

I wanted to see if there was any better hope of the Wind Dancers getting me safely out of the city, and it would be better if Jarka didn't know that. "You go to the market. I'll catch up."

"Watch your back. I've invested too much time in training you to lose you now."

I TRUDGED THROUGH the Shambles, still worrying about Dilly. The Shambles was even noisier than usual that morning. Someone was trying to squeeze a wide chest through a narrow house door. Neighbors shouted advice, and a troop of filthy boys chased one another around the sweating men with the chest on their shoulders. More shouting rose from a street or two over. That sounded like a fight. I marked where it was so I could stay out of it.

When I rounded the corner to Min's, I found her talking to the acrobat Tel. Despite my worry over Dilly, my spirits rose at the sight of him. The Wind Dancers could take me out of town even if they weren't going directly back to the Uplands.

"Fair morning, Doniver," Min said. "How are you?" She looked me up and down. "Other than clean as an empty basin, that is."

I smiled. "I'm fine." It was good to hear an Uplands accent.

"Has the prince been asking about us Uplanders?" Min asked. "Are they going to blame us for that dead magistrate or the threat to Thien?"

"Beran and Grimuld keep asking what the danger is," I said, "but I've been able to put them off, and I've been talking up the Wind Dancers."

"Great!" Tel said. "We want to perform in New Square tomorrow. The whole troupe and its equipment are hidden around town now, so we're ready. We've asked for the king's permission to perform and are waiting to hear if he grants it. Your praise should help stir up people so he agrees. Now I have another request. Do you think you can get King Thien to come to our performance?"

My hope took a nosedive. Cat hissing at a king was all very well, but the old proverb never said how intimidating a king like Thien could be. "I don't know. Why?"

"We're going to act out a play that shows the king what Grimuld's Ringmen are doing in the Uplands," Tel said. "We want to remind Thien that we may be Grimuld's people now, but we're the king's too, and he owes us his protection."

"It would be public, you see?" Min put in. "We could convince more people that Grimuld is stealing people's land. Thien would have to listen then."

"If he's there," Tel said, "and that's where you come in, Doniver. Living in the castle, you have access to the king."

"Sort of," I said. "I see Prince Beran really."

"You can talk to Prince Beran," Tel said. "Ask him to talk to Thien."

If I'd been right about iron ore heading for Lac's Holding, the king and Beran should both be willing to do me a favor. "All right. I'll try."

Tel patted my shoulder. "Good. We're counting on you." He walked to the alley's far end and vanished.

I found Min looking the other way, her brows drawn down. "What's that noise?"

I cocked my head. "A fight? I thought I heard it on my way here, but it's closer now."

Three men ran past the end of the narrow street, and I caught a flash of green. Surely those were some of Grimuld's Ringmen who'd passed Jarka and me on our way down from the castle. I trotted toward them. Min's shop door slammed, and I heard her on my heels.

"Here!" shouted a man's voice. "Down here!"

I rounded the corner in time to see Grimuld's men duck into the alley behind Min's. As I scrambled into the alley, something flew out of the little yard and smashed against the wall opposite in a shower of water and broken crockery. I skidded to a stop just in view of the shrine. One of Grimuld's men kicked at the rocks that had held the water bowl. A second chopped at the mountain laurel with a short-handled ax. The last man held the pinwheel in his hand. He flung it to the ground and crushed it under his boot heel.

"No!" I cried.

Min grabbed at my arm, but I broke away and ran toward the men.

"Stop!" I wrestled with the man wielding the ax. He drove an elbow into my gut, and as I doubled over, trying not to puke, I spotted the pinwheel lying smashed at my feet. My heart twisted at the breaking of something so sacred. "Why are you doing this?"

"You want Mountain Fever here?" demanded the Ringman.

"But I told Grimuld the shrines were harmless," I cried. "They aren't hurting anyone."

The Ringman spat into the dirt. "Savages. Let's go." He and the other two ran back along the alley.

I looked to be sure Min was all right and found her frowning at me. "What do you mean, you told Grimuld? What did you tell him?"

"Grimuld said the Fever was in the Uplands because of the shrines." I stood up, fighting to draw air into my bruised belly. "And I said the shrines were here too and there was no Fever. I was trying to help!"

"You told them? Are you stupid or a traitor?"

"I can fix this," I said.

"You'd better." She sounded close to tears. "They're our link to the Powers, our link to home!"

I turned and ran.

Chapter 17.

Guests

I TORE OUT of the alley and shoved blindly past three women in front of a butcher's, knocking a basket from the arm of one of them. It rolled into my path, and I leaped over it.

"Here!" the basket's owner cried.

"Rude boy," said another.

I could think of only one place where I might get help to save the shrines. I had to get to Beran as fast as my feet would carry me. But when I rounded the next corner, two Ringmen were struggling down the street. Between them, they clutched a wrestling, screaming Tava.

"Doniver!" she cried. "They're breaking everything. My boy tried to stop them, and they killed him!"

Boy? Tava had no family in Rin.

I teetered on the balls of my feet, then veered toward

Tava and her stoning Ringmen captors. "Are you sure she doesn't have the Fever?" I asked the one with a scar on his cheek.

Simultaneously, both Ringmen dropped her arms and moved off. "Fever?" The scarred one sounded as if he were strangling.

"If you caught her, I'd be worried," I told him. "She's usually pretty lively."

Tava skipped backward, spun, and hotfooted away, her gray hair streaming around the edges of her scarf. The Ringmen swayed and exchanged a look. Then the one who had spoken aimed an arrow sharp look at me.

I launched myself up the street, and when I glanced over my shoulder, they were gone. I could do nothing more for Tava now, and I had other things to think about. I zigzagged through streets and alleys, tucking my left hand away and doggedly choosing the upward path. I emerged at last on Kings Way a short distance from the castle. A startled gate guard lowered his pike to block the entrance.

I braced my free hand on my knee and bent over, panting. "Please," I choked out. "Prince Beran said he would tell you about me. I'm Doniver."

The second guard nodded to the one blocking the way. "Let him pass. I've seen him with His Highness."

The guard raised the pike, and I ran through the gate. I tore across the courtyard, dodged a line of servants sweeping the paving stones, ducked through the door I'd been using, and plowed straight into the solid form of Carl.

"Do that again, and I'll smack you silly." Carl scanned my face and frowned. "Trouble?"

"I need Beran."

"You need His Highness. He's busy now."

"Please!" I said. "This can't wait."

Carl gave me the same look Da had when he was deciding whether to send me to sell three goats on my own. "All right, but this better be important." He led the way up the stairs, knocked on Beran's door, and entered when Beran answered.

I pushed past Carl to see Beran standing with arms extended as a valet laced up his tunic. "Your Highness, you need to stop Lord Grimuld," I blurted. "His men are running wild through the Shambles, destroying all the wind shrines."

"Wait until His Highness invites you to speak!" Carl cried.

The valet looked amused but didn't stop fussing with Beran's collar. I had an instant's wild vision of Beran as an oversized doll with the valet in the role of one my two youngest sisters.

"It's all right, Carl," Beran said. He turned his face toward me while keeping his body still for the valet. "After we left the council chamber yesterday, Grimuld convinced His Majesty the shrines were dangerous and asked permission to deal with his own people."

"But the shrines aren't dangerous." I felt trapped in one of those nightmares where you can't make yourself wake up. "Please! I'm the one who told Lord Grimuld about the shrines in the city. My people think I betrayed them, and if I can't stop this, then I did." I clenched and unclenched my fists, even the hidden one, willing Beran to see how important this was. "Please, sir. My honor's at stake."

Beran exchanged a look with Carl.

"Boy's concerned about his honor." Carl smiled faintly. "I've seen that in a boy before."

Beran gave a short laugh. "He and I think alike. Must be that time in the Uplands. I'll speak to His Majesty, Doniver. He should be receptive because you were right about there being iron ore on that boat."

"Thank you!" I let out a long breath. "Please, it has to be right away. Lord Grimuld's men are tearing things up now."

Someone rapped on the door. At Beran's invitation, a servant stepped through. "The king awaits you, Your Highness."

From a carved box, the valet lifted a circlet and lowered it over Beran's hair, turning it so a single red gem gleamed in the middle of Beran's forehead. He wore richer clothes than I'd seen before too. His tunic was scarlet silk.

"I have to attend on His Majesty now, Doniver," Beran said. "Lord Suryan's ambassador is arriving." He stepped back from the valet, who was reaching to adjust the circlet again. "We wouldn't want my future bride to hear I was late and think I was less than enthusiastic. Apparently Lac's Holding women take offense at that kind of thing."

Carl shot him a sharp look and grimaced. I could see why. He was as joyless a future bridegroom as I'd ever seen. I shivered. When I got married I wanted to feel about the girl the way Da felt about Ma. "Can you speak to the king about the shrines first?"

"If there's time, I will," Beran said. "You come along and wait with Carl in case His Majesty has questions. Wait quietly, mind you."

"When fish fly," Carl muttered.

I jumped for the door, but Carl caught me by the back of the collar. "His Highness goes first."

Beran led us out of the room and through another set of senseless corridors. I had to dance from side to side to keep from running up his back. The end of a hallway widened into a small antechamber, where the king waited, surrounded by courtiers. I started toward him, but Carl grabbed my collar again and hauled me aside to stand among a group of attendants.

Beran bowed to his father. "Have you a moment, sir? I'd like to speak to you about something." His voice and face were carefully neutral. Thien hesitated, and Beran added, "It's not about today's ceremony."

Thien's mouth twisted. He raised an eyebrow at a thin courtier. Interpreting the silent question, the courtier said, "The Lac's Holding party is still at some distance, Your

Majesty."

"What is it then?" Thien asked Beran.

"Perhaps we could speak more privately." Beran gestured to the small group of watchers, who were trying to pretend they weren't dying to nose into the prince's business. At Thien's dismissive wave, the attendants shuffled through a doorway, the ones moving slowest looking over their shoulders. Finally, only Thien and Beran and their guards were left.

"I understand Lord Grimuld's men are in the Shambles, destroying whatever wind shrines they find," Beran said.

"I was surprised to learn the shrines were in the city," Thien said.

"As Doniver pointed out yesterday, they don't seem to have caused any problems," Beran said. "And he says they matter to the Uplanders. So I ask you to stop the destruction at once, sir."

Good. Well put.

"Grimuld tells me only a few Uplanders care about them," Thien said. "Despite the sympathy you gained for Upland ways when you lived there, you must know the pinwheels are blasphemous. This is a king's responsibility, Beran. The Powers can't be bound in such a *thing.*"

"Of course not!" I cried.

Carl shook my arm. "Speak when you're spoken to."

Beran's face had stiffened when his da scolded him, but he did his best for me anyway. "Doniver, perhaps you should explain what the pinwheels are for."

I licked my lips. How could I explain what all Uplanders felt in their muscle, blood, and bone from the day they first opened their eyes between Earth and Sky? "Your Majesty, they show us the Powers breathing over the land and take our words back to them. That's not binding the Powers. It's just touching them, maybe, and letting them touch us."

"If they're innocent, why do your people hide them?" Thien gestured toward the place where my left hand should have showed. "One doesn't touch the Powers—any power—without cost. You must know that. Your people fool themselves when they think that they can. What's more, when they trifle with such objects, Uplanders imperil the rest of my people, and the Powers trust me to keep my realm safe. In the end, the Uplands will be better off without the shrines and certainly the city will. You gave us useful information today, Doniver, for which I thank both you and His Highness, who insisted that I listen to you. I'd grant you both favors if I could, but it can't be this one." He exchanged a long look with Beran. "Truly, I would."

"I know," Beran said.

Despair churned in my stomach. I had set Grimuld's men smashing their way through the Shambles, and there was nothing I could do to stop them. I'd faked wind reading and sent Mag to his death, and now I'd betrayed the existence of the wind shrines to Grimuld. If I ever managed to get home, no Uplander who heard what I'd done would have anything to do with me.

"Your Majesty," said a courtier standing in the doorway, "the ambassador has arrived."

"We will greet our guests." Thien smiled a wolf's smile. "We have matters to discuss that should allow us to alter some of the terms of the marriage contract." He swept through the doorway, trailed by his guard.

"I'm sorry, Doniver," Beran murmured. He started after his father, then turned back. "Don't leave the castle again today. If trouble's underway, I don't want you caught up in it. I need you." He followed the king.

"It'll be all right," Carl said with surprising gentleness.

"No." My voice shook. "It won't."

Carl guided me through the doorway to stand among people gathered along the sides of a large room. Tabletops hung in brackets on the wall behind me, and I realized I was back in the Great Hall. The room smelled of sweat and perfume in a sickening mix. Thien seated himself in a large chair on a low platform, while Beran stood at his father's right hand. Beran set his jaw and straightened his back. At least I wasn't the only miserable person in the Hall.

"Carl," I whispered, "since Suryan was smuggling ore, will Beran still have to marry his daughter?"

Carl sighed. "Probably. If the girl's here, her father will think twice before he angers the king."

"Gladoc, ambassador for Lord Suryan of Lac's Holding," a voice announced. A red-haired man strode down the center of the Hall and dropped to one knee before Thien. I'd thought Thien and Beran wore fancy clothes, but Gladoc made them look like sparrows eyeing a peacock. Jewels glittered on his velvet doublet, and gold hoops the size of king coins dangled from his ears. I tried to think what Dilly might like to hear about him so I could notice it, but then I remembered that if she took work in the Lac's Holding house, she'd likely glimpse him for herself. And if she stayed there, I wouldn't be able to tell her anything anyway. Surely we'd been through too much together for her to cut me and Jarka out of her life completely. Not as long as we were all here in Rin.

Across the Hall, Lord Grimuld's nose twitched as if Gladoc had farted hard enough for Grimuld to smell it. Lineth stood next to him, her face pale, her eyes on Beran, who never looked at her. She touched her father's arm, and he bent to let her speak into his ear.

Thien motioned for Gladoc to rise, then beckoned Beran forward. "I present Beran, Prince and King's Heir of Rinland."

Gladoc bowed, then looked Beran up and down the way I'd seen housewives examine chickens at a market. Beran put up with the inspection with a face like stone. When I looked to see how Lineth was reacting to the scene, she no longer stood at her father's side. "Lady Elenia charged me to greet you in her name, Your Highness." Gladoc spoke in the same lazy drawl Dilly used. "And to bring word of you and of Rin back to her."

"I hope you're able to give her a favorable report," Beran said dryly, "both on me and on the city. I've heard that people from Lac's Holding sometimes find Rin and its people equally dull."

Gladoc's smile broadened. "I see from posters that you have the Wind Dancers in town. I saw them in Lac's Holding last year. A performance by them is sure to be entertaining."

Thien glanced at one of the courtiers on the other side of the Hall. "Have we granted these acrobats permission to perform?"

"Not yet, Your Majesty," the courtier said.

And there it was—a chance to make up for what I'd done, and maybe get out of Rin before I did more damage to myself or someone else. I hesitated only an instant before thinking *cat and king* and slithering between the two women in front of me. "Your Majesty, you said I might ask a favor. I ask one that will please both the ambassador and you." Everyone turned to look at me, and my heart apparently decided I might have spoken out of turn, because it scrambled around frantically inside the cage of my ribs.

Behind Thien's right shoulder, Beran actually grinned. I heard heavy footsteps and was unsurprised when Carl's hand clamped on my shoulder.

"I beg your pardon, Your Majesty." Carl bowed, his hand tightening as if he meant to squeeze me dry.

Thien did his trick of lifting a single finger from the

arm of his chair, and Carl instantly stopped trying to drag me away. "You have earned a favor with the insight your Power's mark allowed you to give us. What is it you ask?"

The king's words were cordial, but his voice held a note of warning. When that edge had come into Da's voice, I'd found it best to back down, and my feet wanted to retreat into the crowd. But I was desperate to please my fellow Uplanders and especially the Wind Dancers. "The Wind Dancers are very fine acrobats. What's more, they'd be deeply honored by your presence at their performance. And Uplanders would take it as a sign of your good will toward them despite anything else that's happened."

"I can attest from my own experience that you would enjoy yourself, Your Majesty." Gladoc's oversized earrings danced when he nodded.

"What do you say, Lord Grimuld?" Thien asked. "Would your people like it if Ambassador Gladoc and I attended this show?"

I twitched my shoulder, ready to pull it out of Carl's grip and protest when Lord Grimuld said no, but Grimuld cocked his head. "Perhaps so, sir." He nodded as if making up his mind. "Indeed, Your Majesty, I go so far as to invite you and the ambassador to be my guests. My house fronts on New Square, where I believe they want to perform."

I was left with my mouth open and, for once, nothing to say. Who would ever have expected Lord Grimuld to agree? It didn't make up for him ordering the destruction of the wind shrines, of course. Grimuld probably just wanted to keep an eye on the Lac's Holding ambassador and sniff out any treachery he could use to talk Thien out of this marriage for Beran, but I'd take his help anyway.

"Then, Doniver of the Uplands, we grant your request. We will go to this performance." Thien rose. "Come, Ambassador Gladoc. We have matters to discuss." He smiled his wolf smile again, making Gladoc blink and for the first time look less than cocky. When the royal party had left, the others in the Great Hall drifted toward the doors at the opposite end, chattering about Gladoc or the Wind Dancers.

"Did you see how he inspected Beran?" one man asked. "I'm surprised he didn't ask His Highness to strip."

The woman with him sniffed. "Elenia has nerve to send him. She doesn't appreciate how lucky she is to be marrying the prince. She needs to learn her place."

The man laughed. "I hear all those Lac's Holding women have trouble with that." They moved out of hearing.

"Elenia's not the only one with nerve," Carl said. "You want to take more care about when you speak, lad. You have enough nerve that one day someone's going to decide you need it knocked out of you."

"I'm a cat, Carl, and I'm allowed to hiss." I ignored the way he rolled his eyes. The Wind Dancers didn't know it yet, but today, I'd put them in my debt. Maybe I'd get out of this Powers-forsaken city before someone stopped my supposed divination by killing me.

"Doniver?" said an unfamiliar voice.

I stiffened at the sight of a Tower Guard. Now what? Was that as long as my relief was supposed to last?

The guard shot a sidelong look at Carl, then spoke in a rush. "I wonder if you'd divine my future for me."

An image of Mag flitted across my mind. "I don't have a wind box."

"Your old one's in His Highness's quarters." Carl smiled as if he thought he was doing me a favor. "You can use it. You'll have to do it on the castle wall, though. You're not going out."

I gave in. I'd just have to be careful in what I said. "That won't be as good, but I might be able to see something."

"Behave yourself, or I'll hear about it." Carl strode toward the big entrance doors, while the guard shooed me out the Hall's side.

"This will be useful." The guard chattered as he guided me to Beran's quarters. "I have my eye on some fancy vambraces, and I don't want to wait too long to buy them because another fellow's looking at them too, so I need to know if my promotion's going to come through."

"Ah," I said. Really, Jarka was right. People were so loose-mouthed it was astonishing their tongues didn't fall out and flap around on the floor. "What's your captain say about it?"

I WATCHED THE guard descend from the castle wall and gathered up the paper bits for the stable boy to toss. A cook and a maid waited their turns. I'd not been up on the wall inside the castle before. From here, I could see workers scurrying across the courtyard and watch the wind ripple the tops of the apple trees in Grandda's orchard. Beyond the castle gate, the city sloped away, smoke rising from chimneys to smudge the sky over a golden sea of thatched roofs. It looked peaceful and even pretty, but what was happening in the Shambles?

"I'm ready," the stable boy said.

I forced my attention to the wind box. I told the stable boy that the scullery maid would welcome a visit (she'd stopped to talk to him in the courtyard the day before), told the cook to check her flour delivery because as she suspected the merchant could be cheating her (if she suspected it, she was probably right), and told the maid she'd regret it if she didn't go visit her mother (the mother sounded like an old biddy, but she wasn't getting any younger). After every pigeon, my brain skittered back over what I'd said, trying to see if I'd put someone in danger. I couldn't see how, but then I hadn't seen it with Mag either.

When the maid left, I looked up to find Lineth smiling tentatively, though close up like this, I saw the dark smudges under her eyes. "I think I'm next," she said.

I liked what I'd seen of Lineth, and I liked her for Beran's sake too. I'd tread extra carefully on this one. As she tossed the paper, I invoked the winds and then waited for her question.

She leaned close and spoke low. "You saw danger when you read my fortune before. Do you see it still? If Beran marries Lady Elenia, will he be safe?" Her voice roughened. "Will he be happy?" She blinked and caught her lower lip between her teeth.

Would Beran be happy? Would he ever again glow like he did when he walked with Lineth on the wall? All my life, Da had said a man had to live with honor. He'd just never said how much honor like Beran's could cost. My heart twisted at Lineth's obvious pain. "His Highness will be kind to his wife," I said slowly, "and he'll be honorable. So he'll be happy in himself." I raised my gaze to meet her troubled one. "I don't see any danger."

Lineth gave a sharp nod. "Thank you. I'm glad." She dropped a tower in my hand and hurried away, head down.

Stone it.

I looked around the walkway. I'd thought several more people waited for their futures, but only Wyswoman Adrya lurked, watching me with one hand on her pendant and the corners of her mouth crimped. I scowled, glad to be irritated with Adrya instead of myself. The Wyswoman had probably scared everyone else away.

"You want me to divine your future?" I asked.

"Don't be impudent." Adrya stepped closer, and once again I smelled her unexpectedly sweet perfume. "Your friend Morka."

"Who?"

"The one with the crutch," Adrya said impatiently.

"Oh." I looked down into my wind box and gathered paper bits. "What about him?"

"Do you know if he can read?"

My head shot up again. "Read writing, you mean? Yes."

"Marred twice over, that one," Adrya murmured. "His foot and his mind, though if he can read, that last can't be too bad."

"What do you want with him?" I asked.

Adrya shook herself, clinking her Wyswoman's chain. "That's none of your concern." She waved at my rickety wind box. "You should be ashamed of yourself." Before I could answer, she stalked away.

I glared after her. I was already ashamed and worried enough. And why was Adrya interested in Jarka? I folded up my wind box, shouldered my bag, and clattered down the steps. I really wished I could let Tel and the other Uplanders know I'd gotten the king to go to their show.

The gate guard lowered his pike. "Sorry, Doniver. Carl's left orders not to allow you out."

So Carl had assumed I'd try to leave even when Beran said not to. I had enough annoyance left over from Adrya to resent that assumption even though it turned out he was right. I scanned the courtyard and brightened. I'd go see Grandda in the orchard. I'd ask him about Carl and Maras, and I could learn about grafting too. That would take my mind off my troubles and be useful when I got home, assuming I ever did, and assuming anyone there was still alive to care.

Chapter 18.

A Fall

T HE NEXT MORNING, Beran halted in the shadow of the gate. "Carl asked that we wait for him here."

"Do you always do what Carl says?" I asked.

"I let him think so." Beran grinned, then surprised a laugh out of me by saying, "You should understand. It's a cat and king thing."

I felt a moment's warmth that was almost like friendship. *Careful*, I reminded myself. *You're…well, lying to him.* I shifted from foot to foot, watching the castle door for Carl and Wyswoman Adrya to appear with the glass wind box. Once I finished the morning's show with the wind box, I'd hustle to the Shambles and see how bad the damage was to shrines and people both. Min would probably listen before driving me off, so I'd go to her place first and tell her Thien was coming to the Wind Dancers' performance. She'd tell the other Uplanders, and maybe they'd forgive me for my blunder about the shrines. I prayed they would anyway, or I *would* have if I could find an intact shrine and dared to use it. My heart squeezed at the thought of the Uplanders in Rin turning me away. Was it possible to die of loneliness?

"I regret the king felt the shrines needed to be destroyed." Beran's voice startled me from my concentration on the castle doorway. "Your desire to right the situation with the shrines shows a fierce sense of honor. That's a prize for any ruler to find in a subject. And I never saw harm in them when I lived in the Uplands."

I caught myself smiling. I probably shouldn't care what Thien's heir thought of me. Still, Beran was the second best castle person I'd met so far, coming right after Grandda. "Sir, why didn't your da listen to you? Why did he even send you there if he thought Uplanders were savages?"

He shrugged. "He sent me everywhere. His Majesty believed living in various parts of the kingdom would help me understand them. It turned out that he was correct, though with matters like the shrines, he's not always pleased when I tell him what I've learned. In that case, I'm the cat, but he's still the king."

I pictured living the way Beran had as a boy. Everything I did these days was aimed at getting home. Had Beran felt like that?

"Did you like living all over?" I asked, watching to see

if he'd resent my prying so I could make apologetic noises. "I'd have missed home if my da sent me away."

"When I was young, I was lonely, but I learned to manage." His tone was like the one Jarka used when he didn't want to talk about his cousin's husband. It was preposterous to pity a prince, but pity was what I felt.

A voice called, "Sir!" The stablemaster jogged across the courtyard with some concern about Beran's horse, just being led from the stables. Frowning, Beran followed the man back to the stable doorway, then bent to look at the mare's leg.

Someone tapped my shoulder, and I turned to find a Ringman, standing between the gate guards, holding out a folded paper. I backed away, but he thrust the paper toward me. "For His Highness," the Ringman said. "From the Lady Lineth."

I took the note, and the Ringman trotted away. I turned the blank paper in my hand. The writing must all be on the inside.

"What's that?" Carl appeared at my side, clutching the wind box. Wyswoman Adrya stood behind him, mouth pinched up like her morning ale had gone sour.

"It's for Beran," I said, "from Lineth."

"His Highness, not Beran." Balancing the box on his hip, Carl snatched the paper and tucked it in his belt. "Why aren't you wearing the clean shirt I gave you?"

"I like this one." The new one had no drawstrings at the cuffs.

"You have to let someone wash it. Otherwise people will shy away from your stench. They'll think you're street trash." Carl smiled, which meant this was a joke. Sweet Powers, the man was bad at them.

Beran reappeared, took in we were all there, and strode through the gate and along the street to the town wall. My anxiety rose over giving a convincing but non-lethal reading. I trudged up the stairs after him, the worry I'd tamped down leaping to life again. It would be all right, I told myself. I'd told Beran a believable fortune twice now. I could do it again.

At the top of the wall, Jarka waited with a bruise on his right cheek, a souvenir of our trip to the docks. No sign of Dilly, but in the night, I'd had an idea for how to keep her out of the Lac's Holding house and the grip of the revolting Huryn. Suryan's daughter, Elenia, was going to marry Beran. Not right away, it seemed. From what I could tell, the timing was uncertain, but that didn't matter because eventually the wedding would happen, and Lady Elenia would come to live in Thien's castle. Since Beran seemed to wish me well, I could ask him to hire Dilly as a castle servant, with the understanding she would serve Lady Elenia when the time came. Dilly claimed to hate Rin, which I understood, but maybe she'd be happy if she were with Elenia.

I tried to picture Jarka living in the castle too, but he was so fierce-tongued about keeping out of the grip of the powerful that I just couldn't see it. Even now, he was edging away from Adrya, putting a castle maid between them. Lots of castle folks crowded the walkway this morning, people whose fortune I'd divined the previous afternoon, their friends, and others who wanted to hear more about the threat to the king.

"Fair morning, sir." Lord Grimuld stepped from the crowd and bowed to Beran, his ringed hand over his heart.

"Fair morning," Beran said. "I assume you're here to ask about your magistrate again." He gestured for Carl to set up the wind box.

I clenched my teeth to keep from shouting how evil this lord was for sending his soldiers to trample all over wind shrines that had never hurt anyone. As soon as Carl had the box set up, I jumped toward it. The sooner we finished, the sooner I'd be out of Grimuld's sick-making company. Beran flung the paper bits into the box and blew on them.

"Do you see danger to the king or recognize the killer of Lord Grimuld's magistrate?" Beran asked.

I scanned the inside of the box, thought of Mag, and tried to be careful. "A king is always in danger," I said, "especially in an unquiet kingdom like Rinland."

"In other words," Lord Grimuld said, "you know nothing."

"I'm still looking," I said sharply. I glanced at Jarka, who had edged close enough to peer into the box. And then, clear as a cockcrow, he sucked in his breath. He raised a pale face and quickly looked away, but I saw how his lips whitened as he pressed them together. His hand clapped to his chest, but he jerked it away.

The hair rose on my neck. Maybe it was because we'd been apart for most of the last couple of days, but it was as if I was seeing him for the first time. Jarka had told his cousin that her husband would hurt her. And he'd known that rats were eating the city's grain. And he'd told Tebryn of the Basket that his wife was "managing."

How could I have been so blind? Jarka knew far more than could come from simple guesses. My world tipped around me.

I took a step forward, dizzy with what I suspected, and my too-big boot caught on a raised stone. I pitched face-first toward the stone walkway, but I threw my hands out and only just managed to stop my fall without cracking my head like a walnut.

"What's this?" Lord Grimuld lunged and grabbed my left wrist.

My left one.

We all stared at the hand that shouldn't have been there. I'd scraped it when I shoved it out of my sleeve and used it to break my fall. A drop of blood oozed across it.

Lord Grimuld shook the hand. "You see, Your Highness." His voice rose in triumph. "I told you these Uplanders weren't to be trusted. The boy is a swindling beggar who's lying to your face."

"A sense of honor, Doniver?" Beran's voice had lost every bit of the warmth it had just a few moments ago. "Is this what an Uplander's word means to you?"

"Arrest him," Grimuld offered my wrist to Carl, the only one there in a uniform.

Jarka hurled himself toward them, toppling into Lord Grimuld's back. Grimuld whirled, shaking Jarka off and letting go of me.

"Sorry! Sorry! My crutch slipped," Jarka lied from flat on the walkway.

I bolted for the stairs.

"Stop!" Carl shouted.

Flinging his arms up to protect his head, Jarka rolled into Carl's path. Carl swore and jumped over him. I leaped down the first three stairs. My heel shot off the edge and I fell, tumbling halfway down the stone steps and banging my shoulder before I caught myself. I felt something jam in the wrist of the hand I'd hidden for days now, but ignored the pain and scrambled up.

"Let him go, Carl." Beran's voice came from overhead.

"No!" Lord Grimuld said. "Falsifying the Powers' mark is blasphemy."

I was too far away to hear any more, but I didn't slow until I reached the streets of the Shambles. I ran blindly, darting around corners, trying to lose anyone who might be following. I stumbled into a dead end street and saw I'd headed straight for the Rat Hole.

My left wrist throbbed in what felt like a bad joke of a punishment for shamming the Powers' mark. I choked on a laugh. Apparently my instinct to go home held even when home was a stinking, rat-infested bolt-hole. Shoving the door open, I stepped into the dim room. I hadn't expected anyone to be there, so I jumped when something moved. Dilly had been lying down, and now she pushed herself up to sit against the wall. Tuc uncurled from her side, shook himself so his ears slapped the sides of his head, and trotted to me.

"You scared me." Dilly sniffled and dragged her hand under her nose.

I scratched Tuc's ear. "Same here. Are you sick, Dilly?" It was unlike her to be inside during the day. No money was made that way. Besides, she was supposed to be working in the Lac's Holding house.

"I'm all right."

I approached, fumbling in my bag to draw out bread and cheese and thrust it toward her. "I got this for you and Jarka."

"I'm not hungry."

My own problems fell out of my head. No street kid turned down food. Ever. You stowed it away if you'd just eaten, but you always took it. I dropped down to sit beside her and put the bread and cheese in her lap. Tuc lay down, nose quivering, eyes on the food. She broke off a corner of the bread and gave it to him. Her hands and face were the cleanest I'd ever seen, but she still wore her filthy old dress.

"Are you sure you're not sick?"

"I ate at the Lac's Holding house," she said dully. "I

spent last night there."

I sat up straight fast enough that my boot heels cut scrapes in the rotting wood floor. "What happened?"

She turned the hunk of bread over and mumbled something.

"I beg your pardon?" I said.

The words burst out of her. "Huryn is a snake."

I opened my mouth to say I'd told her so but glimpsed her tear-streaked face. "What did he do?" I asked instead.

For a moment, I thought she wasn't going to answer. "The steward said he'd try me out working in the kitchen. So I was scrubbing the porridge pot this morning." Her voice trembled. "Huryn waited until I was alone and backed me into the pantry and started grabbing me and kissing me."

I felt a murderous desire to "grab" Huryn in ways that would leave him howling. "Did he hurt you?"

She shook her head. "I hit him with a pot of pickles." She gave a twisted smile. "Then I kneed him. He'll be walking funny for a week."

"Good for you." *Howling accomplished.*

A shudder ran through her, and I realized she was crying. I wrapped my arms around her and pulled her against me. "Don't cry. Oh, Dilly, don't. He's not worth it."

"It's not him," she choked out. "It's everything. I'll be here forever." Her fingers knotted in the cloth of my shirt.

"No, you won't." I stroked her hair, my heart

thudding.

She pulled away. Her voice dropped to a whisper. "I don't want to live like my mother. I won't. I'd die first."

I froze, struggling between the desire to pull her closer and the knowledge that I'd be violating her trust. With an effort as great as any I'd ever made, I let her shift away, though I kept one arm around her shoulders. I cleared my throat. "You won't have to." I started to say I'd ask Beran to let her serve Lady Elenia at the castle but realized I couldn't ever go near Beran again. "We'll think of something. You can come to the Uplands with me."

"I don't want to go to the Uplands. I want to go home to Lac's Holding."

"Then that's what you'll do."

We sat in silence for a moment. I felt her take a deep breath before eating some of the bread and tossing a bit more to Tuc.

"My mother wasn't a bad woman." She looked at me anxiously, as if worried I'd been judging her ma. "She didn't mean for things to happen the way they did. She just trusted the wrong person."

"The man you lived with."

"No," she said. "Well yes, him, but really me."

"I don't understand."

"I saw him with a woman who lived up the street." She spoke so softly now that I had to duck my head closer to her face to hear her. "He went after anything in a skirt, and I'd got old enough that—well, I wanted him gone." She drew a wobbly breath. "So I told the woman's husband. The next day, he took off."

"You feel bad about that? You were better off without him."

"Mama didn't think so. She didn't know I'd made it happen, and she was flattened by him leaving. And then, we had no money, and things got—bad. And then she died, and I never had a chance to make it up to her."

I squeezed her shoulder. She was letting me into her dark space. In that place, the wrong word could break her. Things sounded as complicated between mothers and daughters as Carl said they were between fathers and sons, but how to say that to Dilly? "I understand," I said slowly. "Guilt can eat your heart out. My father was on that boat only because I talked him into it." A whiff of smoke clogged my nose.

Dilly lifted her head and stared at me with parted lips. "He's your hard memory."

"My dark place."

"Jarka and I will keep you company there." She nodded once. "That way it won't feel so dark."

Inside me, something broke loose and floated away. "Past is past. We can't undo it. We can't bring them back. All we can do it live like they'd want us to. I bet your ma would have wanted you to be happy."

She rested her head on my shoulder, and I took a chance on asking her something I'd wondered about for weeks. "Dilly, that day I met you on the docks, I was just a strange boy to you. Why did you trust me?"

I felt her cheek round in a smile. "You saved Tuc."

"Oh, come on."

She shrugged. "It's hard to explain. You seemed separate from everything around us, like you were in your own world, and maybe it was a better one. You were starving, but when I said Jarka and I would feed you, you still told me you had no coin. I could see you believed there were rules that good people followed. You weren't the kind who'd just take what he wanted. To me, you felt innocent."

I thought about Mag and wanted desperately to still be the person she'd thought I was. My wrist throbbed. I twisted it, but that only made it worse.

She straightened. "What's wrong with your wrist?"

"I fell and jammed it."

"We should bind that to keep the swelling down." From her pocket, she produced a knife I'd never seen before. She saw me eyeing it. "Huryn's," she said, and I caught her in a glimmer of a smile. "I trust you're not fond of that ruffle." She cut the ruffle away from my sleeve, snapped it straight, and began tying up my wrist.

"And Huryn? Why did you trust him?" I tried to keep from sounding like I was criticizing.

For a moment, she concentrated on tying off the bandage. "I didn't. Not really. I wanted to go home so badly, and I thought I needed him to do it. Wanting and needing can make a person do stupid things."

"You got that right," I said fervently.

A hurried step sounded in the street. I got ready to jump up to run, but I recognized the uneven step-drag and relaxed.

Jarka hobbled through the doorway. When he saw me, he sagged on his crutch. "Well, that was clever. I'm sure our lives will be much easier now."

"Stone you, Jarka. I didn't do it on purpose."

"Why couldn't you have been more careful? There goes an easy mark for food. They'll be after you. They'll be after *us*. We can't even stay in this cesspit any more because Carl knows about it." Jarka's voice shook as I'd never heard it do.

I snatched up the rest of the bread and cheese and flung them at him. He fumbled to clutch them to his chest. "Just shut it. It's a knot that can't be untied."

"That's the truth." As he pushed the food into his own bag, his gaze settled on where my hip touched Dilly's, and his jaw hardened. "Am I interrupting something? Maybe you two want me to clear out?"

Heat flared in my face. Now I did stand up, my fists opening and closing. "I'm comforting her. Haven't you ever seen anyone do that? You should try not grouching at the people you live with. Maybe they'd listen to you better."

He lunged, and I hit the floor with a thump that knocked all the wind out of me. His fist flew toward my face, and I barely got my arm up to block it. I grabbed his wrist, braced my other hand on his shoulder, and heaved until we rolled over in a tangle of legs. I tried to pin his arms with one hand and punch him with the other, but my jammed wrist screamed and a lifetime of hauling himself around on a crutch had left him with a strong right arm. I needed both hands to hold it away from me. Somewhere Tuc barked like the house was on fire.

"Stop!" Dilly hauled at my shoulders. "Stop it!" She tugged me over. I managed to keep hold of Jarka's right wrist, but Dilly dove between us, landing on top of Jarka. "Stop!" I let go. We all lay there for a long moment before Dilly rolled off Jarka and shoved to her knees. The first thing she did was snatch back the cheese and bread that had fallen from her lap under Tuc's nose. Then she snapped, "What's *wrong* with you two?"

I sat up, wrapped my trembling hands around my knees, and caught my breath. What was wrong? Jarka had jumped me, which was wrong in more ways than one. But I knew that wasn't all. Jarka was always confident about finding a way for us to live, and now he seemed as lost as me and Dilly. It felt like the ground had given way under me.

Jarka struggled to sit. "It's been a bad morning, Dilly," he said wearily. "Lord Grimuld knows Doniver has two good hands. He's sending his Ringmen to find him."

"No!" Dilly looked horrified.

"Lord Grimuld's men?" I asked. "Not Beran's?"

"Beran wouldn't do it, but Grimuld argued you were

one of his people, and I could see Beran didn't feel he had the right to fool with Grimuld's rule over an Uplander."

I pushed shakily to my feet. "I should go then." I glanced around the room. "Did Tava come home last night, Jarka?" He shook his head. Another person I'd failed. I shouldn't have left an old woman on the streets without help.

"Where are you going?" Dilly asked.

"The king is going to the Wind Dancers' performance today," I said. "So first I'll go tell Min, so she can tell the others that at least I managed that. After that, I don't know."

"I ate at Min's last night," Jarka said. I envisioned Jarka eating alone and knew from the tightness in his voice that he'd hated it. For someone who claimed to look out for himself alone, Jarka went to a lot of effort to gather friends around him like a little family, replacing the one he'd lost. "Some other Uplanders were there," Jarka went on, "and they weren't too happy with you."

"That's why I need to tell them," I said.

"Suit yourself." Jarka crawled to where his crutch had fallen and levered himself erect. "If you need help, I'll be in New Square, working the crowd. We'll need the money. If you find a place to hide, let me know. I'll look around too."

"I should stay away from you and Dilly. You'll be safer that way."

"Stay away, and I'll hunt you down, farm boy."

"But Carl—"

"Stone Carl."

My throat swelled at the chance Jarka was willing to take for me. So the three of us were together again. Dilly and I had tried to break loose, but in Rin, street trash stayed street trash. Maybe Jarka was right. Maybe this was better.

"I'm sorry for what I said about you grouching. I'd miss it if you stopped." Halfway to the door, I paused. "You saw something in that wind box this morning, didn't you? Something about Thien."

Jarka stopped, face turned away. "Don't be daft. Want to come with me, Dilly?"

I tore my gaze away from Jarka. "You should go, Dilly. The acrobats I told you about are performing."

Dilly's face brightened, which made me feel better too. "I'll go then. I don't know why I was here moping." She brushed at her dirty gown like that would do any good, then lifted her chin. "They gave me a Lac's Holding blue dress, but when I left, I decided this one was better." She, Jarka, and Tuc followed me out of the Rat Hole. At the corner, we parted, but I felt their company long after they left.

Chapter 19.

Wind Dancers

I PICKED MY route carefully, avoiding places where Uplanders gathered. I hadn't needed Jarka's warning to know they might not be friendly. I tried to stay with other people, so I'd be harder for any stray Ringmen or men with knives to spot, and that turned out to be easy because the streets were full of folks heading toward New Square. As I wove my way between them, I thought about the quiver in Jarka's voice, the tears on Dilly's face. Things were going to be tough for a while. I needed to think of some way to get us a little coin and a place to hide out.

At the corner to Min's street, I paused to draw a deep breath, then stepped out where she would be able to see me. I'd have talk fast so she wouldn't have time to throw a cook pot at me. She was talking to Tel, the acrobat, and he spotted me first. His eyebrows lifted, and he cocked his head.

Min leaned out over her counter. "You have nerve showing up here, Doniver."

"I'm sorry," I said. "I didn't mean for that to happen."

"You should have kept your mouth shut."

I'd heard that one before.

"You shouldn't have been in the castle in the first place," Min went on. "Thien and his lords can't be trusted to deal fairly with Uplanders."

"But it turns out to be good I was there. Not for me, but for the Uplands. You wanted Thien to come see the Wind Dancers today, right? Well, he's going to."

"Is he now?" Tel slapped me on the back. "That's good news."

"I suppose it is," Min said grudgingly. "You still shouldn't be hanging about the castle."

"You'll get your way on that," I said. "I can't go back. Lord Grimuld's men are looking for me because they found out I was faking about the missing hand. I don't want to get you in trouble, so I'll keep away from you now. I just wanted to tell you about Thien."

"Sweet Powers." Min's brow wrinkled as the anger melted out of her face and voice. The tension in my shoulders eased. At least there was no doubt where her loyalties lay. "Where will you hide?"

"I don't know." I clutched the edge of her counter. The smell of Uplands cooking drifted out of the shop. I pictured Ma at the stove.

"Come with me," Tel said. "The troupe is setting up its equipment and needs help. We can make sure you're not spotted. Or at least not recognized." He grinned.

Hope sprang back to life in my head. Even with the quarantine still in place the Wind Dancers could get me out of the city and away from Grimuld's men. But wait. Hadn't I just been thinking about how Jarka, Dilly, and I had to help one another? My brain started spinning tales with happy endings. Dilly could decide to go with the Wind Dancers too, despite what she'd said. Maybe even Jarka would go. I pictured Jarka and his crutch among acrobats. Maybe not, but surely I could think of something.

Tel started toward the busier of the two streets bracketing Min's lane. "Our equipment's in the carter's yard."

"All right. Not that way though. The Ringmen are more likely to be there." I led him on a roundabout path to the carter's yard where half a dozen men leaned against the wall outside the front gate.

"About time, Tel," one of them said. "We need to set up."

Tel unlocked the gate, and the men pushed in. A horse cart and two handcarts took up most of the space in the yard, but against one fence was a pile of ropes, boards, pulleys, and boxes. The men began heaping the equipment into one of the handcarts. I grabbed a pair of gigantic sheep horns and a drum.

"This is Doniver," Tel said. "He talked the king into coming today."

"Well done, lad," an acrobat said. He exchanged a look with Tel. "We get a crack at him after all."

"We do indeed, so let's give the best show of our lives," Tel said. "In the meantime, we need a disguise for Doniver. Lord Grimuld is looking for him."

At the name of the lord of the Uplands, the man grimaced. "An enemy of Grimuld's is a friend of ours." He rooted around in a box and pulled out two masks, a green one with a yellow bird's beak and feathers, and a blue one with red streamers down the back. He tossed me the green one. "Wear that. We'll all be in costume and masks once the heavy work's done, so you won't be the only one." He hung the other mask from the side of the cart, ready for when he needed it.

The beaky mask wouldn't exactly leave me inconspicuous. On the other hand, it would make it harder to recognize me, and Lord Grimuld's men would never expect me to be nervy enough to wear something so flashy. More fools they. Da always said I had more nerve than sense, which made me pause only for a moment before stuffing the mask in my belt and helping the Wind Dancers load the cart. Sometimes you needed nerve more than sense. At least I didn't have to keep my hand hidden any more.

When we finished loading, Tel took the handles and pushed the cart out of the yard, maneuvering it carefully around the corner into the street. I pulled my mask on and followed the men through the Shambles to New Square, where a crowd of folks were giddy as fair goers. The posters and Uplanders' praise had drawn even more people than I'd hoped. The square swarmed not just with Uplanders, but also with well-dressed merchants, housewives, and tradespeople. In front of Lord Grimuld's house, men pounded nails into a wooden platform. I guessed the king and Ambassador Gladoc would watch the performance from there. The holiday mood was catching, and the feathers on my mask bounced with my walk. At the very least, I was going to see the Wind Dancers perform.

Tel stopped at the foot of the bell tower. Not far away, Jarka peered into his wind box while an elderly woman waited with puckered brow for him to give her good news. With Tuc at her heels, Dilly wandered nearby, eyeing the food-hawkers' trays, though that had to be out of street kid habit since I'd just seen her eat.

A ripple of movement ran through the crowd, and it parted to let two Ringmen through. No one who could help it stayed within a yard of them, which told you something about how even city folks though of them. I hopped into the cart and lay down behind the shelter of its wooden sides. Mask or no mask, I couldn't afford to take chances. One of the acrobats must have felt the same way because a hand lifted the blue and red mask from the cart's edge.

I got my knees and looked cautiously around. The Ringmen were gone. One of the acrobats took a rope with a hook on the end from the cart, slung it over his shoulder, and trotted off toward the bell tower. A few moments later, I glimpsed movement at the tower's top. The acrobat leaned out, attached the hook to the window ledge, and let the rope down.

"Hand me that anchor," Tel said from the cart's open gate.

Nothing in the cart looked like an anchor to me. I picked out an unidentifiable lump of metal and offered it to Tel, but he grinned and stretched to grab a metal loop attached to a spike. He seized a mallet and departed.

A Wind Dancer in the blue mask with red streamers wandered through the crowd, talking up the show. When he crossed Dilly's path, he detoured to block her way and lean close. She gave a quick, apologetic curtsy and slipped past him, but I saw her quick fingers dip into his pocket.

I was entitled to interfere on that one. I vaulted to the cobblestones and caught up with her. She whirled at my touch on her shoulder, then gave me a sweet smile. "Yes, sir?"

"It's me. Give me whatever you took from that Wind Dancer."

She took a step back and laughed. "I like the beak. It suits you."

I put out my hand and repeated, "Give me what you took from the Wind Dancer."

"Who?"

"The other fellow in a mask. Didn't that give you a hint he was with the show?"

She shrugged. "He was way too friendly. What does it matter who he's with?"

"It matters to me. I'm helping them, and I'm hoping they'll be grateful. So I won't stand by and watch you steal from them. Now give." I thrust my hand under her nose.

She sighed, pulled something out of her belt pouch, and laid it on my palm. "I haven't even had a chance to look at it yet. Is it valuable?"

I frowned at the object in my hand. It was a jointed ring that would run halfway down the finger of anyone who wore it. Its face bore a sketch of a raven.

Dilly craned her neck to look. "Isn't that the ring Lord Grimuld and his men all wear?" She elbowed me. "Maybe your acrobat stole it in the first place."

"Maybe." Something nasty fluttered in my stomach. What was it the Ringmen had said when they demanded to know if Min had any news of the killings in the Uplands? Someone had killed Lord Grimuld's magistrate and his guard and robbed them both. The guard would have had a ring like this. The person who killed him would have it now. An Uplander had attacked me. And the Wind Dancers had been eager to have the king out of his castle and sitting in New Square. I knew all that, but the Wind Dancers had figured in my dreams for years, and I was apparently unwilling to part with even one more illusion. I looked around and found Jarka still in the same place, though the old lady had moved off. I picked my way through the crowd with Dilly and Tuc following.

"Would you like—" Jarka started, then slowly smiled. "Lovely look on you. Improves your face no end. Lord Grimuld's men were just here. You want to be careful."

"I know," I said. "I need your help, Jarka. I want you to read the wind for me."

Jarka gave a short laugh. "You've spent too much time with the pigeons, farm boy. You know what I'm really doing."

"By all that's holy, Jarka, I do." I held out the ring. "Dilly found this on one of the Wind Dancers. It's Lord Grimuld's, the one he and all the Ringmen wear. So where did a Wind Dancer get it? One of them said they'd have a *crack* at Thien since I talked him into coming to the show. Something's wrong, Jarka. I have to know what I've done." I thought of Mag and amended, "What more I've done."

Jarka prodded the ring with a black-tipped fingernail. "You think I can tell you?"

"I *know* you can."

His eyes met mine and held for a long moment.

"What's going on?" Dilly's brows drew down. "Are you saying Jarka really can divine things?"

"Please, Jarka," I said. "I wouldn't ask if it weren't important."

Jarka grimaced. "Your blasted honor?"

"Yes, but also Thien's life. I promised Beran I'd help

protect his father. Think about how you want to protect your cousin. Or me and Dilly, for that matter." I plowed on over Jarka's grunt of protest. "I'd have done anything to protect my father, and Beran's been knocking himself out just to please his. Thien is his only family, Jarka."

Dilly had frozen beside me. "If you can help him, Jarka, you should," she squeezed out. "You know how he feels about keeping harm away from his family."

For a handful of heartbeats, Jarka didn't move. Then he held out the cup of paper bits.

I shoved the ring into my belt pouch and snatched the cup. "Thank you."

"Just throw them," Jarka said.

I tossed the paper bits into the box and blew on them while Jarka invoked the Powers in the wind. "Is Thien in danger if he comes here? Have I betrayed Beran's trust?"

Jarka looked briefly into the wind box. He licked his lips. "Yes."

"Thien's in danger from the man who had this ring?" *Say no, say no. He's an Uplander. Say no.*

"Yes." Jarka still frowned at the paper bits. He drew his elbows in tight to his ribs as if he were being tied up. "Beran...you didn't betray *him*." He sounded confused, but I didn't have time to ask more questions.

"I have to warn them," I said.

Jarka straightened. "What? And get your Uplander acrobat friends in trouble?"

"How could you, anyway?" Dilly asked. "You can't go

back to the castle. They'll lock you up."

Sweat slicked my face under the mask. Could I turn the Wind Dancers in? I'd already angered my fellow Uplanders by telling Lord Grimuld and King Thien about the shrines. If I told Beran or anyone else that Thien would be in danger at the show, Uplanders would take the blame, and I might never be able to go home. Sure as babies cried in the night, the Wind Dancers wouldn't take me, couldn't take me if they were locked up. But how could I not warn Beran and Thien? In my head, I heard my father's voice: "The rock solid center of a man is his honor, Doniver. You lose your honor, you lose yourself."

Misery wrapped a cold hand around my heart.

"I have to do it," I said.

Jarka blew out his breath in exasperation. "You're the biggest fool I've ever met."

He was probably right. I started for the castle.

Chapter 20.

Taken

FOR THE SECOND time in two days, I pelted toward the castle entrance. The last time, I'd been looking for help to save Upland shrines. This time I was accusing Uplanders of plotting to assassinate King Thien. How could things have changed so much in such a short time? Had my loyalties really changed? I didn't know. But I was doing what I'd told Dilly we should do, and living like Da would want. I guessed that meant my loyalty wasn't to the Uplands or the king, but to something bigger than both. And curse whatever it was because it was making my life stoning hard.

At the gate, both guards stiffened, and the one with the pike lowered it, blocking my way. "Show your face," one of them said.

I raised my hand to take off the mask I'd forgotten I

still wore, but then thought better of it. Dilly was right when she said they'd arrest me. "No. I'll wait here where you can watch and see I'm no danger, but I have to talk to Prince Beran."

The guards exchanged a quick look. The one with the pike stayed put. The other moved around behind me.

My breath caught. "Please. There's no time to lose." The pikeman nodded to the guard at my back, and iron-hard hands grabbed my arms and yanked them up behind me. I lunged against the grip. Pain tore through my shoulders, strong enough to make me cry out. "Let go! I have to see His Highness."

The pikeman stepped forward and ripped off my mask. "You!" He looked over my shoulder at the man holding me. "Hold tight. I'll get Grimuld's man." He ducked through the gate.

"Grimuld's man?" Panic flooded through me. "Let me go, please," I said. "I have important news."

"Would this be the news that you've two good hands?"

"I know it looks bad, but this is about danger to King Thien."

"Divined it, have you?" He spat on the cobblestones.

A soldier ran out through the gate, bearing not the Tower, but Lord Grimuld's raven sigil on his chest. I recognized him as one of the men who'd been wrestling with Tava. He hurried up to where I stood, grinning widely enough that the scar on his cheek twisted. "Look at that! It looks like an extra ten towers for me."

"He's all yours." The man behind me shoved me into the scarred Ringman's grip.

He grabbed my arm. "Let's go."

I wriggled to look back at the gate guard. "Tell Beran I need to see him!" I squinted at Scarface. "I think I know who killed Lord Grimuld's magistrate too."

Scarface laughed nastily. "I'll wager you do."

"You have to listen to me."

He tightened his grip. "Shut it, or I'll shut it for you."

Shut it? Was that all anyone ever wanted?

With my arm still clamped in a grip like an iron manacle, I stumbled down Kings Way, scarcely seeing it or the people streaming toward New Square. Near the square, Scarface steered me off into a series of side streets until we came alongside a high, wooden fence. A hubbub of voices spilled up the street from nearby. We must be at the back of Lord Grimuld's house.

Scarface shouted and pounded on a gate. After a moment, it swung open, revealing another Ringman. Scarface hustled me across a small stableyard, up two wooden steps, and through the house's back door into a kitchen. A cook and scullery maid turned toward us from the hearth and table. A Ringman rose from a stool against the wall.

"What have we here?"

"The boy Lord Grimuld is looking for," Scarface said.

The one in the kitchen gave a ferret's smile. "Is it now?" He shambled across the room to open a door directly in front of me. "Lord Grimuld will be happy to hear that, once he's back from the show in the square. Down he goes."

Scarface shoved me through the open door and down a narrow stairway. I tripped and would have gone nose first down the stone steps if he hadn't hauled me back onto my feet with a wrench of my arm. My shoulder screamed a hot protest, and I bit down hard to keep it from coming out of my mouth. At the bottom of the steps, a stone corridor stretched straight ahead, pierced on one side by heavy wooden doors and on the other by high, small windows covered in wooden shutters. We must be in the undercroft, where the household stored its goods. Judging by the bedrolls spread in some of the alcoves, the musky smell, and the Ringman idly tossing knucklebones, some of Lord Grimuld's Ringmen were quartered here too.

The knucklebone player rose. "Another *guest*?"

"Please," I tried again. "Tell Prince Beran I need to talk to him. The king's in danger."

Scarface laughed. "The little snake's been claiming to read the wind. He was lying, of course."

"That so?" the knucklebone player asked me.

"Yes, but I'm not lying now. Please!"

"Let's just throw him in with the old bat," Scarface said.

The knucklebone player bared his teeth. "Got to search him first." He yanked my belt pouch free and tossed it to Scarface, then ran his hands over my body. I tried to shift away from his lingering touch, but he held me firm. "No weapons," he finally said. "No valuables either."

"There's this." Scarface held up the ring Dilly had taken from the Wind Dancer. "Where'd you get it?"

I tried to make my mouth open. Now that I was faced with telling what I knew, my tongue was reluctant to wag. I'd pictured myself telling Beran what I suspected, and I trusted him to work justice no matter how angry he was with me. Could I betray a fellow Uplander to Grimuld's men? I had to. Thien's life was at stake. "A Wind Dancer had it. He's in the square right now." My knees weakened. I'd done it. Now they'd have to investigate further. It was out of my hands.

The knucklebone player's mouth thinned. "I think we'll ask you again later. I'm wondering if you stole it, and if so, who from. There was a Ringman killed in the Uplands not long ago."

I moaned. "I was here then, not in the mountains. An acrobat had that ring. He's the one you're looking for."

"We already know what a liar you are," Scarface said. "I look forward to making the truth run out of your mouth like drool."

The knucklebone player led the way to the last door and lifted the bar. That door might once have closed a storeroom, but unless Grimuld's carrots and onions had been trying to escape, the new looking bar on the outside meant it now shut in something more lively. A dark emptiness waited, perfumed by the unmistakable stench of rat droppings. I knew it was pointless, but I braced my feet anyway. Scarface put a hand in the middle of my back and shoved. I stumbled into the room, the door thudded shut behind me, and the bar descended with a crash.

I grabbed for the bars in the little window and pressed my face against them. "Send word to Prince Beran," I called to the two departing backs. "Tell him I need to talk to him."

Scarface clumped up the stairs. The knucklebone player slouched into his chair, and I heard bones rattling on the table. The guard was evidently gambling against himself, a sure way to win. Or lose, depending on how you looked at it.

"Hey!" I called.

"He won't come," a quavering voice behind me said.

I whirled. Against the wall, someone sat on a low shelf. Even in the murky light, I recognized my fellow prisoner. "Tava! Are you all right?"

She nodded, sending her stringy hair dancing. "You won't believe how nice it is here. They bring food twice a day, and there's blankets and a soft mattress." She patted the shelf beside her, raising the dusty scent of straw.

I'd never have predicted I'd be so happy to see her. She was locked up, but unhurt. As my eyes adjusted to the gloom, the room took form, showing itself even smaller than I'd thought. I thumped down onto the wooden shelf opposite Tava's. What sounded like claws scurried under the bench, and I drew my feet up off the floor and hooked my heels on the edge of the shelf. "Why did they arrest you?"

She gave a jaw-cracking yawn. "Someone saw me leaving my bag of dung on Grimuld's doorstep."

I barked a surprised laugh. "Tava, I think I might love you."

Her broken teeth flashed in the dimness. "Either that, or I killed his magistrate and the guard too."

My breath stopped, then choked in again. "What do you mean, *killed his magistrate*?"

She wrapped a strand of hair around her finger and coyly ducked her head. "You know, Doniver. Those guards were talking about it just now. Anyway, I already told you. They were thieves. They were taking my farm, and when my boy tried to stop them, the guard hit him over the head and killed him. So I took the butchering knife from the barn and stabbed the guard. Then I went into my house and did for the magistrate too." She frowned. "He tracked mud all over my floors."

Her words hung in the dim air between us, waiting for me to take them up. The tappity-tap of thrown knucklebones echoed in the corridor. My thoughts broke and swirled like snow in a blizzard. I kept my voice to a whisper. "Tava, you didn't really kill them, did you?"

She blinked. "Didn't I?"

I shook my head. "How could you? Two grown men,

one of them a soldier? It was a Wind Dancer."

She shrugged. "Well, I wanted to anyway."

In the corridor, the Ringman coughed and spat.

Tava turned her head toward the little window in the door. "If you sit tight, the food will come pretty soon. I suppose you can't do that though. Not if you're looking for that Beran."

I relaxed against the wall again. "I wish he'd come," I said, speaking more to myself than Tava.

"I dreamed he was praying at a wind shrine." She brightened. "The one behind the blacksmith's shop with the blue streamer."

"Not likely," I said. "The Ringmen smashed all the shrines, remember? And Beran wouldn't pray at one anyway."

"No?" She shrugged. "Not praying then. Sleeping." She flopped over onto her side and pulled up the blanket bunched at the shelf's end. "Wake me when the food comes." She sighed, drew three soft breaths, and then let out the gurgling snore I'd plugged my ears against in the Rat Hole.

I watched her hair flutter in her snoring breath, more bothered than was sane by what she'd said. *Be reasonable. She's not right in the head.* A chill ran down my spine that had nothing to do with the cold wall behind me. Adrya had said a muddled mind was as much a maiming as Jarka's foot. What if Tava's mind was muddled because she'd seen her son murdered and then killed the murderers? That would knock almost anyone's mind off balance. What if the Powers had given Tava seeing dreams in payment for what they'd taken? Just because some things she said were crazy didn't mean they all were. She'd dreamed of Beran "sleeping." What if he was unconscious or, the Powers help us, dead?

But she couldn't have killed the magistrate and the Ringman. She was so frail that a strong wind would push her over. An acrobat had killed the magistrate and now wanted to kill King Thien. I jumped to my feet and went to the door again. The Ringman was cleaning his fingernails with his knife. "Hey! Are you listening to me? Let me out, and I can explain everything."

The Ringman sighed, sheathed his knife, and pushed to his feet. He strolled toward me.

I shifted from foot to foot. "Hurry it up. I tell you, Thien's in danger."

The Ringman lifted the bar, opened the door, and delivered a backhanded swat that knocked me to my knees. The room spun. I stayed on my knees, clutching my throbbing jaw. The door slammed shut again.

"Stop your noise," the Ringman said. "Next time, I'll get rough." His steps faded.

"Not too bright, are you?" Tava mumbled. She rolled over so her back was to me and started snoring again.

I struggled to my feet, swallowing away the salty taste of blood. Cautiously, I poked my tongue at my teeth but none of them wiggled. This was what I got for scamming.

No one was going to believe a thing I said for the rest of my life. Clever-tongue, my arse.

I kept moving, like maybe that would get me closer to where I wanted to go. Four steps to the wall, four back to the door. I had to get out of here. I peered through the bars at the small, high windows on the other side of the corridor. If I could get out of the cell, maybe I could scale the wall, open the shutter, and squeeze through. I'd pretend to be sick or pretend Tava was sick and then jump the Ringman when he came. My jaw let out a throb of pain. I needed a better idea. I paced some more, timing my steps to Tava's snores.

A door banged and noise exploded in the hallway. "Is the boy Doniver here?" barked a familiar voice. "I heard he was shouting for His Highness."

I leaped to the door. Carl stood near the knucklebone player, and at the sight of him, I felt an unlikely surge of joy. "Carl, get me out of here! Someone has to listen. Thien is in danger."

"I want to talk to the little worm," Carl flung to the Ringman as he strode down the hall. He stopped in front of me, face red, fists clenched. Despite the door between us, I took a step backwards. "Where's Beran?" Carl asked.

The knucklebone player panted up to stand at Carl's shoulder, but he lacked sufficient guts—or death wish—to interfere.

The bottom of my stomach fell out. "I don't know. Is something wrong?"

"He gave me the slip, the fool," Carl said. "What was in that note you had?"

I frowned. "The one from Lady Lineth? You know I can't read."

"She says she didn't write one," Carl said. "Whatever it was, Beran read it and took off. He hasn't been seen since."

"Written words with no one behind them. What do you expect?"

Carl grabbed the bars in the window. "Don't get smart with me! Where's Beran?"

"I said I don't know." I hesitated, then thrust a thumb to point behind me. "Tava says she dreamed Beran's praying at a wind shrine."

Both men looked through the bars at Tava, who sat up and gave us all a loony grin. "That's helpful," Carl said dryly.

"Carl, it's Thien you have to worry about," I said, "not Beran." Sweet Powers, I hoped that was true. I smothered the sound of Tava saying *sleeping*. "I think the king might be in danger at the Wind Dancers' performance." I gabbled out my tale of a Wind Dancer having one of Grimuld's rings. At first, Carl tried to interrupt with questions about Beran, but as I went on, Carl's brows drew down in concentration.

"Uplanders," the knucklebone player said when I finished.

"You think this acrobat murdered Lord Grimuld's men and stole the ring?" Carl asked.

"Yes, and I think he's planning to hurt Thien."

"Your evidence?"

I squirmed. I could hardly say Jarka read the danger in a wind box. Carl would drag me right through the bars. "They really wanted the king to come see them."

"So they're all involved?"

I shrugged, unable to force myself to say yes.

The knucklebone player spat on the stone floor. "The boy had the ring. Seems to me he's the most likely killer of the magistrate."

Carl blew out his breath. "Describe this man you say had the ring."

"He's wearing a mask. When I saw him, it was blue with red streamers, but they'll all be wearing masks. Let me come with you. I can pick him out, I'm sure." For a moment, I wondered if I really wanted to be on the same side of the door with Carl.

Carl ran his hand over his face, then reached for the bar closing the door. The knucklebone player hipped him aside and leaned on the bar to keep it in place. "What do you think you're doing?"

"I need him," Carl said. "Let him out."

"Not a chance. I value my hide too much. The boy faked the Powers' mark and might have killed a magistrate and a Ringman. He's to stand trial before his lord."

"This is more important. Let him go."

"On whose authority? Yours?"

Carl drew himself erect and looked down his nose at

the shorter Ringman. "The king's."

"You have the king's authority? Don't make me laugh."

Carl leaned over the knucklebone player. "You calling me a liar?"

The undercroft grew so quiet, I heard the Ringman swallow.

"If he goes, I go too," the Ringman said. "I'm responsible for him."

"No argument from me. You can help me keep a grip on the little weasel." Carl heaved the bar out of its brackets.

I jumped out into the corridor, careful to put as much space as I could between me and Carl. I looked back at Tava. I'd abandoned her once. I didn't want to do it again. "Can Tava come too?"

"No, no!" Tava clutched her blanket around her shoulders. "Don't make me leave."

"Tava, Grimuld could hurt you," I pleaded.

She shook her head.

The knucklebone player rolled his eyes and barred the door. I couldn't keep from looking back as I let Carl push me down the hallway. We mounted the stairs and crossed the kitchen, drawing startled looks from the cook and maid.

In the stableyard, the knucklebone player asked, "Where are we going?"

"To New Square to warn the king," Carl said. "Lord

Grimuld too. If a Wind Dancer really did kill the magistrate, Lord Grimuld is at least as likely to be in danger as the king is."

I'd left Tava in jail and was on my way to save King Thien and Lord Grimuld, the two men I'd thought about with loathing on the *Rose of Rin* before Mountain Fever burned through my life, taking with it any belief I might ever have had in myself as a decent person.

Chapter 21.

In New Square

A S WE DREW near New Square, the knucklebone player's grip on me tightened. The show must be underway because the throb of drums bounced along the street, accompanied by a long "Ooh!" as hundreds of people thrilled to whatever the Wind Dancers were doing. A wall of backs blocked the way, but over the heads of the crowd, I glimpsed a Wind Dancer, and for a moment, I forgot they were a threat.

Wing-shaped cape flying behind him, a man in a feathered mask hurtled toward the ground from the top of the tower. In brown and black, he looked like one of the eagles that soared over the Uplands. On either side of him flew men in Grimuld's green tabards, swinging at him with whips ending in balls of fire. They all rode lines running from the tower to the ground, I realized, each man with his foot in a stirrup of rope suspended from a pulley skimming the line. The men vanished behind a screen of gaping townsfolk.

An instant of joy flooded through me. These were Uplanders telling an Uplands story. They were mine, and the story was too. We were eagles, sailing the wind. All Grimuld's cruelty couldn't change that.

When Carl shoved his way into the crowd, people glanced over their shoulders and shuffled aside to let him through to the platform in front of Grimuld's house. "Hold him," Carl told the knucklebone player and climbed the steps.

"Carl, I need to get up there too," I called. "I need to see over everyone's heads."

Carl hesitated, then nodded to the knucklebone player. I dragged him up the three steps and found myself just behind a line of chairs, the nearest one holding Gladoc, the Lac's Holding ambassador. He was applauding enthusiastically, his huge earrings dancing. No love lost between him and Grimuld, I'd guess.

With the knucklebone player breathing down my neck, I scanned the crowd. Near the foot of the tower, red streamers blew from the back of someone's head. "There!" I cried. "No, wait."

Halfway to the king's chair, Carl froze.

Yellow streamers fluttered among the red. The other mask had only red ones, didn't it? The crowd shifted, and I got a better look at a man in a red and yellow tunic rocking along on sheep horns strapped to his feet. He held a striped stocking into which someone dropped a coin.

"It's not him," I said.

Carl slid farther along the chairs to where the king and Lord Grimuld sat, Grimuld's mouth pressed in a hard line. He apparently didn't appreciate having men in his colors shown attacking an eagle with whips and fire. I just hoped Thien understood and believed what he saw. Carl bent and spoke into the king's ear. Thien shot me a doubtful look. Even over the clamor of the crowd, I heard him say, "The boy's a fraud." I tried to ignore the scornful tone and concentrate on spotting the Wind Dancer who'd had the ring.

"Doniver!" Dilly slipped out of the crowd in front of me and pointed back toward the tower. "He's there. Jarka's watching him." One of the guards pushed her farther from the platform. She cringed at his touch but kept pointing and saying, "There!"

To one side of the bell tower, Jarka stood chest-to-chest with a Ringman. Jarka was red-faced, talking excitedly, and gesturing behind the man. He tried to move, but the Ringman blocked his way. I followed Jarka's jabbing finger. At the foot of the tower stood a man in a blue mask trailing red streamers. A wide cape covered his arms and hands.

My breath stopped. "There!"

Carl straightened to look where I pointed. "Which one?"

"In the blue and red!"

Carl started to wriggle out of the narrow space behind the chairs, but there was no time to waste. I wrenched free from my guard's grip and leaped off the platform. Dodging guards, I barreled toward the bell tower where I burst out of the crowd to see the Wind Dancers all on the ground now, tossing lit torches back and forth from the ends of teeterboards. The one closest to me jumped, driving his end of the board to the ground and hurling the other somersaulting into the air, still juggling the torches. I ducked around them and must have startled the man in the air because he missed a catch and the lit torch bounced into the crowd, sending people squealing backward.

The man who'd had the ring skittered away, his cape fluttering open. My heart clawed its way up to my throat. Under the cape, the man held a bow, and in his belt, he'd tucked arrows that hadn't been among the Wind Dancers' equipment. He vanished around the corner of the tower.

"Stop him!" I charged. People turned from the show to watch me, mouths open. I dashed past to find Jarka, still struggling with a Ringman. The acrobat was nowhere in sight.

"He went into the tower, Doniver." Jarka shoved his face into the Ringman's. "Go after him, you fool. He's going to shoot the king."

I shouldered the tower door open and ran in to find a staircase twisting up the walls. I sprinted upward. Someone entered the tower, and I peered over the rail to see the Ringman who'd had hold of Jarka.

"Halt," the Ringman called.

I sped up, taking the stairs three at a time, feet sliding in my boots. The Ringman pounded after me. From above, light filtered through an open trap-door. I dragged in my last gasp of air and scrambled up through the opening to emerge in a low-walled room surrounding a bell. The crowd in New Square stretched below me, and beyond them was the platform holding the royal party. They were all on their feet now, moving toward the door of Grimuld's house with Carl and the king's guard shooing them along.

Then my eyes slid into focus on the horror right in front of me. At the wall stood a man, bow in hand, arrow on the string. He'd taken off his mask. I'd never seen him among the Wind Dancers, but I had seen him. It was the deerskin-clad man who'd tried to kill me. He aimed his bow toward the platform.

"No!" I leaped toward him, but a hand clamped around my ankle, flinging me to the floor. The Ringman had climbed just far enough out of the stairwell to seize me. I kicked at his face. "Look! Look, you fool! He's shooting!"

The deerskin clad man's bowstring twanged.

I gave a despairing cry.

The bowman cursed.

I couldn't imagine a sweeter sound. I yanked loose from the Ringman's grip and lurched halfway to my feet.

As the bowman reached for a second arrow, I drove my shoulder into his knees, knocking him off his feet. The arrow clattered to the floor, but the man swung the bow, and pain exploded from the top of my head. My fingers flew open, and he pushed frantically with his heels and slid away.

The Ringman holding my ankle jumped the rest of the way into the room, grabbed my arm, and yanked me to my feet. Sweet Powers! I'd never seen anyone so stupidly single-minded. He heaved me into the air, and I found myself dangling far out over the low wall, watching the churning crowd below. My breath stopped.

On the platform, Thien had reached the house doorway, but was half turned to look at his guard who had sagged to his knees with an arrow in his neck.

The shooter's bow twanged again. An arrow whistled toward the platform.

"Stop!" I cried, as if the arrow would heed me.

The arrow buried itself in the left side of Thien's chest. Blood flowered on his gold tunic.

The sight of Thien being hit must have shaken the Ringman from his obsession with me at last. He hauled me back into the tower and lunged at the shooter, hitting him square in the middle of his back, and sending him wheeling over the edge of the wall. The crowd beneath turned their faces upward. Then someone must have realized the man's fall wasn't part of the show and screamed. The scream wasn't quite loud enough to cover the thud of a body hitting the cobblestones.

THE RINGMAN TIGHTENED his hold on my arm as we emerged from the bell tower into the square. Tower Guards and more Ringmen swarmed through the crowd, seizing Wind Dancers and shoving people away from the shooter's body. My vision closed around him, so he was the only thing I saw. The top of his head was squashed in and blood puddled around it. Bile rose in my throat. "You threw him to his death," I said to the man holding me.

"He shot Thien," the man said.

"But you killed him." I couldn't seem to take it in.

"Who's he?" shouted someone in the crowd, and my vision expanded again to see the rest of the square. "Is he the one who shot the king?" The man who'd spoken stood, wide-eyed and white-faced, blocking the path. An uneasy rumble rose from the throats of the people around him. I shrank against the suddenly comforting bulk of the Ringman.

"Out of the way." The Ringman pushed the man aside and hurried me toward Grimuld's house, where a crowd of Tower Guards and Ringmen were shoving Wind Dancers through the door into the antechamber. Dilly and Jarka were also being urged along, though a Ringman kicked Tuc out of the way when he tried to follow.

"Don't hurt him!" Dilly cried.

"Shut it, slut." A Ringman prodded her.

Jarka turned to snarl at the man. "Watch how you talk to her."

The Ringman yanked Jarka's crutch out from under him and dragged him, toes scraping on the floor, through the antechamber and into the Hall.

"Don't!" Dilly ran after them.

The man holding me tried to haul me straight through to the Hall, but I glimpsed still figures lying to one side and grabbed the door frame to stop myself so I could see what was happening. On the antechamber's floor, Thien sprawled on his back, face turned toward us, pale as snow, eyes closed. Someone had snapped off the arrow shaft, but the stub still protruded from Thien's chest. Lineth knelt beside him, with Lord Grimuld and Carl hovering next to her. Beyond Thien lay the king's guard. A Tower Guard pulled a cloth from a side table and covered the poor man's face. Ambassador Gladoc lingered in the shadows, watching. The smell of blood washed through the room.

"It has to come out." Lineth's voice shook. "Did someone go for the surgeon?"

My knees sagged. Beran's father was still alive.

"I'll send someone." Lord Grimuld stepped back. "Let's get His Majesty upstairs."

"Are you sure we should move him?" Carl asked anxiously.

"We need to get him out of all this." Grimuld waved a hand toward the men milling in the antechamber and the uproar coming from the Hall. He pointed to four Ringmen, who sheathed their swords and cradled Thien between them, groaning as they lifted him.

Lineth ran up the narrow stairs, and the Ringmen followed, carefully maneuvering Thien around the corner.

"I'll take my leave." Ambassador Gladoc bowed and left the house, probably on his way to send a report to Lac's Holding.

Grimuld watched him go with narrowed eyes, then started toward the Hall. He stopped when he spotted me still clinging to the doorframe. "How did—? This boy escaped from the undercroft. Take him back there."

I struggled in the grip of the man who'd killed the shooter. "I'm the one who tried to stop the bowman! I'd have done it too if this idiot hadn't kept me from him. And I'd have done it without shoving him over that wall." My stomach heaved at the memory of the shooter's broken body. I yanked my thoughts away.

"I beg you to let the boy stay, sir," Carl said. "Until we find His Highness, I need him in hand."

I didn't exactly want to be in Carl's hands just now, but it was better than being locked away in Grimuld's undercroft where I'd be useless.

"The boy tricked His Majesty into going to New Square today," Lord Grimuld said. "He has to be part of the plot."

"I don't think so," Carl said. "He was the one who warned us of danger. Even a lying little weasel doesn't lie about everything."

Words for my tombstone, I thought bitterly. I just hoped they wouldn't be needed any time soon.

Lord Grimuld took a moment to consider his answer. "You're right. He has to be thoroughly interrogated. Bring him." He strode into the Hall, trailed by Carl. I let go of the doorframe and stumbled in.

In the Hall, Carl joined the other Tower Guards gathered to one side, a sea of gold tabards across the room from the green ones worn by the Ringmen. I had the crazed thought that in their different uniforms, they looked like armies facing one another across a battlefield. Thien's Tower Guards were restless and muttering to one another, clearly worried and eager to act, in contrast to the Ringmen, who were at home in Grimuld's Hall and stood in a tidy line.

The man holding me shoved me to stand with Dilly and Jarka, behind the Wind Dancers in the Hall's center. Between the two armies; a bad spot where folks were likely to get crushed once the battle started.

Lord Grimuld stalked to the chair on a platform at the Hall's end. The air seemed to chill as he swept a stone-hard gaze over the acrobats. The Ringman who'd thrown the shooter to his death spoke in Grimuld's ear, then went to join his fellow Ringmen. Grimuld put out his hand, and an attendant stepped forward to lay a birch rod in it.

I stopped breathing. At home, I'd seen a magistrate hold the same symbol of judgment at the trial of a drunken neighbor who'd burned down a barn belonging to his brother-by-marriage. If Grimuld decided the Wind Dancers were all traitors, they'd be hanged. I clenched and unclenched my fists. If the Wind Dancers had killed a Tower Guard and conspired to kill the king, then they deserved to be punished, but I'd loved the Wind Dancers since I was six years old and first saw their show. And they were Uplanders.

"On your knees, all of you," Lord Grimuld said.

A Ringman shoved me, and I landed on my knees with a painful crack. I started to jump up again, but Dilly sank gracefully next to me and took my hand in her shaking one. On my other side, Jarka too was pushed to his knees, though neither he nor Dilly owed Lord Grimuld the slightest fealty. Jarka punched me softly in the side. I wasn't sure whether he and Dilly were giving or asking comfort, but it seemed right to stay where I was between them.

"If you have a defense, you may give it," Grimuld said.

Tel raised a bruised face. "Whatever the shooter was doing, we were no part of it. We don't even know him."

Lord Grimuld swept his gaze over the Wind Dancers, his head turned just slightly to put his good right eye to the front. "He wore one of your masks. You expect me to believe you maneuvered His Majesty into coming to see you, and yet weren't part of the plan to assassinate him?"

"I say again, we didn't know the shooter," Tel said. "I'm not even sure he was an Uplander. Clothes are just a costume. What's more I'm not sure he was trying to assassinate anyone, though your man felt free to execute him."

Compelled by truth, I said, "He was shooting at the platform. I saw him."

Tel glared at me. "Whose side are you on?"

"Good question." Lord Grimuld turned to me. "My man told me you impeded his attempt to stop the shooter."

"That's not true!"

"You've wormed your way into Prince Beran's good graces," Grimuld said, "and he's apparently missing. Have you and your friends here harmed him?"

"Of course not!" I cried.

"His friends?" Tel said. "I think not."

Carl stepped out of the group of Tower Guards. "It's true His Highness is missing. A message came from Lady Lineth early this morning, or so the gate guard said." He took another step toward Grimuld. "His Highness vanished without telling me where he was going." Carl's hands gripped his belt so tightly that the tough leather crinkled.

"He never came to this house," Grimuld said, "and my daughter would not have been so shameless as to send for him. The boy probably wrote the note himself."

"I can't write," I said.

"So you claim, but we've seen how honest you are." Grimuld turned back to Carl. "If the prince has been gone that long, you and your men need to search for him, probably in the Shambles." He pointed to the Wind Dancers. "That's where they've been lurking, and that's probably where their countrymen hold the prince, assuming he's still alive."

Carl shifted from foot to foot. If ever I'd seen a man torn in two, Carl was it. "I hate to leave His Majesty," Carl said.

"I stood by Thien's side at the Battle of Lac's Holding," Grimuld said. "I defended him against an army, so I think my men and I can hold off these scum."

Carl's gaze went from the line of Ringmen to the Wind Dancers.

"Besides," Grimuld added, "given the seriousness of the king's wound, the search for his heir is crucial." An instant of sober silence blanketed the Hall. "Take the other Tower Guards. My Ringmen will guard the prisoners until we know what's happened to His Highness and I can hold a trial."

"Very well." Carl sounded as if he were in pain. "But I want Doniver as a guide in the Shambles. It's a maze in there."

"He stays here," Grimuld said.

Carl met and held Grimuld's gaze. "His Majesty has given me absolute authority and responsibility in matters of His Highness's safety. I judge Doniver's presence is necessary."

Grimuld hesitated, then said, "Very well."

Carl gave me a look that would have cut through armor. "I don't believe he meant harm to the king, but he knows the Shambles and he knows Uplanders. He'll tell me who's most likely involved and guide us to them or he'll be sorry." He pointed to Jem, the Tower Guard who'd come with him to seize me in the Rat Hole, and strode toward the door.

I cringed. Were Min and the other Uplanders *involved*? How much betrayal of my own people could I undertake in one day?

Jem hustled me after Carl, who vanished into the antechamber with a swarm of Tower Guards. I looked back to see Dilly and Jarka both trying to rise to follow me, but Ringmen closed in on them.

Carl and his men poured out of the house and down the steps. A Ringman shut the door behind us, but not before Tuc wiggled in through the narrowing space. I expected the door to open again long enough for Tuc to be tossed out. Instead, I heard the bar slam into place inside. In the back of my head, Jarka's voice whispered, *Notice things. Figure out what they mean.* And I heard Mag saying a bar on the inside was meant to keep people out. I frowned, then glanced at Carl, frantically giving orders to the assembled Tower Guards.

"Wait," I said. "Why did they bar the door?"

"Shut it," Jem said.

"The Wind Dancers are on the barred side," I said. "And the man who shot the king is really, really dead. So who are Grimuld's men keeping on *this* side?"

My thoughts spun like a pinwheel, blowing the bits of information inside my head into an entirely new pattern. Lord Grimuld's men all wore his ring.

Maybe the shooter hadn't stolen the ring from a slaughtered Ringman in the Uplands.

Maybe it had been his to start with and, as Tel said, he wore Upland clothes as a costume.

He could have shot the king because someone else told him to, and then the someone else made sure he couldn't squeal.

The Ringman in New Square had made every effort to let the shooter into the tower and keep everyone else out. And then he'd killed the shooter.

"Carl!" I cried. "The Ringmen barred the door. The danger Wyswoman Adrya saw—it's not the Wind Dancers. It's Grimuld. The shooter had Grimuld's ring because he *worked* for Lord Grimuld."

Chapter 22.

For the Uplands

"CARL!" I CRIED. "It's the Ringmen." From the corner of my eye, I glimpsed Jem's fist slicing through the air. I ducked, and the blow glanced off the top of my head, still hard enough that I'd have gone sprawling if he hadn't kept hold of me. Through a blur of tears, Carl's face swam toward me.

"I don't have time for nonsense," Carl said. "The only thing I want to hear from you is where someone could hide Beran in the Shambles. Hold out on me, and I swear I won't leave enough of you for Grimuld to lock up."

I writhed in Jem's grip. "They barred the door, Carl! They barred it on the other side." Jem yanked my arm up behind my back, and I cried out at the wrench. The fine fabric of Beran's old shirt ripped at the shoulder. Its maker had undoubtedly never pictured the young Beran being manhandled by the Tower Guards.

"Wait." Carl was still as a stone.

"Surely you're not taking the little liar seriously," Jem said. "He's just trying to keep us from searching for His Highness."

"Why would they bar the door?" Carl asked slowly. "The Wind Dancers are supposed to be the danger, and they're inside." He scrubbed his hand over his jaw, then jogged up the stairs and pounded on Grimuld's door. Jem shoved me closer to the steps so we could hear.

"Who is it?" someone called.

"It's Carl. I want to leave some of my men with the king."

Men muttered to one another inside. Carl was just raising his fist to knock again when whoever had answered the door said, "Lord Grimuld's left orders not to let anyone in."

"Why?"

"We're protecting the king," the doorkeeper said.

"We're the king's men," Carl said.

"No one comes in. No one."

Carl came back down the steps, chewing on his lower lip. "I don't like it. We need to get His Majesty out of there and do it quickly."

"How?" another Tower Guard asked. "Who's going to question Lord Grimuld's orders?"

"Maybe a council member?" Jem suggested.

"Lord Grimuld is chief councilor," Carl said.

Pieces of ideas still fluttered around in my head. When you suffer a loss, sometimes the Powers give you insight in return. Maybe my loss made me able to understand even Tava's insight. "His Highness could do it."

"We don't know where he is." Carl narrowed his eyes. "Or do we?"

"If you mean I did anything leading to his capture, I didn't," I said. "At least, not on purpose. But I still think I know where he might be."

"Where?" Carl's voice drilled into my skull.

Too late to keep quiet now. "A wind shrine. Where else?"

I POINTED DOWN the narrow gap between the fence behind the blacksmith's yard and the blank wall of a house. I could just see a blue streamer fluttering from a fence post. "There's a gate at the back corner of the yard where the streamer is," I said in a low voice. "The shrine is through there. I'm guessing the Ringmen missed it, maybe even on purpose because they wanted an Uplands place to stow Beran." Sweet Powers, I hoped Tava was right about this, because I had no other ideas.

"Will it be locked?" Carl asked.

I shook my head. "Grimuld wants us Uplanders to take the blame for Beran's disappearance. The gate will be open all right."

Carl gazed down the alley. "There'll be guards though, assuming he really is there. You wait here." He beckoned to the half-dozen Tower Guards following him.

"I want to come," I said.

"You're unarmed and don't know what you're doing. You'd just get in the way."

"Give me a knife or a bow. I swear I can help."

Carl actually laughed. "Not likely. Stay here."

With Carl in the lead, the Tower Guards slipped toward the gate. I waited until they were nearly there and crept after them, moving as silently as I did when I hunted in the mountains. I imagined cold, pine-scented air filling my lungs and tingling over my face. Then I slid on a slick of rotting tomatoes, remembered where I was, and told myself to pay attention. Grimuld's men had killed and would be willing to do it again.

The Tower Guards all drew their swords. Carl put his hand on the latch and swept one last glance over his men. He raised three fingers and lowered them one by one. As the last one folded, he flung the gate back, and they burst through.

Shouts sounded inside the yard. I broke into a run but skidded to a halt when a head popped over the fence. A man in Uplands clothing vaulted out of the yard and into the alley. Half turned to look back at the gate, he came flying toward me. In the narrow space, I couldn't have moved out of the way if I wanted to. He barreled into me, crashing me into the garbage-strewn dirt and landing on top on me with the force of a sack of grain dropped out a barn's loft. For a startled moment, his nose hovered an inch away from mine. Then he scrambled away, driving one knee into my stomach and narrowly missing my face with the other. I grabbed and managed to get hold of an ankle. The man hopped, dragging me on my back along the filthy alley. Beran's shirt ripped farther. Threads and patches of my skin scraped off into the grit.

"Carl!" I shouted.

Jem and another Tower Guard pounded out of the yard and struggled to seize the man without trampling me. I let go of the man's ankle and rolled into a ball, arms up around my head. When boots no longer landed a finger's width away, I cautiously uncurled. The Tower Guards each held one of the man's arms.

"For the Uplands!" the man cried. "We did it for the Uplands."

I climbed to my feet. "He's lying." At least I hoped he was. If Uplanders now turned out to be guilty, my life had just started down a new and lonely path.

The man sneered. "Death to Thien the Tyrant! Death to Lord Grimuld!"

"Liar," I said, putting as much conviction as I could in my voice. "You can't even talk like we do. You run your words together like mush."

Jem and the other Tower Guards gave me impassive looks, then dragged the shouting man through the gate. Jem jerked his head for me to follow.

Guards jammed the small shrine. They must have tripped over one another going in because I could see no other way they'd have managed to let the man escape. One of them pinned a second man against the fence.

"You're all useless," Carl's voice boomed. "I'll be telling your captain that. And you! Don't you ever disappear on me like that again."

A Tower Guard moved aside, revealing Carl pulling ropes off Beran's ankles. The prince was ignoring Carl's scolding and rubbing the red lines on his wrists where more ropes had evidently been tied. When Beran's eyes met mine, he stiffened.

"I see you have him," Beran said.

Carl's angry face turned to me.

I took a step back. "I swear I had nothing to do with this."

"It wasn't him," said the man who'd smashed into me in the alley. "It was Doniver. He helped us lure the prince into the trap." We all looked at him. "For the Uplands," he added.

"Shut it," the other man said. The fake Uplander who'd been spewing my name stuttered into confused silence.

Beran gave a short laugh. "My apologies, Doniver."

The knot in my stomach loosened a little. "I'm sorry about hiding my hand," I said. "I didn't mean to deceive you." I frowned. "Well, I did. But I'm sorry."

Leaning on Carl's arm, Beran struggled to his feet.

"Who really put you two up to this?" he asked the men who'd been holding him. They edged as far away as they could given the crowded yard and the men holding them. At that moment, Beran looked as menacing as his father ever had.

The throat-knot bobbed on the man who'd run me down. The other man threw him a warning look. "Keep quiet. We'll be taken care of."

"Like the man who shot the king was taken care of?" I asked. "A Ringman shoved him out of the bell tower." Both men turned pale. "If I worked for Lord Grimuld, I'd think about that."

"My father's been shot?" Beran asked sharply.

"He's alive," Carl said, "but only just. And his guard is dead. The boy claims Grimuld's behind all this, and I'm beginning to believe he's right."

Beran nodded to the guards holding the men. "One of you, give me your sword. Then take these two to the castle cells. I'll deal with them later." Buckling on the guard's sword, he limped out through the gate with Carl at his side, still explaining what happened.

I started after them, but a smear of color underfoot made me pause. A blue paper pinwheel had been trampled into the dirt. I picked it up. The bent wings were still attached to a stick, although the end of the stick was broken. I straightened the wings as best I could and stuck the splintered end of the stick into the little mound of dirt under a straggly yew where it usually stood. I puffed at it.

When it spun, my whole body lightened.

I bent and spoke into the whirling blades. "I'm all right. I was ailing, but I'm better now. Tell them, please."

I didn't have time to wait for the pinwheel to stop spinning. I ran out of the shrine and after Beran.

Chapter 23.

A Matter of Honor

A T THE EDGE of New Square, Beran called a halt in the shadow of a house across from Grimuld's. Carl waved the other Tower Guards against a shop wall where they'd be less visible. The square was strewn with nut shells and orange peels. The crowd had thinned, but people still stood in small groups, talking in hushed voices and watching Grimuld's door for news of the king. The Wind Dancers' equipment littered the space near the bell tower, and people skirted around it, as if the Wind Dancers had poisoned it with their touch. Flies buzzed over the streaks of blood where the shooter had fallen. I swallowed bile.

"If you ordered them to bring His Majesty out, they probably would," Carl told Beran.

"Alive?" Beran scanned the square. "If he still is, of

273

course." Under the coolness in his tone, I heard the tension. No boat was burning here, but I smelled charring anyway. "Who's in there?" Beran asked.

"His Majesty," Carl said, "about a dozen Ringmen, the Wind Dancers." He nodded toward me. "Doniver's two friends."

"Lineth?" Beran asked, voice tight.

"Yes, sir, and Lord Grimuld, of course." The "sir" told me Carl had regained enough grip on himself to stop shouting at his prince.

We studied Grimuld's house. Like those around it, it stood three stories tall, with high narrow windows. I tried to think. If this was Jona's house back home, and I wanted to sneak in, how would I do that? Not that I would sneak into her house. For one thing, her father had arms like logs, and I wasn't ready to stand in a marriage circle and say the vows yet. But if I would, how would I go about it?

"We need to get in and take charge of my father before they stop us," Beran said. "Maybe I could knock, be invited in, and open the door for the rest of you."

"You're not going in there alone," Carl said. "Think, sir. With His Majesty injured, you can't risk it. Do you want to leave Lord Grimuld as ruler of Rinland?"

I edged closer to Carl. "I might be able to get in."

Both heads swiveled toward me. "How?" Beran asked.

"There are windows into the undercroft. I saw them when the Ringmen locked me in one of the storerooms."

Carl eyed me up and down, frowning. "I saw them

too. You're skinny, but you're still likely to scrape off useful parts if you try to squeeze through one of them. And there was a guard."

"I can do it. Besides, you haven't thought of anything better."

Carl rolled his eyes. "Street trash, did your father never try to beat some respect into you?"

Beran sliced his hand through the air between me and Carl. "Doniver's right. We have no better plan."

I snapped my mouth shut. It was Beran's da, not mine, who needed to be defended now. Him and all the others still caught in Grimuld's power, including Jarka and Dilly. Saving them wouldn't bring Da back, but it might make me feel more like a whole person again.

"Are you sure you can fit, Doniver?" Beran asked.

"I have to," I said. "My friends are in there."

"What about the guard?"

My stomach felt remarkably like it had after three cups of wine.

"There might not be one now," Carl said. "The one who was there came to the square with us, and there'd only be the old woman to guard. She didn't look eager to escape to me. Surely Grimuld has every available man in the Hall."

Last chance to shut it, warned a voice in my head. "Let me try," I said out loud. A man spoke up when it would do some good.

"We'll circle around behind Grimuld's house," Beran

said to Carl. "You stay here. Wait until we signal that we're ready, then make enough of a fuss at the front door to draw as many Ringmen as you can." He studied the square. "Get the crowd involved if you can."

"I'm coming with you," Carl said.

"I need you here. They'd ignore one of the other guards, but everyone knows you're my bodyguard, so you can squawk about me being missing. They have to tread carefully with you." Beran gave him a small smile. "You'll have to let me out of your sight again sometime, Nanny."

Carl looked very unhappy, but said, "Get yourself hurt, and I'll make you sorry."

Beran laughed and beckoned me and the other Tower Guards to follow him. He led us along back streets to Lord Grimuld's side of New Square. We crept up next to the fenced stableyard behind Grimuld's house. Beran and the guards looked as cool as if they were out for a stroll, but if we had to stand still too long, I might accidentally launch myself over the fence.

The prince waved one of the Tower Guards to the street's end, where he'd be able to signal Carl in the square, then gripped the latch on the gate and tried to ease it up. It didn't budge. He motioned to two of his men. One of them formed his hands into a stirrup into which the other stepped. The first one heaved, and the other disappeared over the fence.

"Hey!" someone cried.

A muffled crash followed. A moment later, the gate

creaked inward, and I scrambled into the yard after Beran and the Tower Guards. A man in Lord Grimuld's green tabard lay sprawled in the shadow of the woodpile next to the back steps. The guard who'd gone over the fence let go of the gate and returned to the unconscious Ringman. He pulled off the Ringman's belt and used it to bind his hands.

Beran moved lightly up the steps and tried the back door. Like the gate, it was locked. The window it was, then. Beran slipped back down into the yard as I moved along the house to what I was pretty sure was the right low window. Beran raised an eyebrow. "It's small," he whispered. "Can you do it?"

I crouched. When I braced my hand on the sill, the top of the window was no higher than my elbow. It had looked bigger when the Ringman was dragging me toward the store room.

"Sure," I said. What was the point of doubting myself?

Beran motioned to one of his men who leaned out the gate and waved to the man at the corner of the house. We all waited in silence while my heart tried to kick its way through my ribs and escape.

A loud banging rose above the murmur of the crowd in the square. "Open up," Carl's voice shouted. "Let me in. I want to see the king."

The banging thundered on. The sound of the crowd grew louder. "What's wrong?" called an unfamiliar voice, a bystander probably.

"They won't let me in," Carl cried at the top of his lungs. He banged on the door some more. Surely even Carl's hand wasn't hard enough to produce that racket. He must be using the hilt of a sword or a knife. I jiggled one knee, silently begging Beran to get this show moving.

"Open up! Let me in!" Carl bellowed.

"Let us in!" shouted someone in the square. Other voices took up the cry in what quickly settled into a loud chant.

Beran drove his heel into the shutter. The top board splintered with a noise like a tree falling. I waited for the Ringman guard to run down the undercroft hallway and poke a sword up at me, but no one came, and the house's back door remained encouragingly shut. I supposed that little short of the bell tower collapsing would draw the attention of the people in the house away from Carl's din. At least I hoped so.

Beran thrust his hand through the hole in the shutter. Something wooden clattered to the floor inside, the bar probably. He pushed, and the shutter flapped open. A dark space yawned. He pointed at me.

I flopped onto my belly and shoved my legs through the opening. Braced on my forearms, I wriggled backward until the wood of the sill bit into my hipbones. I hesitated, shaking my feet to kick away the imagined feel of hard hands grabbing my ankles and yanking me into the rat-infested darkness.

Nodding encouragingly, Beran crouched to grasp my

wrists. The one I'd sprained throbbed in his grip. I eased my hips off the sill. The top of the window frame slid lightly along my back, pulling my already shredded shirt out of my belt and adding more scrapes to my skin. One more wriggle sent me popping through the window like a cork exploding from a bottle. I dropped to the floor, catching my ear at the last instant on the top of the window frame. For a moment, all I could do was rock with pain and try to gather my scattered breath and wits so I could make sure Tava didn't give me away. I watched for a guard who didn't appear.

"No guard?" Beran's face peered through the window.

"No." I put one hand on the wall and struggled to my feet.

"Go on then." Beran pulled his head back and vanished.

"Tava, it's me." I staggered down the hall.

Her withered face bobbed up at the window in the store room door. "Oh, Doniver. I thought I heard something. Are you going upstairs? Would you please tell the cook to put less salt in tonight's soup?"

"Shh." I patted the air with my hands. I considered letting her out, but she was as unpredictable as a ball bouncing down a hill. "If you're quiet, I'll tell her."

Tava twiddled her fingers in front of her mouth, like kids did to show they were buttoning their lips. I felt her eyes on my back as I crept toward the stairs. "Less salt," she hissed.

I hunched my shoulders and tiptoed up the steps toward the door into the kitchen, sliding my mind over what might lie on the other side of it. The last time, a guard had been in the kitchen, but surely Lord Grimuld wouldn't leave one of his men snitching food and flirting with the kitchen maid. Not with Thien and the Wind Dancers in the house and Carl bellowing in the square.

I pressed my ear against the door, but even here Carl drowned out all other sound. When I cracked the door open and peered through, no one was in sight, and the back door loomed a tantalizing two yards ahead of me, a heavy bar jammed across it. Drawing a deep breath, I lunged into the kitchen, grabbed the bar, and heaved. It didn't move.

"Here!" said a voice behind me.

The cook and the kitchen maid stood near a short hallway that probably led to Grimuld's Hall. They'd evidently been trying to see what was happening with Carl and his assistant rioters in the square, but now they turned to face me. I heaved again. The bar popped loose, flew past my jaw, and landed with a crash. Instantly, the door burst open, and Beran and his men spilled through, swords in hands. The kitchen maid squeaked. The cook opened her mouth wide, but before she could scream, Beran was there with his hand clamped over the lower half of her face. A Tower Guard hovered at his shoulder, the point of his sword at the maid's chest.

"Look at me," Beran said.

The cook and maid obeyed. Both sets of eyes widened. The cook's hands plucked at her skirt as she tried to curtsy while still in Beran's grip.

"You know who I am?" Beran asked.

"Yes, Your Highness." The maid sounded faint. She too gave a quick dip of a curtsy.

"You will stay here and keep quiet," Beran said. "No harm will come to you." Slowly, he lifted his hand from the cook's mouth, nodding approvingly when she stayed silent. A Tower Guard herded both women to the other side of the table. Beran beckoned the rest of his men toward the hallway. They slipped after him, then waited crowded together in the hallway while Beran silently lifted the edge of a curtain and peered through the gap. Beneath Carl's cries, the murmur of male voices drifted from Grimuld's Hall.

Dilly's voice pierced the masculine rumble. "Listen! We had nothing to do with shooting the king. Those people out there are worried that you're threatening him. Let them in and prove you mean him no harm."

As she spoke the last words, Beran yanked the curtain aside and charged through, his men boiling after him. I ran to join them.

Beran and his men descended like a rockslide on the Ringmen's backs. The Ringmen's weapons were out but pointed toward the space along one wall where the Wind Dancers, and Jarka and Dilly were huddled, with Tuc tied to a nearby bench. Lord Grimuld shot out of the chair on the platform. Beran ran toward him, but Grimuld sprang behind the wall of turning Ringmen, drawing his own sword.

Ringmen and Tower Guards rushed together. Steel clanged. Tuc barked like a mad thing, dragging against his tether.

The instant the Ringmen turned to meet the Tower Guards, the Wind Dancers flew into motion in a way that made me proud to be an Uplander. Tel jumped onto a sideboard, then bounced off the wall and landed on a Ringman's back, his arm around the man's neck, his fist knotted in the man's hair. A Tower Guard ran his sword into the Ringman's guts. Blood spurted, and I hastily looked away.

Another acrobat swung on the chain from which one of the oil lamps hung. He drove the heels of his boots into a Ringman's head. The man crumpled to the floor as Jarka lanced the point of his crutch into another Ringman's back. The man stumbled an arm's length forward, and Dilly shattered a vase on his neck, just below the edge of his helmet.

Not far from me, three Ringmen fought off two Tower Guards, one of whom already had a spreading red stain on his tabard. I darted a frantic look around for something, anything, to use as a weapon. I grabbed the edge of a tapestry hanging on the wall behind the struggling men and caught the eye of a Wind Dancer at the tapestry's other end.

"Help me!" I called.

The Wind Dancer grabbed his end of the tapestry. We both yanked at the thing, which turned out to be surprisingly heavy. I braced my feet on the wall and dragged on it with my full weight. It tore loose and slid down the wall in dust-spewing waves. As the top edge fell, the momentum allowed me to throw the bottom edge out and up to land on the backs of the three Ringmen. The tapestry bubbled with their efforts to escape, beating out clouds of dust. The Tower Guards sneezed so hard, they had to back away.

As I danced out of reach, I glimpsed Beran ducking out into the antechamber, going after his father no doubt. Then I saw Lord Grimuld break free of the swarm of battling men and follow the prince. No one went after them. Probably none of the struggling swordsmen even saw them go.

I wove my way through them at a run. Someone needed to watch Beran's back. Carl would kill us all if we let anything happen to him.

I raced into the antechamber in time to see Lord Grimuld running up the steps, his sword in his hand. The door guards were gone, presumably into the melee in the Hall. Carl had stopped shouting, which meant he'd run around to the back door and would soon burst into the Hall, but I couldn't wait for Carl to notice Beran was missing and figure out where he'd gone. I scrambled up the stairs after Grimuld. As I neared the top, I forced myself to slow down and move quietly. Surprise was the only weapon I had.

I climbed far enough to see the upstairs hallway where closed doors lined both sides. Grimuld's back was to me, but Beran faced me with his sword pointed at Grimuld's gut.

"Where's my father?" Beran demanded.

"Are you accusing me of something, Your Highness?" Grimuld sounded calm, but he never took his gaze off Beran's sword and kept his own blade leveled at the prince.

Beran snorted. "Other than trying to kill your king you mean?"

The last door on the left opened, and Lineth stood framed in the doorway, a bloodstained apron over her gown. She must be caring for Thien, thank the Powers. Her presence was probably the only thing keeping Lord Grimuld from having killed the king already. When she saw Beran and her father at sword point, she took an uncertain step toward them. "What's happening? What's that noise downstairs? Has the surgeon finally come?"

The one Grimuld claimed he'd sent for? Not likely.

"Are you part of this, Lineth?" Beran's voice caught. "Were you just following your father's orders when you said you loved me?"

Her brows drew together. "What do you mean?"

Lord Grimuld spoke before Beran could. "See his sword? He's here to kill the king. He wants the throne for himself."

Until the Tower Guards burst into Grimuld's Hall, I would have sworn Grimuld planned to make Beran king, marry him to his daughter, and control Rinland from behind the throne as much as he could, though maybe just until Beran produced an heir of his own who could have Grimuld as his guardian. Now that Beran was supposed to marry another woman, Grimuld had evidently decided his only course was to get rid of both Beran and Thien, probably to seize the throne for himself. I had to hand it to him for being able to think on his feet. He was slippery as a fish.

"I don't believe it." Lineth looked from her father to Beran. "I know his heart like I know my own. He'd never hurt his father. You've made a mistake."

The tension in Beran's face eased. "Go back in the room, Lineth."

Instead she stepped into the hallway. "Please, both of you, lower your swords."

"Go back," Beran said sharply. He glanced over his shoulder at her.

As he did, Lord Grimuld leaped, slapped Beran's sword aside, and flung his arm around the prince's neck. He yanked Beran against him and set the point of his sword under Beran's jaw. "Drop your weapon."

"What are you doing?" Lineth cried.

Grimuld jabbed, and blood dripped from Beran's chin. Beran opened his hand and let his sword clatter to the floor.

I crouched but hesitated to spring. I didn't know where that sword point would wind up if I jumped Grimuld.

"You, boy," Grimuld said, "come around where I can see you."

I looked stupidly around as if he might be talking to someone else.

"You thought I didn't know you were there?" Grimuld gave a short laugh. "Typical Uplands arrogance. Move before I stab him in the throat. Lineth, go into the room."

I mounted the last four steps and sidled past Grimuld and Beran to stand near Lineth. "Your da's the one who means to kill King Thien," I said. "He'll blame it on Beran, though."

"Very good," Grimuld said, "only it'll be Beran and the Wind Dancers he hired."

"No," Lineth breathed.

Beran grasped the arm locked around his neck and forced it a finger's width away. "You hear her? If your own daughter doesn't believe you, no one will."

Grimuld pursed his lips, then slowly smiled. "They will if the boy swears he saw you murder your own father and heard the acrobats talk about working for you."

"What?" I said.

"He's an Uplander," Grimuld went on. "Everyone knows how they stick together. And they make such a fuss about their word. If he gives it, people will believe it."

"I won't," I said.

Beran tried to speak, but Grimuld yanked his arm tighter around the prince's throat. "You want to go home, boy?" Grimuld asked. "I'll send you. What's more, I'll see that your family's provided for. They'll never go hungry, never want for anything. Pick up Beran's sword. We need it."

My breath stopped. I saw the little farm in the valley, Ma agonizing over how long Da and I had been gone, struggling to run the farm and feed and clothe my sisters. Even if I got home on my own, our lives would be hard without Da.

Grimuld watched me, steady as a snake. "And think about the Uplands. If you do this, I'll be king here, and I'll let the town masters choose the next lord. Your people will be governed by one of their own again."

I stared at the sword on the floor, fingers twitching.

"Father, stop it!" Lineth cried. "You've served Rinland your whole life. You can't betray it now."

"It's for the good of Rinland," Grimuld said. "Thien is incapable of dealing with rebels like Suryan."

Beran's face reddened as Grimuld put more pressure on his throat. Grimuld, too, was flushed from his effort. The scar near his left eye stood out stark white.

I glanced over Grimuld's left shoulder and cried, "Get him, Carl!"

Grimuld twisted frantically to look around his blind spot. I jumped across the distance between us and grabbed his sword hand, then hung from it, dragging it away from Beran's throat. With a heave of his chest and shoulders, Beran broke loose. Grimuld's swinging sword hand sent me flying through the air until my back and head struck the wall, and I slid to the floor with black spots dancing in front of my eyes.

Beran scooped up his sword and rushed toward Grimuld, who took a step back, then another as Beran's flashing weapon drove him into retreat. Grimuld edged back one more time, and his foot found empty air at the top of the stairway. He cried out. Arms circling, he tumbled backward. I heard him bump down the length of the steps.

"No!" Lineth ran toward the steps, brushing Beran aside.

"Stop, Lineth," Beran cried. "There's a battle down there." When she ignored him and vanished down the stairs, he ran after her.

I pulled myself to my feet and tottered to the top of the stairway to look down. Carl had finally appeared. Face dark with dismay, he hovered over the trio on the landing. Grimuld lay sprawled, blank face staring at the ceiling, blood trickling from one corner of his mouth. Lineth crouched at his side, sobbing. Beran bent over her, his arm around her shoulders.

"I'm sorry," he said. "I'm so sorry. I know he's your father, but by my honor, Lineth, I couldn't be merciful. I couldn't do that to Rinland."

My throat swelled. *I'm sorry, Ma. I wanted it more than I've ever wanted anything. But you know what Da would say. By my honor, I couldn't do it.*

Chapter 24.

Aftermath

I LEANED BACK against the sun-warmed stones of the castle wall, my legs stretched out before me, with Dilly on one side, Jarka on the other. I twisted my ankles, admiring the boots the castle's shoemaker had given me that morning. They fit as comfortably as boots usually did only the day before I outgrew them.

A rider in Thien's gold tabard trotted through the castle gates. Across the courtyard, a groom emerged from the stables and reached for the bridle. The rider dismounted, unhooked a messenger's bag from her saddle, and strode off toward the Great Hall. A maid emerged from the kitchen with a big bowl on her hip. She sat on the bench outside the kitchen door and began peeling potatoes. *Dinner*, I thought happily.

Jarka shifted on the bench. "It's been a whole week.

How long is Beran going to keep us here?"

"I like it here," Dilly said. For what seemed like the twentieth time, she smoothed the skirt of her new, bright blue dress. "It's clean, and the men are gentlemen." Tuc sprawled at her feet, eyes half closed.

"Jarka and I are gentlemen," I said, then grinned when she rolled her eyes.

"It's not bad here, even though the place is crawling with powerful people." Jarka poked at a cobblestone with the tip of his crutch. "Wyswoman Adrya's a little bossy, but the library's full of books and scrolls, and she's teaching me lots of lore."

"Sound to me like you're teaching her, too," Dilly said, "or maybe just reading the future and letting her take the credit."

"She might say *blame* rather than *credit*. She's a good lore-mistress though. It's a fair trade. Still, if Beran doesn't let us go by tomorrow, I'm going anyway. I'm worried about my cousin." He caressed the leather bag on the bench next to his thigh. As far as I knew, Jarka hadn't let the new wind box out of his reach since Beran gave it to him. Jarka had read the wind at dawn and fretted about his cousin ever since. I had to wonder about how many bad things Jarka constantly learned that he couldn't do anything to prevent. How big was his dark place?

"Beran's just making sure we're safe," I said. "He's worried people might still blame us for the attack on the king. He's worried about you especially because now that people know you're not a fake, they might think you're dangerous. You've told me often enough that being a wind reader doesn't always work out well."

Jarka grimaced. "True enough."

"Being a little dangerous might be fun though, Jarka," Dilly said. "Girls like a little danger, especially in a good man like you."

Jarka and I swung to look at her. "Girls in Lac's Holding?" he asked.

"For sure there, but maybe everywhere." She shrugged. "Don't tell me you didn't enjoy the danger with Grimuld just a little. It's exciting. Why shouldn't girls feel that too?"

Jarka's face was pink. He lifted his lame foot and dropped it. "I thank you for the thought, Dilly, but girls aren't likely to overlook this." He looked at her from the corner of his eye, and I knew as if I'd read it in a wind box that he wanted her to contradict him.

"The right girl will," she said, "once she notices there's more to you than that."

It occurred to me that Dilly might not have been as ignorant of Jarka's feelings about her as she pretended. He frowned at the cobblestones.

"Jarka, you're not really eager to go back and live on the streets, are you?" I said, moving away from a painful subject. "Let Beran keep you as long as he's willing."

Jarka shook his shoulders once. "You planning to stay?"

He knew I too was itching about the length of our stay at the castle. "The difference is I have someplace to go. Maybe I should have gone when the Wind Dancers left for the Vale. I probably could have slipped away from the castle."

"Not from Carl though," Dilly said.

"No, not from Carl." I couldn't help laughing, though I wasn't happy at the idea of any of us becoming street kids again. Any kids really. It wasn't right.

Three men walked through the castle gates, two of them men-at-arms in the blue tabard of Lac's Holding. The third man was Ambassador Gladoc, his face grim. Beran had publicly accepted Gladoc's claim that Suryan knew nothing about the smuggled iron ore, but I suspected no one was fooling the prince. The three men entered the castle, passing the messenger on her way out. She went on to the barracks on the other side of the courtyard.

Dilly had straightened at the arrival of the Lac's Holding group, and her gaze lingered on the door through which they'd gone. "I wonder if Lady Elenia is coming soon. I'll bet the wedding will be beautiful."

"I'm not sure Beran wants her to come," I said slowly. "He loves Lady Lineth."

"Lineth's a traitor's daughter," Jarka said, "and royalty can't just follow their liking when they marry."

"I know, but it's a pity," I said. "Beran must want love as much as a farmer in a cottage does."

"Lady Elenia probably does too," Dilly said. "And if she's going to leave Lac's Holding, the least her husband can do is appreciate her."

Carl emerged from a doorway and came toward us. "His Highness wants to see you, Dilly."

Expecting to be the one Carl was after, I'd half risen. I turned to look at Dilly, whose eyes widened in what looked like alarm. She was still skittish about being alone with a man, even Beran. "Are you sure it's Dilly he wants?" I asked.

"I think I can tell the difference between you and her," Carl said.

"We'll go with you, Dilly," I said.

"You weren't invited," Carl said.

"We'll go anyway," Jarka said, drawing his crutch under him. "We've been looking out for one another for a while now, Carl."

Tuc scrambled to his feet, flapped his ears into place, and raced toward the door Carl had left open.

"Not the dog!" Carl cried.

Dilly kept a yard from him, but said, "Tuc likes you, Carl. You should be flattered because he doesn't like just anyone."

Carl shook his head but smiled and headed back inside with us all in tow. He steered us down a hallway that turned right, descended three steps, and broke into three other corridors. Carl chose the leftmost one, and we emerged in the wide hallway leading to the council chamber. Carl escorted us in, then stood just inside the doorway.

Beran sat at the table in his usual place, leaving the king's chair empty. Thien was out of danger and well enough to have been carried home, but he was still ill. Beran had been conducting Rinland's business for the last week, but he never sat in Thien's place. I guessed Beran didn't want to chance confirming Lord Grimuld's rumor that he'd been after his father's throne.

Across from Beran, Ambassador Gladoc leaned back in his chair, fingering one earring, and studying the prince with a puzzled look on his face.

Beran, on the other hand, grinned like a fool. He blinked at the sight of Tuc, Jarka, and me but quickly shifted his attention to Carl. "Carl, send someone to fetch Maras, please." He reached down to scratch Tuc's ears.

Carl stepped into the hallway, then returned.

"Ambassador Gladoc," Beran said, "allow me to introduce your gallant countrywoman, Dilly, and her two gentlemen friends, Doniver and Jarka." Gladoc raised one eyebrow, but when Dilly dropped a curtsy, he bowed from his chair. "Tell Dilly what you told me," Beran said to Gladoc.

Dilly's face was flushed. I guessed she was excited about being so close to the Lac's Holding representative.

Gladoc cleared his throat. "Lord Suryan regrets it greatly, but he must withdraw his permission for his daughter to marry Prince Beran. The recent attack on the king has led Lady Elenia to believe Rin is too dangerous a place for her to live."

My mouth dropped. Maybe the women of Lac's Holding really *did* do what they liked.

Dilly made a soft, mewing sound, and I saw she was close to tears. She'd counted on Elenia's presence in Rin to rescue her from a life she hated. I made an immediate decision. I'd ask her to go home with me as soon as we were alone.

Beran must have heard Dilly too because he spoke hastily. "So to our regret, we must surrender the idea of marrying Lady Elenia. However, despite my great disappointment—" Gladoc gave him a slit-eyed look, and Beran paused to smooth out his ear-to-ear grin. "I say despite my disappointment at losing Lady Elenia, I can still be of service to at least one person from Lac's Holding. If you wish it, Dilly, the ambassador has agreed to take you home with him and arrange for you to enter into service in Elenia's part of Lord Suryan's household."

Dilly sucked in her breath and took a step toward Beran before stopping herself. "I do wish! Oh, thank you, Your Highness. Thank you!" She bobbed a curtsy.

To my shame, my first reaction was dismay. Then I saw the joy quivering in every line of her body. Next to me, Jarka let out a sigh.

"Very well." Beran thumped a finger on the table. "Ambassador, Dilly will be ready for the trip the first thing tomorrow morning. The dog goes too," he added.

Gladoc opened his mouth.

"You may go," Beran said before the ambassador could speak.

Gladoc recognized his dismissal and took his leave.

Beran beckoned to someone who'd just entered the room, and Maras skirted around me and Jarka. "Come, Dilly," she said. "Let's see what kind of clothes we can round up for you before tomorrow."

Dilly started off with her but stopped to hug Jarka and then me. "I don't want to leave you!"

"This is a good thing." I steadied my voice. "It's what you want, Dilly."

"I know." She sniffled. "I'll have a chance to see them before I leave?" she asked Maras. The servant woman nodded, and she and Dilly started out the door.

"We'll come with you now," I said. "Jarka can pick out gowns for you."

"One moment, Doniver," Beran said. "You can certainly go with Dilly, but I need to speak to you first."

Dilly and Maras went on, Tuc pattering after them. Jarka paused just outside the doorway, waiting for me but watching Dilly until she followed Maras around a corner.

"Before the ambassador came, I had news that will interest you," Beran said. "A messenger brought several letters from different places in the Uplands. The plague has apparently lifted. There've been no new cases of Mountain Fever in a week."

"No new cases?" I felt stunned into stupidity.

"That's right. It should have burned out long before now, but it stopped exactly a week ago today, the same day the rats vanished from our new granaries." Beran cocked his head. "The day Lord Grimuld died."

I grabbed the back of a chair to steady myself. Maybe the Powers had disapproved of Grimuld as much as the Uplanders had. Then the implications of what Beran had said dawned on me, and I sank into the chair I was clutching. The plague was over. "I can go home," I said, testing the words to see if I believed them.

Beran leaned toward me. "I would keep you here, Doniver, if you wanted to stay, see that you're taught a trade and have a decent life. I'm told Grandda would take you on as an apprentice. And you need to know that the loss of life in the Uplands has been great. There's a good chance your family is gone."

I pushed at the edge of the council table, like I could shove the thought away.

"But if you want to go home, I'll send you by river as far as possible." Beran held out his hand to Carl, who'd been glaring at me since I sat without the prince's permission. Carl untied a fat pouch from his belt and laid it in Beran's palm. Beran loosened the drawstring, pulled the pouch open, and showed me what lay within—gold king coins marked with the profile of Thien himself. They glittered in the glow from the oil lamp overhead. I'd seen them at home only when we sold a large stand of timber.

I put out my hand, then pulled it back. "For me?"

"You earned them." Beran pulled the drawstring tight and handed the pouch to me. "You were of great service to the king, which is what I've been telling him whenever we talk about who the new Uplands lord will be. If you go home, I think you can at least be certain that you'll be ruled by another Uplander again. Go on with Dilly now. You can take a day to think about it and tell me tomorrow what you've decided."

The pouch weighed my hand down with the promise of a future. The Powers had blessed me the day Beran strolled up to watch me tell fortunes on the town wall. I rose and shuffled to where Jarka hovered, peering around Carl's substantial back.

At the door, I paused. "What about you, Beran?" When Carl twitched, I hastily amended. "What about you, Your Highness? If Lady Elenia is staying in Lac's Holding, maybe you can marry Lady Lineth."

Carl sucked in a noisy lungful of air, and I braced myself to be told to shut it because I was poking my nose into what was clearly none of my business. But Carl hesitated, then set his jaw and turned to eye Beran. "An excellent idea, Doniver."

Beran gave us both a crooked smile. "His Majesty has final say about such things. We'll see."

Carl's breath seeped out through his teeth. "On your way now. I want to talk to His Highness." He shoved me out of the room and closed the door after me.

Jarka was leaning against the wall, and I didn't need to

be a diviner to read the message in his face and know he'd heard everything. "Jarka—"

"So this is all good. You and Dilly can both go home. Great. I'm glad." He pushed himself erect.

"You should come with me," I said. "My family would be happy to have you, and life is sweet in the mountains."

He briefly lifted the tip of his crutch from the floor. "The mountains are no place for someone who can't run up and down them like a goat. Besides," he added, "I've heard that lions live in those mountains. I'd rather take my chances with pickpockets and rats."

Wyswoman Adrya came around a corner. "There you are," she said to Jarka. "Come along now. You're late for your lesson." She set off in a swirl of skirts that loosed a wave of sweet perfume. I still couldn't make that scent fit her. Whatever made her choose it was well hidden.

"I can't come, Mistress," Jarka called after her. "I have to go see my cousin. Since my friends are leaving, I'm going right now."

I cringed at the pain loading down *my friends are leaving*.

Adrya turned back, her pendant swinging. "His Highness forbade you to leave the castle. And your cousin can wait. An apprentice has responsibilities."

"Apprentice?" I perked up. "You'd be off the streets for good, learning to be a Wysman."

"I can't do that," Jarka said. "My cousin needs me. You've seen her, Doniver. I can't leave her with no one to protect her."

"But you can't go back on the streets," I said desperately, then swung to face Adrya. "Mistress, you could help him, right? Get permission for him to leave and come back?"

"The husband is the problem?" Adrya said. "That's manageable. If you were my apprentice, Jarka, I'd owe it to you to go with you to tell off this husband and anyone else who needed it."

I choked on a laugh. "Mistress Adrya would be good at that, Jarka. Let her help you, and then let her teach you."

For a moment, he looked stunned. Then he pulled himself upright. "She has to let me keep the wind box."

Adrya threw up her hands. "I take back what I said about the box. You can keep it. Now, come. We can talk on the way."

"That would be good. Would you please tell her husband the castle is keeping an eye on him?" Jarka hoisted the strap of his bag higher on his shoulder and hobbled toward the Wyswoman.

"Absolutely," Adrya said. "I'll make sure the guards check on her regularly too."

In the back of my head, I heard Jarka reading from *The Book of the Wys* on the day I met Prince Beran: "*Wysmen and Wyswomen arise in every generation,*" Jarka had read. "*The faithful know them by the Powers' mark upon them, by their courage and wisdom, and by their selfless care for the weak and the needy.*"

"Wait," I said.

Jarka turned.

"I don't need time to think," I said. "I'm leaving as soon as I can, and after that, I'll probably never see you again. But I'll never forget you, Jarka. I think maybe you're already a Wysman."

Jarka looked away, blinking. He patted the bag holding his new wind box. "I'll check on you once in a while." His voice was rough.

"I'll keep that in mind and behave myself."

"You shouldn't travel alone though," Jarka said. "With Ringmen still around, that's dangerous."

I smiled. "I wasn't planning to go alone."

I LEVERED MYSELF up the rocky hillside, breathing in noisy gasps that told me I'd lived on the flatlands too long. No matter. My lungs and muscles would soon toughen up when I started on the work waiting at home. Assuming home was still there. I licked my dry lips, lowered my head, and struggled up the last yard to the small plateau. From near at hand came the sound of water plunging over stone. I shouldered soft-needled branches aside and emerged at the foot of a narrow waterfall.

Near the edge of the stream that flowed away downward, a pinwheel spun in the breeze that always blew here—here where the Powers' breath always moved and people lived close to Father Sky, wrapped in the arms of Mother Earth's mountains. The scent of pine and earth and clean water perfumed the crisp air.

I watched the painted wooden blades spin. Did I have words to send somewhere? Assuming I found my family still alive and on our farm, what I wanted most to say would be said face to face. I pictured Ma and my sisters, and with a pang of loss, I knew there were things I wouldn't say, too. There were things I'd never tell them, dark places that would live inside me, maybe for the rest of my life. And if my family was gone, well, I'd already lost my childish belief in a safe world, but this was where I fit. I was in the Uplands. That had to be better than where I'd been.

A thought occurred to me. No, two thoughts. I bent over the pinwheel and added my breath to the rush of air. "Tell Jarka to be careful. Folks don't always welcome the Wys. And tell Dilly—Well, tell her I'm happy for her."

And I was. Mostly, anyway. I was glad for my friends' happiness, but I felt Jarka's and Dilly's absence like snow down the back of my shirt.

The pinwheel spun on. I waited. A flickwing trilled from a branch just over my head, then sailed like a loosed arrow straight toward my family's farm. The knot in my stomach eased a little. I picked my way back across the plateau and skidded down the hillside to the path where my companion drowsed in a patch of sunshine.

I laid my hand on her shoulder. "Wake up, Tava."

Her eyelids lifted, showing cornflower blue eyes that looked at me blindly before they focused. She climbed to her feet while I picked up my pack and shrugged into it.

"Not much farther now," I said.

"When we get there, I'll cook," Tava said. "I'll make you soup. I always made soup when my boy came home from taking our goats to market."

"My ma cooks," I said.

Tucking wispy gray hair behind her ears, Tava turned away. "I'll do it."

Was she trying to tell me something? I wiped sweaty palms on my trousers, then hooked my thumbs through the straps of my pack. "Let's go."

I led her up the last twisting bit of trail. Just ahead was the shoulder of the mountain from which we'd be able to look down into the valley. I spotted the blotch of sunshine marking the end of the tunnel of trees. Leaving Tava behind, I lengthened my stride and then broke into a run. I burst out from between the walls of trees and leaped to stand next to the big rock that had marked the top of the trail for as long as I could remember.

Below me, in the green of the valley, nestled the house, the fields, the barn, the sheds. I swept my gaze back and forth but saw no sign of life other than the white dots of goats on the opposite slope. The only sound was the tinkle of the wind chimes along the roof edge. The only things moving were the cloth streamers blowing at each house corner. I squinted. Were the goats so far away that they'd gone wild? Or did they still belong to the farm? Was anyone there for them to belong to?

A door slammed, and a girl ran into view between the house and the chicken coop. I put a hand on the rock to steady myself. My middle sister carried a basket and was no doubt on her way to gather eggs. She vanished behind the chicken coop.

Wheezing, Tava labored up behind me. "Your little brother will need someone to keep an eye on him. I can do that too."

I snapped her a look. "I don't have a little brother."

She pointed down into the valley.

I turned back. At the well stood Ma, cranking the handle to draw the bucket up. She caught it and poured the water into the pail she carried. Then she straightened, hands braced in the small of her back.

My breath caught. She was pregnant.

"Five months gone, I'd say." Tava nodded. "It's a good thing we didn't stay away any longer."

In a move that looked well-practiced, Ma put a hand over her eyes and lifted them to look directly at the top of the path. I was sure she'd never know me at that distance, not changed as I was. But she froze for only an instant before she dropped the bucket and flung a shout over her shoulder. "It's him!" Before she'd had time to turn back, I'd skittered halfway down the steep path, running toward family and work and care, running toward the future I had chosen and the man I wanted to be.

Then Ma had me in a hug. I realized that in the three months I'd been gone, I'd grown tall enough to tuck her under my chin. "Ma, I have to tell you about Da."

"Hush," she said. "I know. I heard him on the wind. It's you we've been waiting for."

Then I was wrapped from the chest down in little kid arms, and my new life unfolded in front of me.

I was home.

Acknowledgements

Like most of what I write, *The Wind Reader* had a long gestation, almost ten years in fact. When I went back and tried to identify everyone who gave me feedback and support along the way, I was overwhelmed by how many people I found.

So let me thank Karoline Ellis, Elizabeth Desmond, Bonnie Brunish, E. M. Kokie, Jenna Nelson, Jennifer Schmit Adam, Kelly Andrews, Jane Ostrander, and Lisa Levine, all of whom gave me great critiques.

Thanks to the writer group at the Hearst Center, particularly Felicia Babb Cass. When I needed cheerleaders, you were there.

I thank Sarah Prineas, Deb Coates, and Lisa Bradley. Dragons of the Corn were fierce but clear sighted and full of good suggestions.

Thanks to Sara Yake, who helped me believe in myself.

Particular thanks to Carol Houliston, whom I have missed on each day since her death.

Thanks to Marco Pennacchietti for the gorgeous cover.

Finally, thanks to Sara-Jayne Slack for her support and editing. May Inspired Quill thrive.

About the Author

Dorothy A. Winsor is originally from Detroit but moved to Iowa in 1995. She still blinks when she sees a cornfield outside her living room window. For about a dozen years, she taught technical writing at Iowa State University and served as the editor of the *Journal of Business and Technical Communication*, but then she decided writing middle-grade and young adult fantasy was more fun.

She lives with her husband, who engineers tractors, and has one son, the person who first introduced her to the pleasure of reading fantasy.

Find the author via her website:

www.dawinsor.com

Or tweet at her: @dorothywinsor

Lightning Source UK Ltd.
Milton Keynes UK
UKHW01f1049051018
330017UK00001B/39/P